Also by Ted Olson

A STRANGER AND AFRAID

HAWK'S WAY

Ranch on the Laramie

Ranch on the Laramie

by Ted Olson

AN ATLANTIC MONTHLY PRESS BOOK
Little, Brown and Company—Boston—Toronto

FIRST EDITION

T 03/73

Library of Congress Cataloging in Publication Data

Olson, Ted, 1899-
    Ranch on the Laramie.

    "An Atlantic Monthly Press book."
    I. Title.
PZ3.O525Ran [PS3529.L7]   813'.5'2   72-8985
ISBN 0-316-65052-8

ATLANTIC–LITTLE, BROWN BOOKS

ARE PUBLISHED BY

LITTLE, BROWN AND COMPANY

IN ASSOCIATION WITH

THE ATLANTIC MONTHLY PRESS

*Published simultaneously in Canada
by Little, Brown & Company (Canada) Limited*

PRINTED IN THE UNITED STATES OF AMERICA

To Oscar and Louise
and, in memory,
Father and Mother,
Hattie, Martha, Lee, Harry,
Vay and Mary

Preface

SOME YEARS AGO, in a book whose name and author I have regrettably forgotten, I encountered a description of life on the American frontier toward the end of the last century. It was a grisly picture of loneliness, drudgery, privation and squalor. Men and women worked from dawn to dusk, and longer, in bitter cold or blistering heat, day after day, week on week, year after year. There was no respite, no recreation, except for infrequent excursions to some scruffy little town to replenish the larder and wheedle an extension from the bank. They had no luxuries and few amenities. They drew their water from well or stream. Their sanitary facilities were a chamber pot under the bed and a malodorous privy outside. At night they huddled around a wood fire, too exhausted for conversation, reading — if they read at all — by the flicker of a kerosene lamp.

As I read I became perplexingly aware of a sense of recognition. I grew up on a Wyoming ranch, in the first two decades of this century, along with my older brother and two sisters. My Norwegian-born parents had settled on the Laramie River, in southeastern Wyoming, in 1890. My father had been a sailor on windjammers and an engineer on the Union Pacific; my mother had come to America in an immigrant ship and had worked as maid, cook, and housekeeper. The ranch was our home until my mother sold it in 1917, five years after our father's death.

In many particulars the life described by my unidentified historian was the life I had known as a child. But the feeling-tone, to borrow a word from the psychologists, was altogether different. I had never thought of our life, then or afterward, as pinched or squalid. I had never considered myself disadvantaged. On the contrary, those years on the Laramie River seemed in retrospect good years — harsh, perhaps, in some physical aspects, but richly rewarding.

Retired now, after a life that took me a long way from Wyoming — to newspaper offices in San Francisco, New York and other cities, to wartime London, to Foreign Service assignments in European capitals — I still feel grateful that I was privileged to start out as I did. In this book I have tried to put down some recollections of a way of life that has vanished — partly from a need to verify my own recollections, to reassure myself that I was not romanticizing what that historian had attempted to describe with clinical objectivity; partly with some notion that the other side of the story — the way it had looked to someone who was there — ought to be on the record.

Contents

Ranch on the Laramie

1

House, River, Mountains, Plains

BEGIN AT THE BEGINNING.
But what was the beginning? Childhood memory is a dubious witness. Its focus blurs; forms shift and dissolve. A picture emerges momentarily and then disintegrates. How much is actual memory, how much hearsay transmuted into the illusion of memory?

Out of the flux one scene materializes, and stays. I am sitting in the kitchen astride my rocking horse. It must be afternoon; the sun slanting through the western window is warm on my face, the window's outline sharp on the worn linoleum. My shadow and the horse's, merged into one shadow distorted and elongated, rock with us. We rock and we rock and we rock.

And that is all. I have a dim recollection that my mother is busy on the other side of the kitchen, but that may be only assumption. Mama is always in the kitchen, busy with something, except when she is outside, busy with something else. There is no one there but us two; I assume that my brother and sisters are at school, that Papa is busy in the fields or the stables. I have no idea what the season is. Late autumn or early spring, by the slope of the sunlight.

That, at any rate, is the first memory I can be reasonably sure of, my first awareness of a personal identity and a setting in which that identity existed. I have no idea how old I was; old enough to sit on a rocking horse, but it may have been a very small rocking horse. It has no emotional significance or symbolism, like that which attached to Citizen Kane's "rosebud" sled. It makes that one brief appearance and then vanishes.

Anyway, the kitchen is a good place to begin. That is where I began, as a conscious being. And many of the important activities of ranch life, for grown-ups as well as children, go on in the kitchen. It is of course a great deal more — dining room, living room, library, workshop.

My picture of the kitchen on a winter night is a composite of many memories. Supper is over, the dishes are washed and dried, the towels (flour sacks opened out and hemmed) hung neatly up to dry. The hot-water reservoir at the back of the range has been replenished. Two pails of fresh water stand beside the sink. The table is set for breakfast; the oatmeal is simmering in the double boiler on the back of the stove.

A glow seeps through the open draft and flickers on the linoleum. It is cozily warm in the low-ceilinged room, though the windows are already brocaded, a crystal jungle of ferns and fronds. The wind growls outside, sniffs for a chink, a clawhold. Now and then it sends a sinuous icy tongue under the door; the strip of carpet lifts and bellows. A white fungus is growing in across the linoleum. My brother puts two more sticks in the ravenous fire.

My father sits on one side of the table, within reach of the big cupboard that holds pipes and tobacco, maga-

4

zines, books, and a great deal more. He is reading: the *Laramie Boomerang,* perhaps, or the *Breeder's Gazette,* or perhaps *Brann's Iconoclast.* On the other side of the table Mama is darning stockings. She likes to read, too, but has precious little time. There is always darning or mending or patching or clothes-making. We children are occupied in various ways, with our toys, our books, perhaps with a three-handed game of casino.

In winter our schedule is luxuriously relaxed. We don't get up until seven, we stay up as late as ten, the grownups even later. Sometimes when the mending is done there is still an hour or more of leisure. Then Papa may take down the cribbage board. "Fifteen-two, fifteen-four, fifteen-six . . ." He pegs out their scores. If neighbors should drop in — and even in this country of great distances it does happen, though not often — they are likely to play solo — a game somewhat resembling bridge, except that one successful bidder takes on the others single-handed.

The clock snicks off the seconds and the minutes. As the youngest I am the first to be bustled off to bed. In winter we dress and undress in the sitting room, in front of the heater, a squat four-legged iron structure with a maw cavernous enough to ingest an eight-inch chunk of wood. With the draft closed the log will smolder quietly all night and blaze up quickly when the draft is opened. The bedroom is unheated. The blankets (sheets would be unendurable in winter) are not exactly cozy, but I burrow down into the little nest thawed out by the hot flatiron that Mama has tucked in a few minutes before. I thrust my feet against it, pull them back. Even through its swaddling of rags it is too hot yet to touch. I sniff the smell of scorched cloth. Mama tucks the blankets around my shoulders and up to my chin. I ask, "Time to curl down and go to sleep?" "Time to curl down and go to sleep," she assures me. It is the nightly ritual. (Why "curl down" instead of "curl up"? I have no idea.) I am drowsily conscious of the wind snarling and clawing outside the thickly furred window. I am luxuriously confident it can't get in.

Slowly my horizon expanded — to the yard, the corrals and stables, the fields, the woods along the river, the plains and mountains beyond. There must have been moments of adventure and discovery, quantum leaps in the exploration of my environment and my perception of my place in it. But the picture that comes to me now is all in one piece.

Our house was of logs, unpainted and weathered gray, with white plaster chinking; the shingled roof was gray too. It sat low, on a foundation of bigger logs. It had five rooms — kitchen, parlor, two bedrooms, and a milk cellar. Separating parlor and bedrooms from the kitchen was a hall, which led to the seldom-used front door. When I got too big to sleep three-in-a-bed with my sisters I was moved to a couch — "the lounge" — in the hall. It wasn't exactly private, but I don't recall being bothered by the traffic, late or early. At five or six who worries about privacy?

Built against the east wall of the kitchen was an enclosed lean-to which we called "the shed." It was porch and foyer, where we stamped or broomed off snow or mud before coming into the house, hung up dripping slickers and icicled sheepskins. It was the laundry, with washing machine, tubs, wringer and washboards, clotheslines and clothespins. In summer we washed up there before meals. Every kind of paraphernalia was stored there: fishing rods, creels, hip boots and other outdoor gear, garden tools, utensils, buckets. Here the dog and cats got their milk and whatever food they did not find for themselves; they were rarely admitted to the house proper. Here I played on stormy days.

I have not, you may note, mentioned the bathroom. Like most ranches we had none. The versatile kitchen served that purpose in the narrower sense of the word. The sink doubled as washstand for big and small, except in summer; then washbasins and towels were moved outside. On Sundays Papa would fill a basin with hot water, hang a mirror above the window, strop his razor and scrape away the week's crop of reddish beard, wiping off bristles and lather on a scrap of newspaper. On Saturday nights Mama set a round, galvanized-iron washtub on the floor, filled it with hot water from the reservoir, tempered with cold from the buckets by the sink, and soaped and scrubbed us one after the other. When I was small enough, I squatted in the tub; after my legs lengthened I had to perch on the edge which was hard on the backside. Having no acquaintance with any other shape of tub I was not unhappy, nor did it ever occur to me to wonder how Mama and Papa managed.

For other needs we had to go outdoors. The privy (we called it the closet) was attached to one end of the icehouse, fifteen or twenty yards from the kitchen door. In summer it was a rather pleasant place. You could sit for a quarter hour or more, if nobody hollered at you, daydreaming or poring over the inexhaustibly fascinating pages of Sears Roebuck or Montgomery Ward (more familiarly Monkey Ward), who provided the toilet paper. (A story current in those days told of the sheepherder who, having inherited a million dollars, sat down and wrote laconically to Montgomery Ward: "Please send me one of each.") In winter it was different. Your skin shrank from the icy boards; the frigid wind blew up around your buttocks. You did your business in a hurry and scampered back to the kitchen.

For a humiliatingly long period after I graduated from chamber pots I had to be escorted to the closet at night. I was scared of the dark. Mama, or occasionally Martha, my mentor and protector, went along uncomplainingly as bodyguard. Oscar jeered: "Scaredy-cat! Dassn't do his business without Mama holding his hand."

"*Ti stille, du Oscar,*" my mother would command, in her no-nonsense voice, and Oscar would shut up, until next time.

I should like to make a dramatic vignette of my eventual triumph over cowardice, but it would be fiction. All I remember, dimly, is that there came a night when, shamed by my brother's taunts and my own self-contempt, I marched quakingly out to face the terrors of the dark, and returned cured. If anybody said anything — "That's my brave little Teddy," for instance, or " 'Bout time, Kid!" I don't remember it.

The area in front of the house was paved with smooth slabs of stone. A few steps from the door was the well. It was enclosed in a wooden housing with a hinged lid. Above was a framework supporting a pulley through which the well rope passed. You could look down and see yourself in miniature, silhouetted against a disc of sky. When you lowered the bucket the image splintered. You joggled the pail until it filled, hauled it up, emptied it into the kitchen pails. The water was always cold, in July as in January, and delicious. In winter the spillage froze on the flagstones and made footing precarious; every so often someone had to chop the ice away. Once in a while the bucket got loose and plunged into the depths, taking the rope with it. Then Papa or Oscar would work his way perilously down the moss-encrusted rocks and grapple with a rake until he recovered it.

Shadowing the well and the doorway was a great gnarled Methuselah of a cottonwood. The trees on the west and north sides of the yard were younger, just the size for a beginning climber. They were my jungle-gym, until I graduated to the big cottonwood, which offered more variety. To the east, a currant hedge separated the yard from the vegetable garden. In early summer it was a bank of yellow blossom; the fragrance filled the yard and the house.

We had no lawn; meadow and upland grass and wild flowers grew as they chose, scythed down when they got too dense and tall. There were flower beds along two sides of the house and another at one end of the root cellar. The house itself was festooned in summer with hop vines and morning glories. Half a century later I marvel how exuberantly everything blossomed in that harsh high-altitude climate, where the span between frost and frost was never more than three months. We had no chemical stimulants, only stable manure and rich black humus from the river banks. We used no pesticides; the threat of a silent spring was unimaginably remote.

Along the south side of the yard were the satellite buildings — bunkhouse, icehouse, smithy and carpenter shop, root cellar, privy. To the west were barns, chicken house, pigpen, wagon shed, granary, corrals, cattle sheds, feed lots. The buildings stood on a rise of land in a bend of the creek. (We pronounced it "crick.") A quarter of a mile to the south the river wound, mostly sheathed in cottonwoods. In the spring it would break over its banks, flood the lower meadow, and bite off a few cubic yards of our precious hay land.

Many ranch houses were grander, a few more humble. Ours seemed to me eminently satisfactory. I was outraged when a schoolmate from town made some reference to "the cabin," and I realized that he was talking about our house. Sure, it was built of logs, but that didn't make it a cabin. "The cabin" was the one-room structure on the homestead claim across the river. I didn't have wit enough to appropriate the word as a status symbol. Hadn't Lincoln been born and reared in a cabin? I, alas, had been born in my aunt's small frame house in town, a sad oversight on the part of my parents. But I did live in a log house, and with more imagination I might have made something of it.

The river that cradled and nourished and for a few days each year tried to terrorize us was the Big Laramie. (There is a Little Laramie River, too; they merge north of Laramie, our railhead and market town.) Our ranch lay a few miles below the gap where the Big Laramie, originating in northern Colorado, breaks through the mountains and begins its long meander toward the North Platte. In mid-Nebraska the North Platte picks up the South Platte, coming up from Colorado, and together they flow into the Missouri. The Missouri, a couple of states farther eastward, joins the Mississippi. When I was old enough to understand maps and comprehend that majestic sequence of confluences I used to flip sticks into our creek and imagine them bobbing out, months later, into the Gulf of Mexico.

In three directions we looked out to mountains. South of the river the land tilted up to the westward, gently at first, in long swells and furrows, then more steeply, until it became a mountain. We considered it our own special mountain, though our neighbors farther upriver might have asserted equally valid or perhaps superior claims. Its name was Jelm.* It was big enough — 9,665 feet — and

---

* There are conflicting views on the origin of the name. Nora Field, writing on "Old Cummins City" in the *Laramie Boomerang,* says: "New miners, promoters . . . changed the name to Jelm, which in Scandinavian means a crown." (It doesn't, actually; *hjelm* means helmet.) But George R. Stewart's *American Place-Names* says firmly it's "an adaptation of Gillam, from an early tie contractor for the railroad." Take your pick.

close enough to make an impressive bulk against the sky. It was gracefully shaped, rising steeply on the south to a rounded crest, then sloping northward in a long, languid gradient. The ridge and the crest were blackly stubbled with pine, the lower slopes gray or tawny with sage or scanty grass. There were three deep vertical gouges below the ridge, wooded with quaking asp, luminously green in summer, yellow in the fall, bone-gray in winter.

Our mountain caught the first sun in the morning, while the plains were still smoke; it kept a scalloping of gold long after the sun had disappeared; it propped up the evening star, icily white in the apricot afterglow. For a few days one summer an awesome itinerant pitched camp above the ridge: Halley's Comet, outward bound after one of its rare visits to earth. I was watering the horses at the creek the evening I saw it there. I remember adding seventy-five years to my age — I must have been ten — and speculating whether I would be on hand to welcome it back. Mathematically possible, I decided, but unlikely.

To the west and northwest, and farther away, was Sheep Mountain, a long, sheer, saw-toothed, densely wooded wall. Beyond its northern tip we could see the flash of snow, in winter a massive compact glitter, in summer a thing of shreds and patches. This was the Snowy Range, more correctly the Medicine Bow Mountains, with 12,005-foot Medicine Bow Peak as their sovereign. They were thirty miles away, and many years were to pass before I knew them at close hand.

East from Jelm, forming our southern horizon, stretched a succession of lower elevations: Ring Mountain, so named because of a gigantic circle on its western flank, presumably of Indian origin; Red Mountain, with a sheer northern face of a color between vermilion and firebrick; Bull Mountain, Boulder Ridge. And far to the east, no more than the rim of a saucer holding the plains from flowing down to Nebraska, the Laramie Mountains, popularly miscalled the Black Hills, but not to be confused with the proper Black Hills in South Dakota.

This was historic country. Indians had hunted buffalo on the plains since time immemorial, until the white man came. They had fought gorily — among themselves as well as against the invader — over what a contemporary writer has called the territorial imperative. A sharp eye may still catch the gleam of an arrowhead on a pebbly slope. A few names survive. The Medicine Bow Mountains and the Medicine Bow River were so called because their timber provided a tough, straight wood for bows; they were in the Indian idiom "good medicine."

The first white men had come through here nearly a century before I made my entrance. More than one of them left his scalp and his bones. One left his name as well. Laramie — the town, the fort on the Platte that long antedated it, a peak, and three rivers — all commemorate Jacques La Ramie, a young French-Canadian trapper who started up the river in 1817, or thereabouts, ignoring Jim Bridger's warning that the Indians were unfriendly, and never came back.

Bridger was here, and Kit Carson, and John Charles Frémont. Francis Parkman, riding out from Fort Laramie to get better acquainted with the Indians, probably looked down into the Laramie plains from the crest of the hills to the east, but came no farther. The Overland Trail cut across our basin, diagonaling northwest around the outriggers of the Snowy Range. When the light is favorable — early morning or late afternoon — you can still in a few places make out the ruts gouged by the covered wagons.

Hunters, trappers, mountain men, gold seekers, emigrant trains, the Pony Express, the soldiers garrisoned to protect them — they add up to a considerable traffic, although nobody thought to count them. These were transients, most of them probably glad to leave the Laramie plains behind them. Not until the railroad arrived, in 1868, did many people come to stay.

All this I was to learn later. At the time of which I write I lived in the present, and was quite satisfied to be where I found myself in the first decade of the twentieth century.

There can be no more perfect setting for a ranch than in the crook of a river, with mountains on two sides, plains on the third and fourth. A ranch on the prairie always seems a little bleak, even after fifty years of labor have conjured into existence meadows, a sheltering cottonwood grove, a lawn, flower beds. A ranch in a mountain valley, with no horizon but mountains, must give one — would give me, certainly — something like claustrophobia, anyway a sense of being fenced in. Our ranch, I felt, was just right.

2

Meet the Family

MY FATHER MUST HAVE THOUGHT SO. He had first seen the Big Laramie in the late '70s or early '80s. Though it was more than a decade before he came there to stay, I like to think that from the beginning he may have felt, "Here is where I belong."

He had come a long way to find it — from a farm in southern Norway, on the west side of the Oslo Fjord. Like so many other Norwegian boys, he had taken to the sea at the age of fourteen. For seven years he sailed the oceans of the world in windjammers — Norwegian, English, American. On a winter night he could spin fascinating yarns. In Calcutta he had seen cobras swaying in time with a snake charmer's flute. He had watched a fakir thrust a sword repeatedly through a basket in which his small brown assistant had been tucked, draw the blade out dripping with blood, and then — just as the horrified seamen were thinking of lynching him — open the empty basket while the grinning lad trotted out of the crowd. He would show me a picture of a full-rigged ship and name every mast and yard and sail and sheet — at sea a rope, he would explain, isn't a rope; it's a sheet.

Then, one dreary Christmas Eve, while he was holystoning the decks of a Yankee vessel, he decided he had had enough seafaring.

"Never before," his diary recalled twelve years afterward, "did I realize so fully how cheerless a sailor's life was, how barren of those little joys and pleasures that commonly fall to the lot of man be his station in life ever so humble, and I resolved right there and then to quit it and seek some occupation on shore."

He found it in Wyoming Territory, about as far from salt water as a man could get — 2,000 miles from one ocean, 1,000 from the other, and 7,200 feet aloft. He had headed there, beating his way from New Orleans, because he had an uncle living in Laramie City. "Uncle Christie" — his first name was Evan — had arrived ten years earlier with a Union Pacific construction crew and stayed to work in the railroad shops. With his help my father got a job as fireman — after a discouraging period during which he was at the point of pushing on to the Pacific and signing up again as an able seaman — and worked up to engineer.

He rode locomotives for twelve years, mostly between Laramie and Rawlins, 120 miles to the west. It was no doubt better than holystoning decks, but his journal suggests that it was monotonous and arduous. Routed out by the callboy at any time of day or night. Sitting hour after hour at the throttle, peering into a smother of sleet and snow, and sparks and cinders spraying up from the bell-mouthed smokestack. Shuttling back and forth past a bleak succession of stations, most of them not much more than a water tank, a signal tower, a dingy clapboard building, a cattle-loading chute. Lookout . . . Rock

15

Creek . . . Medicine Bow . . . Rawlins . . . Medicine Bow
. . . Rock Creek . . . Lookout . . . Laramie; the names fill
page after page of the pocket-sized *Daily Assistant for
Locomotive Engineers, Firemen, and Mechanics in General* in which he kept his records and jotted down his
reflections.

"This close written page you see opposite represents
fifty days of hard work," he wrote in April, 1887. "Fifty
days in thirty, if I go on at this rate I shall have lived 65
years when I am only forty. Thats piling up years behind
one self rather hurriedly, but then thats the way here in
America. Oscar Wilde hit it about right, when he said
that Americans were in a continual hurry to catch trains;
thats what I have been doing all month, and I have
caught them pretty regular too."

There were breaks in the monotony, of course. One was
grisly. Bringing his train into Rawlins one morning he
saw a body dangling from a telegraph post. When he
stepped down from the cab he learned, from other railroad men vying to be first with the news, that lynch law
had finally caught up with Big Nose George.

George Parrotte was one of the last of the road agents
that harassed the Union Pacific and the stages bringing
gold out of South Dakota's Black Hills in the '70s. When
posses closed in on the gang, cleaning out one hideout
after another, he had escaped to Montana. There he was
captured. Returned to Wyoming for trial, he got the same
kind several of his colleagues had received previously.

"I didn't eat much breakfast that morning," Papa
recalled.

Throughout these years he had been exploring the
mountains west of the little prairie town. They were not
much like the gentle landscape of farmland and forest he
had known as a boy. But they had trees and water and
meadows; they were a happy contrast to the lunar vistas

he saw from his cab window. He kept going back whenever he could, to hunt and fish.

When he learned that a ranch on the river, twenty-two miles west of town, was for sale, he pooled his resources with those of an acquaintance and they became co-owners.

He drove locomotives for several years more, giving the ranch whatever time and money he could spare. Finally he felt able to make the break and become a rancher fulltime. At the end of his methodical tabulation for December, 1894, I find, in his neat small print-clear script: "Goodbye UP 3 meals a day and every nights sleep from now on. Good meals too."

He had then been married for six years, and had a son, Oscar, five years old, and a daughter, Hattie, just turned one.

My mother had grown up on a farm high in the mountains of eastern Norway, where the summers are short and capricious, the winters long and harsh. The house where she was born is still there; the date on the corner fireplace is 1805. It stands in a placid valley traversed by a little river that widens here and there into a lake. Behind it the mountain rises steeply to a treeless plateau — *vidda* in Norwegian — which sweeps westward in crests and troughs until it drops into Norway's central valley, Gudbrandsdalen. To the northwest the *vidda* is broken by a cluster of snow-inlaid peaks, known collectively as Rondane.

This is Peer Gynt country. It was to Rondane that Peer fled with the stolen bride, and there he met the Troll King's daughter and her hideous family, and grappled with the Böyg. In some cranny on Rondane's western slope he built the cabin where Solveig waited a lifetime for his return.

From Mama's stories of her childhood and youth I

judge that they were a happy time. There was work, of course, plenty of it, but there was frolic too — sleigh rides, berry-picking expeditions, dancing — the acrobatic dances that tourists see at folk museums. She remembered, with nostalgic warmth, summers at the *saeter* on the edge of the *vidda*, where she tended the cows and goats, milked them, churned butter, made cheese. The life of a *budeia* was spartan and the hours were long, but she loved the sense of space and independence. There were other *saeters* nearby; the girls visited back and forth. And of course young men found errands on the *vidda* from time to time.

A happy life. Why then had she left it?

"There were too many of us."

Her parents had sent her to the nearest town to learn the craft of a seamstress. But when an opportunity to emigrate to America appeared she decided to take it. She was twenty-two years old.

An earlier emigrant had returned to Sollien with seductive tales of "gold and green forests," to translate literally a Norwegian phrase. He must have been a persuasive salesman. He recruited a flock of twenty-odd young people, shepherded them on the long journey to Christiania, and loaded them on a ship bound for New York.

Mama did not remember just when she and her companions began to realize that their helpful countryman was in fact an agent, who undoubtedly pocketed a fat commission for rounding them up and delivering them.

It was a horrible voyage. The ship was small, dirty, slow. For three ghastly weeks it lurched westward through winter seas. Crowded like cattle into the filthy steerage — my mother always suspected that the vessel was in fact a cattle ship diverted to immigrant traffic — the passengers were all sick, virtually without intermission. A quarter of a century later Mama's voice as she told of it would tighten with remembered misery.

They reached the promised land at last, were herded through the immigration reception sheds at Castle Garden, and loaded on a train for the West. The enterprising countryman had arranged everything. They were bound not for Minnesota or Wisconsin, where most Scandinavian immigrants had settled, but for the Rocky Mountains.

There the young Norwegian seamstress found work, as hired girl and later cook, first at Virginia Dale, Colorado, a stage station on the Overland Trail, then at Buffalo, Wyoming — a long stagecoach trip across the prairie from the Union Pacific station at Rock Creek — finally at Laramie. And there, five years later, Berthe Jonsdatter Vollum of Sollien, Österdalen, now known as Bertha Johnson, and Hans Olsen Grythe, of Sande, Vestfold, now simply Hans Olson, Union Pacific engineer, were married.

Father was tall — a little over six feet — blue-eyed, aquiline; his close-cropped hair was a neutral color, his moustache reddish. If a son can judge, he was a good-looking man. Mother was small, brown-eyed, brown-haired. Not conventionally pretty, I suppose. But hers was a strong face, a firm mouth, a determined chin; a face that weathered well. At eighty-five it had not wizened or crumpled; the cheek and chin lines were still firm, the mouth set only a little deeper, the gaze direct and serene as it is in the wedding portrait.

In our time it has been the fashion for children to hate their parents (or profess to), for adolescents to defy them, for adults to attribute their own shortcomings to parental and maternal error, whether despotic severity or fawning permissiveness. I loved mine, and so, I am sure, did my brother and sisters.

Because we never questioned their love we accepted their discipline with little question. No doubt there were flare-ups of rebellion. They expected obedience, and they dealt strictly with serious misbehavior. I can still hear Mama's voice, charged with an indignation that could find expression only in Norwegian: *"Stygg unge!"* (Bad, literally ugly, child.) I remember the dread command: "Take down your pants." She used the flat of her hand, not a hairbrush or a shingle; she applied it to my backside with a vigor that set me howling. I suppose for a few minutes, maybe as much as an hour, I hated her. But since I was spanked only when I richly deserved it, and not always then, I could not reasonably nurse a grudge long.

I tagged along with my father whenever permitted, happy if I could hand him nails or fetch a tool. One of my early chores was to tote a pail of freshly churned buttermilk to the hayfield. I would watch Papa drink long and thirstily, knowing my reward was coming. After he had cached the pail in the shade of the stacker, he would pick up the reins and say: *"Nu ska' vi kjøre!"* That much Norwegian I understood: "Now we'll take a ride." I would perch on the low framework at the rear of the sweep, my heels dragging in the stubble, as the wooden teeth scooped up windrow after windrow. When he brought the fragrant moving mountain back to the stack he would let me step in between load and sweep to hold the hay as the horses backed away. When I was a little older he would let me clamber up the slant of the stacker, scared and proud, as he encouraged me: "That's my little sailor!"

He whittled playthings for me: wooden swords and guns, beautifully tooled; a single-masted boat which I sailed up and down the garden ditch; and "Jacks." That was his name, and mine, for a succession of flat wooden men, half or two-thirds as big as I was, which for a long time were my principal playfellows.

On summer evenings we went fishing. I won't pretend that I enjoyed every minute of those expeditions. The mosquitoes swarmed out of ambush as soon as we approached the river, and there was no fending them off. Their hypodermics perforated a calico shirt as if it were gauze. They wriggled through or under the netting we draped over our hats and tucked into our collars. Mosquito dope — citronella, I suppose — repulsed them for only minutes.

I sloshed along, wet to the waist, getting colder and colder, and tired, and discouraged. I tried vainly to imitate Papa's cast; my flies would slap down with an impact to send any fish scuttling, or snag a branch on the other side of the river, or hook a twig behind me. I spent most of my time untangling them.

If some unwary fingerling — the family half-wit — did nibble my fly I would strike either too soon, snapping the hook away, or too late, after even a half-wit had realized that this particular Royal Coachman or Black Gnat (whatever he might be called in trout) didn't look digestible.

Papa was not unaware of my troubles. He always seemed to sense when I was approaching the degrading outlet of tears. He would reel in his own line and come plashing back.

"Come up here on the bank, Teddy. Now let your fly float down to the head of that riffle. That's right. Now reel it back in, very gently. That's the way. Now keep doing that."

It wasn't orthodox procedure, but it worked. When we came blinking into the kitchen I would pipe proudly, "Mama, I got two. Lookie!" Dad, meanwhile, was emptying his catch into an old dishpan, preparatory to taking them outdoors to clean — twenty-five, maybe thirty trout, brooks and a few rainbows, mostly pan-size, a couple that might weigh a pound. Tomorrow's breakfast, and maybe dinner. Hay hands who didn't like fish were out of luck.

Between them, Mama and Papa must have taught us to read. Certainly I was haughtily beyond "See the boy run" when I entered school, the autumn before I turned six. One Christmas, Hattie gave me *Great Expectations*, my first adult book. Papa and I read it together. He was Joe and I was Pip. He would fence me into the woodbox corner with his leg, as Joe fenced Pip into the chimney corner to protect him against Mrs. Gargery when she was on the Ram-page. (Mama did *not* play Pip's sister; she would have been sadly miscast.)

Our parents loved Dickens. Several of our milk cows were named for his heroines — Dorrit, Betsy, Nancy, Nell. I don't know whether Mama and Papa had discovered him separately, or after they met. Certainly a shared love of books must have helped draw them together. There was a ceiling-tall, glass-doored bookcase in the bedroom I shared with my sisters until I or they were too old. I assumed that every household had books, and was astonished when I first visited neighboring ranches and saw nothing but the mail order catalogues, a ceremonial Bible, with brass clasps discouraging casual access, and a few novels of the E. D. E. N. Southworth–Bertha M. Clay–Augusta J. Evans school.

Mama and Papa must have been the delight of itinerant book agents. They had little sales resistance. We had a ten-volume "Library of American Literature from the Earliest Settlement to the Present Time," compiled by Edmund Clarence Steadman and Ellen Mackay Hutchinson, and published in 1889 by Charles L. Webster & Co., New York. Therein I met (along with such now-forgotten minor figures as George Henry Boker, Paul Hamilton Hayne and John Townsend Trowbridge) Hawthorne, Thoreau, Emerson, Parkman, Whitman, Sidney Lanier and Henry James, Jr. (Note that "Jr.") There was an eight-volume "Library of the World's Choice Literature," edited by Ainsworth R. Spofford, Librarian of Congress, and Charles Gibbon, author of *Robin Gray*, etc., and published by Gebbie & Co., Philadelphia.

And a one-volume *Gleanings from Popular Authors*. A massive *Cambridge Book of Poetry and Song*, quarto size, at least three inches thick and surely weighing pounds, which juxtaposed Emily Brontë and Maria Gowen Brooks, John Keats and John Keble, with magnificent eclecticism. The poets — Longfellow, Whittier, Poe, Will Carleton, Byron, Moore, Scott, Rossetti, Tennyson, Goethe (in translation), and all of Shakespeare in one volume of microscopic print. Some of these were in ornately bound octavos, with decorations incised into quarter-inch-thick covers, and a few genuine steel engravings.

Emerson's *Essays*, in six volumes. Macaulay's *History of England*, five. John Lothrop Motley's history of the Netherlands, eight. *Science for All*, five.

And two shelvesful of magazines from the 1880s — *Atlantic, Scribner's, Harper's, Century* — in which I first encountered the work of Howells, Cable, Hamlin Garland, and of others long forgotten.

These books had been bought not for decoration but for content, and they had been used. I often came across Papa's notations in the margins — concurrence, dissent or amplification. Under Elihu Burritt's *A Learned Blacksmith*, in which that scholar-traveler-diplomat relates how he mastered Latin, Greek, French, Spanish, German and Italian, and then progressed to Hebrew and "50 Oriental languages," Dad had remarked, "I love a cheerfull liar." On the flyleaf of *Science for All* there is this penciled comment:

Science worships truth alone; her gaze is steadily fixed upon the real; she never glances aside to follow expediency. Her work is to declare what is; she leaves to others to say what ought to be. Pure, unwavering, serene science walks this world of ours, a grand clear daylight illuminating all dark places, revealing with equal lucidity, beautifull facts and ugly facts. As the rays of sun falls alike on gorgeous palace and filthy hovel, on fair and happy faces, and on those plowed deep with the lines of misery and want, so does the sunlight of science throw clear beams on the glory of nature, and illuminate with equal brightness its stains and its dark blots.

An unattributed quotation, or his own reflections? The florid language suggests the former, but the misspellings and lapses in grammar lead me to believe it is original. He had been practising English composition even as a seaman. His models were naturally the nineteenth-century writers he was devouring. The dry record of hours on the locomotive is frequently interrupted by a quotation — I have noted one from Oscar Wilde — or a comment of his own:

This closes year 1885. Tomorrow we start on a new, hidden in the mysteries of the future lays the new year before us, it may bring joys, it may bring sorrows, whatever may be the case, God grant me strength to bear cheerfully my lot; be it sorrow and disappointments or happiness and joys.

In the first page of the 1884 book:

Our life is made up of funeral knells and is nothing but a gigantic funeral procession, every tick of the clock, every breath we draw, every word we utter, is a step nearer the grave, is that much power lost never to be regained. It ought to bring every reasonable being to serious meditations.

This may have been only the romantic melancholy of the young, an imitation of literature rather than a reflection on life as he had experienced it. But the recurrence of the theme suggests a darker vein. The poem he quoted most often — it was a favorite of Abraham Lincoln, too — was "Why Should the Spirit of Mortal Be Proud?"

Papa was a man of substance and authority in the community. Neighbors asked his advice, and occasionally even followed it. He was a founder of the Albany County Cattle and Horse Growers Association, and its first president. He took an active part in the interminable skirmishing over grazing and water rights. If he hadn't been a political maverick he might have held public office. As one of a very few Democrats on the Big Laramie, he couldn't expect to get far in politics, and he didn't. He ran for the legislature once, but lost.

He hadn't always been a Democrat. He had switched parties in 1896, to follow the banner of Free Silver and the golden trump of William Jennings Bryan, into the wilderness, as it proved. His apostasy caused a schism in our previously close-knit clan. Uncle Christie, like most Scandinavians and every Union Pacific employee who knew what was good for him, was a staunch Republican. He was shocked by Father's defection, and when his own son Hans also registered as a Democrat, he accused Dad of proselytizing. There were words, and Father stalked out of the house with the melodramatic exit line, "I'll never darken your door again!" I don't know how long the estrangement continued; by my time relations were cordial again.

As for Mama, she was the first one up in the morning, the last to bed at night. When we shivered out of the blankets in the winter dawn she had fires going in kitchen and parlor, and breakfast almost ready. Her day began at five in summer, even earlier during the fall wood hauling, never later than seven in winter. It rarely ended much before ten. She was the one who saw that everything was snug before she blew out the lamps.

I find it hard to remember her not busy. Sometimes on a summer Sunday she and Papa would walk out to the fields so that he could show her how the oats were coming along. Neighbors might drop in for a visit (but they had to be given coffee and something with it, at the very least). Occasionally we went visiting ourselves — an afternoon call (coffee, cakes, and perhaps a glass of wine) or a daylong excursion, with dinner. That happened once or twice a year, and these were the only meals, except those my Aunt Kari fed us on our infrequent trips to town, that Mama did not have to prepare.

Her one concession to human frailty was a short nap after our midday dinner. Five minutes, ten, at most fifteen were all she permitted herself, all, she insisted, that she needed.

Neither she nor Papa ever had a vacation of the sort that everybody now assumes to be his right and need— two weeks or more away from alarm clocks, timetables, worries and routine. Sixty years ago ranchers didn't take vacations — at least not small ranchers like us. Who would milk the cows and clean the stables and feed the cattle and take in the eggs and churn the butter? A ranch is a living organism, of which you are a part; you can't click a switch and shut it down. I doubt if it ever occurred to our parents that their twelve-to-fourteen-hour days, seven-day weeks, fifty-two week years might be considered drudgery. They had always worked; they assumed that work was a condition of life. The only words remotely resembling complaint that I ever heard Mama utter were a wistful reference to the years when she had had time to read books, and a confession, many years later, that she had never really liked cooking; if she'd had the choice she'd rather do laundry. And that was when laundry meant tubs filled and emptied by hand, washboards, homemade lye soap, hand-rinsing and -wringing, hanging clothes out in weather so cold that in five minutes shirts and pillowcases were boards. She was, incidentally, a superb cook.

She was small, wiry, quick, and seemingly tireless. She did everything with a quiet competence that made it look easy. Her serenity was rarely ruffled, though, as I have noted, she could deal stingingly with flagrant misconduct.

Her code was simple and strict. Right was right and wrong was wrong; she did not recognize twilight zones. She would have been bewildered and unhappy in an age of permissiveness. Her harshest word was "wicked," but she reserved it for acts that hurt people.

My parents were not among those immigrants who never quite sever the umbilical cord. They spoke only English at home — unless they had something to say that we children weren't supposed to understand. Except for a few phrases — we were expected to say *"Takk for maten"* before leaving the table — we learned no Norwegian. Mama could send us into convulsions of giggles by telling us how American names were pronounced in Norway.

"Mama, tell us how you said 'Iowa,'" we would coax.

"Yo-^vah."

"And the waterfall."

"Nee-_a-gar-_a Falls."

"And what did you call George Washington?"

"Gay-org Vossing tone."

My brother Oscar I didn't know very well in my early boyhood. He was ten years older. He had left school before I entered — to the distress of our parents, who couldn't understand his lack of interest in books. He treated me with the condescension normal to older brothers, teased me without mercy, though equally without malice, ignored me much of the time. Later, after he came back to the ranch, we became friends, and we have remained so.

Oscar is superbly competent at practical things, a doer and a maker, restless and bored when his hands are idle. He might have been an inventor; after retirement he kept busy in his workshop mending and improving appliances and utensils, his own and the neighbors', devising ingenious new gadgets — he calls them "gizmos." He is a craftsman, the kind you rarely see now, exacting in his own standards, contemptuous of slovenly workmanship. He is stubborn (like me), and sometimes wrongheaded (I think). But he has deep compassion, great kindness, an unselfishness that can be exasperating; most of our disagreements have been about his obstinate refusal to take his due. A good human being.

I have never ceased to wonder how children of the same parents, equipped presumably with the same genes, growing up in the same home, can so often be so different. Hattie and Martha, though less than three years apart, were as unlike as Oscar and I. Hattie was deliberate, in motion and decision; it was a family joke that she would stand at the window for five minutes, mooning, while she dried one plate. Martha, quick, deft, competent, would have the dishes done while Hattie polished that one plate. Hattie's mind was methodical. Her best subject was mathematics; she even seemed to *enjoy* it. Martha was imaginative, intuitive; she loathed arithmetic, but loved poetry.

Hattie was sedate. Martha was a tomboy. She frightened even Mama one evening by impulsively jumping on her horse, Patsy, bareback and with only her apron as a bridle, and pelting off up the hill, her heels drumming his ribs to make him go faster. She came back ten minutes later, intact and impenitent. She could pluck a bumblebee out of the air and dash it to the ground before it could sting.

In one chore, however, Hattie excelled. That was berry-picking. She would squat by the currant hedge or in a gooseberry patch and strip bush after bush methodically, getting the lone berries as well as the fat clusters. She never seemed to have to stand up and stretch and see what was going on in the world, as Martha and I did. We may have picked faster, but we picked by spurts. As the minutes passed the spurts got shorter and the stretches longer. So Hattie's pail would be full while ours were scarcely past the halfway mark. Obviously hers was the temperament that makes a good berry picker. She put up more than her share of the jelly, too.

Whether because of age or disposition, Martha and I found ourselves in a sort of defensive alliance against our elder siblings. (We didn't, of course, know that word.) Sometimes we tried to coax Hattie into our play, but she didn't cooperate very well. Martha and I had given romantic names to our imaginary horses; mine, I think, was Bayard, Martha's was Lightning. "What's *your* horse's name, Hattie?" we asked. She reflected briefly, and answered: "Millegs." "Millegs! What kind of a name is that?" "My legs," said Hattie, practically. We gave her up.

Martha and I played Indian in the thickets along the creek, where the web of tunnels trodden out by livestock made good stalking country. We fashioned bows with willows and string, whittled arrows from boards pried off old grocery boxes. We gave our playground a geography and affixed names. Big Bow Valley had an especially luxuriant growth of smooth, straight willows; Little Bow Valley a reserve supply, not quite so good. No doubt we had Indian names for ourselves, but I don't remember them. Our alarm call I do remember. "Black Hawk's coming!" one of us would cry. We would scuttle into the most secret of our hiding places, under the creek bank, with water protecting our rear and a clear fire field in front.

We spent one summer afternoon scooping tadpoles from a rapidly drying pool and transplanting them to a larger pond. I choose to believe that they survived to serenade us later as full-grown frogs. We made willow whistles, and squirt guns — you bore a hole in the closed end of a hollow rush and fit a plunger of cloth wound tightly around a straight stick.

We had fun. Martha didn't condescend, or exploit her advantage of two-and-a-half years in age and several inches in height. She accepted me as I was. We read the same books, had the same capacity for make-believe, stimulated each other to zanier flights of fancy. Without her, and with no boys of my own age in reach, I should have been solitary indeed. I worshipped her, and once in school I shook my fist openly at a teacher who was reproving her.

3

From Each
According to His Ability

I LEARNED VERY EARLY that life was not simply a matter of rocking in the afternoon sunshine while supper smells drifted seductively to my nose. That picture dissolves and another materializes. Again it is afternoon, but somewhat later; the girls are home from school and helping Mama. The door opens, admitting a swash of icy air and a small boy. I am clutching to my chest a battered milk pan, piled high with chips. I set it down carefully on the linoleum and slide it under the stove. The chips are kindling; there is always a mound of them around the chopping block. They will dry out under the stove until Mama lays the fire in the morning — a crumpled newspaper, the chips, then fine-split pine sticks, ready for the match.

It will be a year or two before I am big enough to fill the woodbox back of the stove, more years before I split the wood myself. But already I am a working member of our small but very nearly self-sufficient community.

Much, much later I shall realize that it was in a way like the society envisaged by Karl Marx: from each according to his ability, to each according to his needs. I don't think it was built to the socialist blueprint, although my father had indeed read Marx. In the bookcase there was an English edition of *Capital* borrowed, the stamp indicated, from a seaman's library in Liverpool. (I wonder if it is still charged out to him.) You couldn't run a small family ranch any other way. Everybody has to pitch in.

There can be little slacking or soldiering, either. The family state is self-policing. Every afternoon without fail Oscar — who splits the wood and fills the woodbox — reminds me, "Getcher kindlin', Kid!" It is my pride to reply triumphantly, imitating his derisive chant, "I *got* my kindlin'!" Somehow that sounds incomplete. So I take to adding a nonsense syllable to perfect the echo: "I *got* my kindlin', Rid!" I lisped in numbers, but not very well.

When you're the youngest of four, you learn to be either docile or wily, or, more likely, a combination of both. I calculate I came out about 80–20 — four parts docility, one part wiliness.

I don't recall demurring, for instance, when Martha decided that I should be taught indoor as well as outdoor chores. I learned to wash dishes — standing on a stool to reach the sink — as well as dry them. She was a strict taskmistress, handing back any plate or saucer not adequately sudsed and rinsed. I learned also to sweep and mop and dust, to sew on buttons, even to darn stockings. My early darns were somewhat roughshod, literally. I limped home from school more than one afternoon with a waffle imprinted on my heel.

As I accumulated years and stature my tasks multiplied. I brought the cows in at milking time. I fed the calves and the pigs, and sometimes the chickens, though mostly those were Mama's care and pride. I pumped the bellows in the blacksmith shop. I turned the grindstone, the churn, the washing machine. I ground the coffee. I filled the kerosene lamps and trimmed the wicks. I watered the flowers. When I was big enough to haul the brimming well bucket up from the murkily glittering depths I took over responsibility for keeping the reservoir at the back of the range filled and two pails of water on the bench by the sink.

I try to blink aside the haze of nostalgia; I ask myself whether all this could really have been the fun it seems now, in an old man's remembering. I rather think it was. Not all, but much of it.

Feeding the calves, for instance. Gluttonous little beasts, all bawl and belly. For an hour they have been congregated outside the gate by the bunkhouse, shoving and butting for precedence. When they see me — and the pails — the bawling augments. I poke one bucket after another through the bars, batting voracious muzzles aside, until every one is properly socketed. There is a lull: not silence, but a rich contented slurping, guzzling and bubble-blowing. It doesn't last long. A hungry little Hereford can drain a gallon bucket in about one minute flat. It takes him maybe thirty seconds longer to lick up the oil meal at the bottom — a substitute for the cream we have filched from the maternal formula.

Is he satisfied now? Not by a long shot. Every calf is an Oliver Twist. He butts the pail, he bangs it against the gate, he shakes his head truculently and butts it again. When you pull it back through the fence he turns to his nearest neighbor, grabs an ear and begins to suck greedily. If you happen to be in reach he grabs you. The legs of my overalls and the elbows of my jumper are usually slobbery from service as a pacifier. Obviously my young wards consider me a mother substitute; they never seem to realize that without a pail I am no good to them whatever.

A milk cow's calf is taken away from his mother almost at birth. He is likely to be a little slow in learning that from now on he must get his nourishment from a bucket instead of from a teat. The trick is to push his head down into the pail, moisten a finger with milk and let him suck it, dunking his muzzle from time to time until he begins ingesting by the mouthful. Some catch on quickly; some don't. Mama had seemingly infinite patience with the dullards. Mine frazzled quickly; I'm afraid that sometimes I dunked them more vigorously than was really necessary.

But I liked calves. I was their patron; they appreciated me; we were friends. I never achieved a similar empathy with the hogs. Great unsightly beasts with gleaming slimy snouts, sly little eyes, skin dingily pink through coarse sparse bristles, gross cylindrical bodies awkwardly pegged onto silly inadequate legs, a ridiculous scribble of tail serving none of a tail's proper functions — protection, modesty and the discouragement of flies. And that hideous squealing and grunting!

The pigs were quartered in an enclosure adjoining the chicken house and overlapping the garden ditch, so that they had constant access to water and mud. I toted them armfuls of greens, rhubarb tops, lamb's quarters and dandelions, and slops from the kitchen — soured milk, excess buttermilk from the churning, scraps and leavings, a malodorous mix of everything human beings had no use for. A pig is a portable garbage disposal unit.

Cows, horses, even a hen or a rooster now and then, have personalities, but to me one hog looked and behaved like every other. Not to Martha, though. For one whole summer she godmothered a piglet, and he returned her affection. When the mama sow, foraging for food, led her brood near the house, my sister would squat down and spread out her apron, and Piggie would gallop up and jump into her lap, nuzzling and wriggling and grunting blissfully as she rubbed his ears and cooed endearments.

As he outgrew her lap and his cuteness, the friendship petered out. Just as well. It had no future, while his was predestined and brief. In a few months a piglet becomes pork. We had too much common sense — even Martha — to speculate sentimentally on the identity of the chops and roasts that Mama set before us.

Calves get skim milk because butterfat is a salable commodity, too valuable to be wasted on four-legged animals. (Or for that matter on bipeds. I was reared on skim milk, and I still feel a flicker of surprise when I see it in supermarkets, specially packaged for customers with a weight problem.) Butter is one of our cash crops, and I am not very old before I am helping to process it. We use a barrel churn, which sits in a cradle and is rotated end over end by a crank. I turn the crank — spelled at first by my mother or one of my sisters, later all by myself.

It is a tedious job, and it gets harder minute by minute. As the butter begins to coalesce the churn turns more heavily and unevenly; the contents resist the upward heave of the crank, and then break loose and come down with a slap. Slosh . . . slap . . . thud . . . slosh . . . slap . . . thud . . . Heavier and slower, until Mama stops me, unclamps the lid, peers in and adjudges that the butter has arrived.

Now the buttermilk is drained off through the spigot at the bottom and the butter — cauliflower-shaped golden clots — is scooped into a big wooden bowl, to be beaten smooth and salted, and then packed for storage or marketing. Some goes into stoneware jars, some is compressed into one-pound cubes in a wooden mold that imprints it with a floral design. The Gem City Grocery gets the stone jars; the one-pound cubes are for individual customers, of whom Mama has a small but loyal clientele.

The buttermilk we drink ourselves, and what we can't drink goes to the hogs. Does anybody under fifty know the taste of real buttermilk? Not that heavy, pale "cultured" variety one finds now; there is no resemblance, except possibly in chemical composition. The real article is (or was) only a little thicker than whole milk; the small butter clots that eluded the centripetal pull of the churned mass give it a golden tinge, and crunch delightfully on the tongue. There is nothing like it to quench the thirst. On summer afternoons Mama sometimes sends me to the field with a jugful, ice-cold. I can still see Papa hoisting the jug aloft and drinking and drinking, at last handing it over to Oscar and wiping his moustache with a deep sigh of contentment.

Many years after, driving across Iowa, I tried to get a drink of buttermilk. Surely in the great hog-and-dairy state, if anywhere, that golden nectar must still be brewed. No luck. In restaurants and at soda fountains I met only blank looks and shaken heads. Has technology, searching restlessly for different ways of doing familiar things, learned to extract butter without leaving buttermilk as a by-product? Or do the hogs get it all?

When I was a child we relied on time and gravity to separate cream from milk, as farmers had done for millennia. The milk, warm and foaming from the cows, was strained into big stoneware crocks and left to stand. When the cream had risen it was skimmed off with a perforated metal skimmer. Later we acquired a separator. It was faster, certainly; you emptied the pails directly into the separator tank, wound the crank, and — magic! — cream trickled from one spout, skim milk from another. In five or ten minutes the job was done.

But I prefer to remember the milk cellar as it was before mechanization. "Cellar" we called it, though it was sunk only two steps below the kitchen, off which it opened. Along the wall under the east window was a long bench or trestle for the milk crocks and jars and pails, the wooden bowls in which the butter was worked and the molds that shaped it for the market. The churn stood in mid-floor. The rest of the room was larder and storehouse. Some farms had separate dairies, often built over a spring or a stream. At 7,500 feet we had no need for extra refrigeration. In summer our cellar was delightfully cool, in winter shivery cold.

Another picture swims up from the deep past. Mama and Papa are sitting at the kitchen table having their bedtime snack. Between them is a crock of sour whole milk. They sprinkle it thickly with sugar and cinnamon, and then plunge in their spoons. The cream is a thick golden crust; it breaks to expose a semiliquid pool of clabber and whey. Does that sound unappetizing? I would adjure you to try it, not sparing the sugar and cinnamon, but I am afraid the exhortation would be futile. Where would you find a bowl of sour whole milk? In Norway or Denmark, perhaps; never in the land where yogurt, like buttermilk, is a laboratory culture.

The flower beds become my responsibility as soon as I am big enough to tote a sprinkling can. I fill it from the garden ditch that runs along the north side of the yard. It is brimming now; in the growing season the garden's thirst is insatiable. I squat on the bridge to submerge the can. I lug it, water slopping on my overalls, to the pansy bed that is Mama's special pride. And justifiably. The wooden frame built against the north end of the root cellar is filled a foot deep with soil from the river bottoms, thick black dirt enriched by the decay of centuries of leaves, fertilized every spring with stable manure. In that nourishing culture the pansies grow to enormous sizes — bigger than a silver dollar surely, maybe as big as a teacup — and luscious colors: deepest midnight purple, only a hint warmer than black; blues dark as a thundercloud, blues clear and luminous, bright butter yellows, browns tinged with carmine. Nobody else along the Big Laramie has pansies like those.

It takes several trips to drench them properly; the parched high-prairie air blots up moisture unbelievably fast. Then come the beds nearer the house: morning glories alongside the front door, their blue and scarlet and white trumpets already beginning to furl as the sun finds them; sweet peas clambering up the trellis of string along the north wall of the house; under the living room window a half dozen low-growing varieties, changing from year to year — phlox, pinks, candytuft, sweet alyssum, sweet william. And somewhere there are always nasturtiums. We children nip off the tips and suck the nectar, robbing the bees without a qualm.

Mama has a green thumb. (Doubtless that is only a metaphor for loving flowers enough to learn their habits and crotchets.) Somehow she finds time, in those sixteen-hour days with tasks crowding upon her in never-broken procession, to plan the garden, to study catalogues, order seeds, tuck them in the ground, even to slip out now and then to uproot weeds and loosen the soil around the tender young shoots with an old kitchen fork. Of course everybody helps, one way or another. But the skill, the leadership and the dedication are hers.

I help Papa too. Anyway I tag along, and he lets me run and fetch, hand him tools, hold something while he nails or staples or bolts it. I trot after him when he sets out, wearing rubber boots and carrying a long-handled shovel, to irrigate. That means following the diversion

38

ditches along the grain fields, shutting down one head gate, opening another, building little earth dams or breaking out others to channel the water to patches beginning to dry out. I am not much help at this, surely, but I'm happy to be along. The June sky is immense and blue, accented by only a few tufts of cotton and swatches of scrim. The young wheat, already up three inches, flows in long green indolent ripples. The mud squushes deliciously between my toes. (I don't need rubber boots; in summer I go barefoot.) Blackbirds with scarlet epaulettes, clustered in a young cottonwood, are repeating, always with the same rising intonation of delighted surprise, "Unc-le LEE! Un-cle LEE!"

Turning the grindstone, while Papa sharpens an ax or a scythe, is less fun; when he bears down to smooth out a nick it's work. I like blacksmithing better. The smithy is back of the icehouse, in a log building it shares with the carpenter shop. Papa has kindled a fire in the forge, fed it with smithy coal, pumped it to incandescence. It's my job to keep that central core at the same fierce roaring intensity while he shapes the metal on the anvil. It comes out of the forge as blindingly white as the fire itself, but cools rapidly under the hammer — bright red first, then dulling; it may have to be reheated several times before Papa is satisfied. I learn to pump the bellows handle with a steady rhythm so that the blower snores steadily and the fire never flags.

The smithy is an exciting place: the sooty walls, the blinding radiance, the leaping shadows, my father's gigantic against the low roof, the clang of hammer on anvil, the smell of coal smoke and hot metal, the sizzle and spout of steam when a hot horseshoe is plunged into water to be tempered. Exciting, and perhaps just a bit frightening.

39

There is one job, though, that I definitely do not like —
I cannot persuade myself, even after sixty years, that it
was anything but drudgery. That is weeding.

We have a big vegetable garden — peas, beans, lettuce,
beets, radishes, carrots, parsnips, rutabagas, I don't remember what else. It feeds us abundantly during the
latter half of the summer; the surplus, put down in sealed
glass jars or otherwise stored, carries us through the
winter.

The garden lies east of the house, beyond the currant
hedge. To my eyes, looking out morosely from my thirty-
six inches of altitude, its expanse seems infinite. Row
after row after row after row. And in every row swarm all
manner of uninvited guests, brash, tenacious, each one of
them to be uprooted laboriously.

You might think that weeding would be the ideal chore
for a small boy; obviously my parents think so. He is
close to his target area. His joints are supple; stooping or
squatting is easy for him. His fingers are small enough to
extract the intruder without bruising the sensitive plant.
He has no aversion to dirt; indeed, he rather likes it. And
he is capable, on occasion, of almost inexhaustible patience. He can squat for an hour watching a file of ants —
foraging party or construction crew — or observing the
maneuvers of a flotilla of tadpoles.

The trouble is that his patience is selective. Ants and
tadpoles fascinate him because they are constantly in
motion. Weeds are tediously static. More important,
when he does get tired of watching tadpoles he can leave
them unsupervised and do something else, whereas he is
stuck with the weeds until the last row, 'way out on the
horizon, is liberated. Only temporarily liberated, alas. By
next week there will be a lusty new crop.

The sun scorches down on neck and shoulders. Sweat
trickles stingingly into eye corners. A reconnoitering mos-

quito shouts "Tally-ho!" and drives in for the kill. His cohorts converge from all quarters of the compass, a skirling gray blizzard of tiny hypodermic needles. The quarry slaps, swishes furiously and futilely with his straw hat, smears on more mosquito dope; it seems only to whet their appetites. His hands and neck are splotched with gore, his own. Nobody ever successfully smote a mosquito on the wing; he is vulnerable only after he has spudded in and gorged himself.

After interminable hours the summons to dinner gives the young gardener a respite. But it is shadowed by the knowledge that the weeds will be waiting, minutely taller and tougher, when he comes out again. So will the mosquitoes.

No, I didn't like weeding. How much I didn't like it I realize anew as I write this, from the vividness of detail, the high emotional content of my recollections. But if I ever rebelled, the mutiny was quickly suppressed and not repeated. I learned early on that I could not pick and choose among chores. It was a useful lesson, though I'm afraid it took me a good many years to be properly grateful that I had learned it young.

4

School District No. 8

Still sits the schoolhouse by the road,
A ragged beggar sunning . . .

Ours, alas, is gone, pulled down and cannibalized long ago. Gone, too, are most of the generation that could instantly have identified those lines, and without prompting continued to the poem's climax:

"I'm sorry that I spelt the word.
I hate to go above you,
Because" — the brown eyes lower fell —
"Because, you see, I love you."

Do the pupils at the consolidated school, five miles down the highway toward town, read Whittier? And Longfellow, and Bryant, and Lowell? Or have the American classics, as we were taught to consider them, yielded to writers more "meaningful" and "relevant"?

Our schoolhouse was a one-room log structure, measuring perhaps twelve feet by twenty. It had four windows, two on a side, eight or ten desk-benches, double size but rarely occupied by more than one scholar, a table and chair for the teacher at the far end. A blackboard spanned the wall behind her. The room was heated by a round iron stove; the older boys were charged with keeping the woodbox filled and the fire roaring. Out in back was the outhouse, which served both sexes. When you had to go you raised your hand, one finger extended if your errand was a quickie, two fingers for more serious business.

We had a mile to walk. In spring and fall it was a pleasant mile. Most of the way we took the high road, along the bench, the meadows on our left, the grain fields on our right, lush and rippling, or shorn and sere, according to the month. We could mark the progress of the season in the color of the willows and cottonwoods along the creek and the more distant river, in the flow of the irrigation ditches, brim-full in May, a trickle among the rocks in September, in the blossoming and the fading of the flowers — flags and buttercups in the meadows, cactus and loco along the bench.

In winter it was not often so pleasant. The school was west of our ranch, and therefore upwind. We plodded along, chins buried in collars, earmuffs pulled low, mittened hands stiffening around lunch-pail handles, teary eyes and oozing noses icicled. Sometimes the gusts were so savage that we had to turn and wait until they had worked their tantrums out. The wind did us one favor, however; it broomed the bench clear of snow. Coming home we had it at our backs; it hustled us along, making the journey twice as fast.

In really rough weather Papa sometimes took us part or all of the way, in the hay sled. Not often. Our parents didn't believe in coddling, and we didn't expect to be coddled. I am wryly amused now when I hear the radio announce that the schools in our city and the suburbs will be closed because of a three-inch snowfall.

Though our school was humble in dimensions its span was ambitious — from the first grade through the eighth, from the ABCs to history and civics. That, at least, was its potential, though all eight grades were never populated at one time.

Study and recitation proceeded simultaneously. While a Sodergreen or a Wennerholm was stumbling through the capitals of the forty-five states (forty-six after the admission of Oklahoma in 1907), the youngest Olson sat with eyes shut, stuck in the multiplication table at seven times nine as usual. The scrape of pencils on slates told of others working out more complicated problems, or trying to diagram sentences. It was good training in concentration.

What did we learn? Readin', writin', and 'rithmetic, of course. Geography, physiology, history, civics. A smattering of art: we sketched books and ink bottles in black and white, copied flowers splashily in watercolor. The Perry Prints, handed out to reward punctuality, attendance and scholarship, introduced us to the Masters — Raphael, Rubens, Rembrandt, Murillo, Landseer and Rosa Bonheur.

Our textbook in Language — which embraced both readin' and writin' — was *Stepping Stones to Literature,* in The Riverside Series, and published by Silver, Burdett and Company. McGuffey was two generations back. In between had come Barnes' New National Readers, published by the American Book Company, New York and Chicago. There were still copies of Barnes around; he must have been displaced only a few years earlier. Since I devoured leftover Barnes at the same time I was trudging

44

along *Stepping Stones,* and supplemented both from the family bookshelves, I am not sure which introduced us to "Kentucky Belle," "Curfew Must Not Ring Tonight," "Driving Home the Cows," "Bingen on the Rhine," "The Legend of Bregenz" and similar perishable classics.

There was of course solider fare in *Stepping Stones.* We must have sampled *Hiawatha* and *Evangeline* and *Snowbound* and *Thanatopsis* and *Rip Van Winkle,* at the least, in the later stages of our pilgrimage. Lacking a copy of the Riverside Series I can't be certain which works I first encountered in District No. 8, which were administered to us in high school, and which I discovered for myself.

Martha and Hattie and I inherited Papa's appetite for poetry, and memorized yards of it. Oscar did not. His lack of interest was hardened into lifelong abhorrence by one teacher who oversold the product.

The day's reading included Poe's "Raven," and Oscar's stumbling recital, with frequent pauses for prompting, did not satisfy Miss Pryor, who had studied elocution. I wasn't there, and I can only imagine the dialogue, but it may have been something like this:

MISS PRYOR: Try to read with more *feeling,* Oscar. This is *poetry.* A very *dramatic* poem. Now let me hear that last verse again.

OSCAR (*in the same monotone, a bit more sullenly*): ... Ghastly grim and ancient raven wandering from the nightly shore tell me what thy — thy lordly name is on the Night's Plu — Plu — Plu-to-ni-an shore quoth the raven nevermore . . .

MISS PRYOR: No, *no,* Oscar! Try to *imagine* the scene. There's the raven, up there on the shelf (*indicating, in the absence of a bust of Pallas, the bookcase at the back of the room*) ...

OSCAR: I don't know what a raven is.

MISS PRYOR: Why, it's — well, it's like a crow, only larger. Imagine a crow, if it helps you.

OSCAR: I don't see no crow.

MISS PRYOR: *Any* crow, Oscar. "I don't see any crow."
OSCAR: I don't neither.

Oscar never did see the raven, or its smaller cousin. And never again, throughout his more than eighty years, did he willingly read another poem.

Of physiology I remember a few scraps helpful in crossword puzzles. A bone of the arm? "Ulna" if the space calls for four letters, "radius" if it's six. Of the leg? "Femur" or "humerus," most probably; now and then they sneak in "tibia" or "fibula," just to keep you alert. I pause, and try to visualize that pictured skeleton, with name tags strung around the margin of the page. Two more words surface: "clavicle" and "scapula." I wonder why the puzzlers neglect them.

I recall much more vividly the book's preachment on the evils of intemperance. In livid color it showed three versions of the digestive organs. The first pictured those of a total abstainer; they were clean, wholesome and no doubt superbly functional. The second set, identified as belonging to a moderate drinker, were already disquietingly distempered. The third, horribly contorted and cooked to a furnace red, must have been sketched at the autopsy of a Skid Row cadaver. It was meant to terrify, and it did. When someone, I presume from the W.C.T.U., came around with the Pledge, I signed willingly, and so, I believe, did Hattie and Martha.

I kept that Pledge for a good many years. All through the Prohibition era it protected me against the enticements of fusel oil and wood alcohol. The Eighteenth Amendment had been repealed for some time before I was able to convince my conscience that our childhood commitment was no longer binding.

Geography was much simpler in the first decade of the century; there were fewer of everything. I remember a calendar showing the flags and the rulers of the nations of the world; it was easy to get them all on one sheet. I must have pored over it often, because even now I can picture clearly the faces of Armand Fallières, President of France; Franz Joseph, Emperor of Austria and Hungary; Peter of Serbia, Edward VII of England, Mutsuhito of Japan, Porfirio Díaz of Mexico, Oscar II of Sweden.

We plodded dutifully across the map, memorizing facts: population, capital and other cities, climate, principal products, major rivers and mountains; bounded by what countries or states. Most of this we forgot as soon as our examination papers were graded. It seemed to have very little to do with us.

It was a simpler world, and we had no premonition that even before our school days were over it was to be rocked by the first convulsions of a half century (or more) of fissuring and fragmentation. We could not anticipate the grim lesson that a succession of wars would teach us, and our children and grandchildren: that no place on the globe is so remote that events there may not some day affect them.

The history we learned was equally parochial and simplistic. It was also chauvinistic. Our country was the best of all possible countries. Its wars had been righteous, and we had won them gloriously. Its heroes — Washington, Jefferson, Lincoln, Grant — were several sizes larger than life, and like their portraits remote and marmoreal, despite the fables concocted to humanize them. The founding of the country took up a disproportionate amount of space. The Revolutionary, Mexican and Civil wars were described battle by battle. There was not much room left for social ferment, class conflict, the clash of interests and ideologies, even if the writers and editors had considered those appropriate fare for young minds.

In a term that was to become popular half a century later it was essentially WASP history. It recounted the colonization of the eastern seaboard by Englishmen — with a nod to the Dutch — (their right to subjugate or slaughter the "savages" already resident there was of course never questioned), the breakaway from the tyrannous mother country, the westward expansion of the new nation, still English in language, manners and traditions. The later tides of immigration were treated perfunctorily if at all.

Yet ours was a community of Johnsons, Olsons, Sodergreens, Lunds, Ostermans, Berglunds, with only a small ethnic minority of Anglo-Saxons. Pupils in District No. 8 were likely to enter the first grade speaking the heavily accented English they heard at home, or occasionally none at all. A more imaginative educational program could have exploited that background. History might have meant more if we had been reminded that our own parents, and we ourselves, were examples of the process that had made America and Americans. Geography would have been less dull if the teacher had taken our ancestral countries as a point of departure, and drawn on parental reminiscences to populate Europe, and by extension other continents, with human beings as well as with rivers, mountains, exports and imports.

There was history all around us, indeed, but it hadn't got into the textbooks yet, and to my recollection no teacher thought of fitting it into the curriculum. The immigrant wagons had crawled along the Overland Trail only a few miles away. There had been Indian battles and massacres just across the mountains to south and west. Laramie's own story was history, rather gaudy history. When we went to town we saw men who had helped make it. Surely some of them might have been coaxed to tell us their stories. Old-timers are notoriously garrulous. If now and then one of them had forgotten where he was and who was listening we wouldn't have heard anything worse than we heard around the bunkhouse.

I have already confessed that I have no aptitude for figures. I stumbled through Numbers and trudged on into Arithmetic with no calamitous pratfalls, but it was drudgery all the way. Again I find consolation in the relevancy test. Mightn't the going have been less arduous if the book had posed problems we could reasonably expect to encounter? In the upper grades we learned, or tried to learn, how to figure the quantity of wallpaper or carpeting required for a room with certain specifications. How many ranches in 1910 had wall-to-wall carpeting? And how often, if ever, did you paper a parlor? Once, to my recollection; our parents managed it competently without consulting the textbook, lathering the strips, spread out on a wooden trestle, with homemade paste and matching them snugly. But every winter a rancher had to calculate the number of tons of hay in a stack — hay he was selling, if he had a surplus, or buying, if he found he was running short. No arithmetic book I ever saw contained that formula. But Dad had set it down carefully in one of his notebooks, and if you're curious, here it is:

Add width and overtop, then divide by 4. Multiply result by itself, then multiply by length and divide by 422. The result will be number of tons in stack.

In one other respect our education was grievously limited, lamentably false, though we were cheerfully unaware, then and for decades afterward, of that particular shortcoming. We grew up as racists.

49

The history we studied was the history of white America. The Negro appeared occasionally, to be sure, as a picturesque figure in plantation life, an essential component of the Southern economy. Only once did he move to the center of the stage, and then in a passive role, as a *casus belli*. We were taught, of course, that slavery was evil. We read *Uncle Tom's Cabin*, we shuddered at its horrors, we hated Simon Legree zestfully. We assumed, however, that the Emancipation Proclamation had put an end to all that, and nothing in our teaching or our experience prompted us to question that assumption. Books (*Uncle Remus, The Little Colonel*), music (Stephen Foster and "coon songs" such as "Rufus Rastus Johnson Brown"), the games we played — all these perpetuated the Southern myth of Negro inferiority. Darkey, colored man, nigger, whatever you called him — we had no notion that the words might be offensive — he was basically a comic figure, childlike, obsequious, lovable, loyal, but still comic.

Romping in the school yard we chanted:

> *Eeny, meeny, miney, mo.*
> *Catch a nigger, let him go . . .*

or

> *Smarty, smarty!*
> *Had a party,*
> *Nobody came but*
> *An ole black darkey.*

or

> *Nigger, nigger, never die;*
> *Kinky hair and shining eye.*

We had seen only one colored man in our young lives — Thornt Biggs, foreman at a ranch down the river, regarded generally as a first-rate cowhand and "a damn white nigger." I saw him only once or twice, in the annual County Fair parade. He looked like any other cowboy, only somewhat darker of skin. Had I been more perceptive, I might have wondered how that quiet competence accorded with the Uncle Remus myth figure. I regret to confess that it didn't.*

Teachers came and went. Rarely did one stay more than a year. Some were local girls, recent high school or normal school graduates, who later would marry and rear children and become grandmothers and eventually lie in Green Hill cemetery. Others found their way to District No. 8 from farther away, by what process I never learned. Some of these were old, by a child's measure — desiccated spinsters whose dreary odyssey from one shabby rural school to another I can now recognize was pathetic. Some were young, and may just possibly have read *The Virginian* and headed west in the hope there would still be a few males unclaimed.

The position could have offered few other inducements. The salary was forty-five dollars a month, out of which the teacher paid thirty dollars for board and room. Father argued vigorously but vainly for an increase. "Hell," he

---

* Though Thornt Biggs was the only Negro I knew about, I learned some years later that there were several others in Laramie whose acquaintance I had been too young to make. They were a redoubtable madam named Susie Parker and her associates, whose place of business was one of the most popular on First Street. There was a story, perhaps apocryphal, that Susie was once on the witness stand being questioned about a shooting at her emporium. The county attorney, seeking to establish the circumstances, asked: "Now, Mrs. Parker, would you please describe to the jury how the furniture is arranged in your parlor?"
Susie replied with a fat chuckle: "Why, Judge, you know just as well as I do how my parlor is arranged."

once exploded to the school board, "I pay a man that much for shoveling manure!"

If the new teacher was even moderately attractive word got around. It was remarkable how many fellows, from upriver and downriver and even from over on the Pioneer Canal, would find errands to take them past the schoolhouse at recess time or after hours. It was interesting also to note how skittishly their mounts behaved. Even a staid cow horse will do a few crow-hops if spurred in the flank. Once, two young scamps — I regret to say that one of them was my brother — roped the doorstep and dragged it off across the prairie, though they had the grace, after an interval of teasing, to replace it.

Of the seven teachers who guided me through that many grades I remember only two with any clarity.

One I shall call Miss Hawks, though that was not her name. She was one of the pathetic spinsters, gray and dim. I remember her because she had a favorite poem, and wanted us to appreciate it too. She would start off gallantly, her frail voice surprisingly resonant:

> *I want free life, and I want fresh air,*
> *And I sigh for the canter after the cattle,*
> *The crack of the whip . . .*

There she derailed. She would back up and try again:

> *The crack of the whip . . .*
> *The crack of the whip . . .*

She never got any further. There was a memory block she could not surmount or bypass.

I believe it was Miss Hawks who once enlisted Martha's services as chaperone. The Charles Sodergreens, with whom she was boarding, were to be away overnight.

52

Would Martha come home with her so that she wouldn't be left alone with the hired man? Martha was willing, probably delighted. She liked being helpful, and she was always ready for any new experience. So at four o'clock, off they went together.

Here, I grieve to confess, my recollections and my brother's differ sharply. I was almost sure I remembered the two . . . (I grope for a noun encompassing a ten-year-old tomboy and a woman well into the fifties. Nowadays one would say without hesitation "girls"; the upper limit of girlhood has been extended to infinity. "Damsels," perhaps? It has the proper Victorian flavor. Better still, maybe, James Fenimore Cooper's biologically specific term, "females.") Anyway, I thought I remembered the two of them arriving at school next morning, virtue presumably intact, reputations unblemished.

Oscar says firmly: "No, it wasn't that way at all. When you and Hattie got home and told what had happened the Old Man hit the roof. He went straight up to Sodergreens and brought Martha home with him. I don't know what he said to Miss Hawks, but he sure gave Martha a dressing down."

I didn't, at the time, understand what all the fuss was about. But in retrospect I am reasonably confident that Miss Hawks's good name was not damaged.

Poor Miss Hawks, who panicked at the thought of a night on the ranch unchaperoned, and yet could declaim, with a fervor one would never have suspected in that withered personality, her yearning for free life, fresh air, and the canter after the cattle. Years later, stumbling on Frank Desprez's "Lasca" in some anthology, I learned what happened after that crack of the whip that always brought Miss Hawks up short. Lasca was a Mexican girl whom the narrator had loved rapturously. One day they were overtaken by a bunch of stampeding longhorns, and

Lasca, to save her lover's life, threw herself atop of him and was ground to pulp by the thundering hoofs.

It was only then that I began to appreciate that there may have been more to Miss Hawks than met the mocking eyes of her pupils. And perhaps to her predecessors and successors whom I have characterized so callously. How many of them too were starved romantics? And what fun Freudian psychiatry could have with that memory block that locked tight at the crack of the whip!

Frieda Wagner I remember for quite different reasons. She was an outlander — from Missouri, I think. She was tall. She was handsome. And smart. And tough. How tough I learned in the first day or two, and by the end of the week I was telling Mama dolefully: "Teacher has a pick on me."

My trouble was that, being moderately bright and incorrigibly bookish, I was accustomed to being teacher's pet. Miss Wagner, spotting me immediately as a conceited little prig, must have set deliberately about deflating me. She treated me with cool professionalism, just like my schoolmates. She called me to order just as peremptorily when my attention drifted, as it often did. If at recess time I headed for the bookcase in the back of the room she shooed me outdoors to play with the others.

I was grieved, I was resentful, I moped. But I got very little sympathy at home. In those primitive times it was not the fashion to ascribe Junior's difficulties to the incompetence of the teacher and the archaic inflexibility of the System. So I stopped whining, buckled down to work, and eventually began to realize that Frieda Wagner was the best teacher I had ever had. She even managed to give me some notion of arithmetic, which nobody before her had succeeded in doing.

Good-looking, spirited, self-assured, she had plenty of

54

beaux. Though I never guessed it at the time, Oscar was sorely smitten. She gave him no encouragement. Probably she thought him too young; he must have been about nineteen, and she a few years older. If she was looking for a Virginian none of the candidates measured up. She didn't return next fall and I never knew what became of her.

Teachers boarded at one of the nearby ranches — usually with the Oscar Sodergreens, who had a big house with room to spare. Once a year, protocol required the incumbent to pay ceremonial visits to the homes of her other pupils. These were painful occasions. Mama would scrub and polish us until we glistened and felt as stiff as sheets hung out to dry in January. Dad would come in early from work, get out mirror and razor and shave away the bristles, put on a clean shirt. Dinner would be special — and Mama's special was indeed something. We minded our manners with extra care.

I can't remember the conversation. It didn't, happily, deal with our shortcomings; that would have been impolite. I suspect it was stilted. I know we were relieved when Teacher arose, and said she'd had a lovely time but she must be going.

Getting her home was sometimes a problem. It would be dark by then, and it was a murky mile-and-a-half to Sodergreens — no distance to us natives, but frightening to a lady from Iowa whose imagination could conjure up a redskin behind every willow clump and translate a coyote's evensong into the hunting cry of a wolf pack.

If the visitor hadn't brought her own transportation Papa would hook up a team and drive her home. Papa, or a reluctant Oscar. My brother remembers, with reprehensible relish, one occasion in particular when he was drafted as escort. Oscar disapproved of teachers generally, as a matter of principle, but he did distinguish among various representatives of the category. There were a few he was prepared to tolerate. Tonight's guest was not one of those. She had ridden down on Sonny Sodergreen's horse, Nubbins, who was in the stable contentedly munching oats and gossiping with Oscar's Dan in the next stall. Oscar saddled both horses and took them up to the house. Let him tell the rest:

"The minute she was in the saddle I touched Dan with the spurs and he took off. Of course Nubbins took off after us. We went up the hill hell-bent for election. She was bouncing all over the saddle, hanging on for dear life, and hollering. I bet that was the fastest ride she ever had."

I have to recognize that my brother's behavior before he left school — shortly thereafter his attitude toward teachers underwent an astonishing reversal — bordered on juvenile delinquency. During one Christmas holiday week he and Sonny, his boon companion in scalawaggery, found themselves in the neighborhood of the schoolhouse while hunting rabbits, and decided to look in. The door wasn't locked; nobody locked doors in those days.

It's remarkable how fascinating a schoolhouse, Poe's Pit and Pendulum for five days of the week, can become during holidays. Emptiness and silence. No shuffle of restless feet. No drone of recitation. No scrape of chalk on blackboard or pencil on slate. The familiar room is strange; it challenges exploration. You explore. Furtively at first, treading softly, lowering your voice by long habit. Then more confidently. Then, as the intoxication of defying taboos possesses you, with boisterous delight.

I can imagine Oscar and Sonny that day. They open one desk after another, hold up its hoarded treasures to daylight and ridicule. The teacher's desk does not escape;

nothing is sacred. They scrawl ribaldries on the blackboard. They test the echo with words they didn't learn from any textbook.

Eventually, having exhausted the obvious possibilities, they pause for a reconnaisance.

Sonny says reflectively, "I never did like that picture."

Oscar: "Me either."

In tacit accord they raise their .22s. They fire, almost in unison. They reload and fire again.

When the offending picture (Oscar doesn't remember what it portrayed, or what excess of patriotism, piety or sentimentality aroused his loathing) is adequately perforated, they cast about for further diversion.

"Hey, look!" exclaims Sonny.

He is holding up a miniature wooden keg, no bigger than a boy's fist. In the first decade of the century tacks were packed in such kegs. Sonny sets it on the stove. They back off and take aim. The result is successful beyond expectation. The keg virtually explodes. Tacks spray out like shrapnel.

It is an eminently satisfactory ending to their sport. More would be anticlimax.

When school reopened after New Year the miscreants were quickly identified. The circle of possible suspects was small, and the trail was easy to pick up. I don't know what happened to Sonny, but more than sixty years later Oscar recalled vividly: "The Old Man sure gave me a licking." It must have been something special, that licking, to sting after sixty years.

5

Going Places

THOUGH OUR NORMAL AMBIT was defined by the boundaries of the ranch, and the quarter mile promontory extending to the schoolhouse, it widened now and then: a Sunday visit to neighbors, sometimes as far away as the Berglunds or Ostermans on the Pioneer Canal, or the Nottages, at the far end of Sheep Mountain; a dance, at one of the few ranch houses big enough to accommodate two "squares" — four couples each; a neighborhood rodeo. (We didn't call it that; the word had not worked its way north from the border.)

And once a year, perhaps, a trip to Town.

"Town" is twenty-two miles away. The round trip takes two days — a morning on the road inbound, afternoon, evening and forenoon in Laramie, home next day in time for the chores and supper.

We set out in the spring wagon immediately after breakfast. Mama sits beside Papa in front; Hattie, Martha and I fit snugly into the back seat, elbowing and bickering occasionally, but too excited to be really quarrelsome. (Oscar is left behind to do the chores. He will have his turn later.)

Our route leads across corners of the Hammond place and the Riverside ranch until it climbs out to the prairie and joins the highroad. The meadows are still awash and in flower. Great yellow sweeps of buttercups. Blue flags clustered in the lowlands, erect and stately. Shooting stars, delicately pink, frail and patrician among those sturdier companions. The willow thickets simmer with birds — sparrows, goldfinches, blackbirds — take your pick among three patterns, plain, red-winged, and yellow-throated. A killdeer repeats his name plaintively, insisting on his identity but sounding dubious about its being recognized. Meadowlarks perched on fence posts keep exclaiming "Oh, geewhilliker-whilliker!" We feel the same way.

"Meadows look good this year," Papa remarks approvingly.

Out on the highway the landscape changes: green-gray sagebrush instead of meadow grass, and earth-hugging upland flowers. "Highway" is a courtesy title; it would not be recognized as such today. We jog along double ruts; grading is years ahead, blacktop decades in the future. The ruts are deeper here, though, and hard gravel except for patches of gumbo that turn to grease or glue in wet weather. There are several sets in the wide lane, most of them too deeply gouged to be usable except in meeting or passing.

We check off the landmarks. Nelson's road ranch. Twelve-Mile Hill, from which we catch our first glimpse of Laramie, as yet only a smudge of smoke. The Soda lakes, shallow and fringed with alkali. Papa points out a flotilla of ducks cruising indolently, indifferent to the brackish water.

Laramie is solidifying out of the smoke. Martha shouts, "I see the University tower!" There it is, an inverted exclamation point punctuating the flat sprawl of the town.

The horses quicken their trot. We rattle dashingly by the old penitentiary, across the river bridge, making a satisfactory clatter on the plank flooring, past the abandoned brick plant, left into Cedar Street.

And here we are!

Aunt Kari has been watching for us. She is on the doorstep as Papa pulls the team to a halt. Agnes and Sena are close behind her. We children tumble out of the wagon, gabbling news from the river, questions about life in the city. Mama and her sister greet each other more sedately. Papa unloads our overnight gear and the gifts Mama has brought — butter, eggs, a glass or two of jelly — and drives off to stable the team. Aunt Kari calls after him that dinner will be waiting when he gets back.

Of "town" proper, the business section across the tracks, I can offer not a first impression but rather a montage. More people in one block than we saw in a year upriver. Delivery wagons clattering along behind bony horses. An ice wagon, its gunnysack-swathed cargo spilling dark scribbles in the dust. Carriages, buggies, ranch wagons like ours, bicycles. Now and then an automobile, belching noise and stench. And occasionally one that didn't belch — a Stanley Steamer, hissing along in a wraith of vapor, or an electric, soundless except for the growl of hard tires on gravel.

The electric looks like a sedan chair, and the driver might have belonged to the age of sedan chairs. She — did any male ever drive an electric? — is obviously what I would have called a grande dame had I known the words. I remember her, rightly or wrongly, in the lavender affected, then as now, by elderly ladies, with a small, flowered hat set firmly on white hair. She sits erect and serene at the tiller; moving a stately five miles an hour, she surveys the crowd benignly, and now and then dispenses a gracious bow.

The serious business that brings us children to town is to be outfitted with clothes. Shoes, of course; Papa can resole them as expertly as any cobbler, but we keep outgrowing them. Dresses for the girls, or goods from which Mama can make dresses. And hats; girls still wear hats, and keep them firmly in place with a rubber band under the chin. Sunbonnets, for everyday wear. For me, overalls, the kind with a bib, and pants for dress occasions, knee length, with decorative buttons at the side. Stockings for everybody, long, black, heavy, made for warmth and durability.

I am proud when I can accompany Papa on his errands. He seems to know nearly everybody; he is always being stopped for a chat. I wriggle with embarrassment under the ponderous affability that older people turn upon children, if they deign to notice them.

"This your boy, Hans? What's your name, young feller? . . . Named after Teddy Roosevelt, I s'pose. [I wasn't.] Figger on being President yourself some day?"

I never figger out the answer to that. He doesn't expect one. Having done his duty by me, he resumes man talk with Dad.

Our route leads eventually to the barbershop, where I perch precariously on a board across the chair arms while my pate is mown to a whitish stubble. Papa supervises the job from the next chair, where he too is getting trimmed, not quite so close to the skin, and shaved. For that the barber produces from the open cupboard inside the mirror a shaving mug labeled "Hans Olson" in sweeping Spencerian script. Everybody who is anybody has his own shaving mug, even if it is used only a few times a year. Between trips to town Papa shaves himself on Sunday mornings, and cuts my hair whenever he decides I need it.

Errands completed, we return to Aunt Kari's for supper, and in the evening we go to the movies. (I doubt if that abbreviation was in use yet; I think we said "moving pictures.") Laramie has two theaters, and sometimes, with reckless extravagance, we go to both. At ten cents a head (in a couple of years it will be a quarter) the extravagance isn't ruinous.

For that we get three one-reelers — usually one romance, one thriller, one comedy — and an illustrated song. The romance, more often than not, concerns an Indian maiden and her brave, played by actors properly coppertoned but undisguisably Caucasian of feature. We find no incongruity in this. We are comfortably ambivalent toward the Red Man — as history and literature are ambivalent, counterbalancing Sitting Bull with Pocahontas and Sacajawea, Buffalo Bill's fictional foes with Hiawatha and Ramona. I associate the thrillers with Bronco Billy Anderson and the comedies with Flora Finch and John Bunny, though I suspect they came along a few years later.

And after this double portion of entertainment Papa and Mama, in a final flourish of extravagance, sometimes treat us to ice cream before we wobble drowsily back across the tracks to bed.

Two of my enduring memories, however, have nothing to do with the glitter and glamor of city life. (Laramie's population was about seven thousand.)

One is of standing outside my uncle's house watching the trains go by, two blocks away, and being able, if I was lucky, to run into the house shrieking, "Mama, Mama, I saw 1288!" That was the locomotive Papa had driven many times between Laramie and Rawlins, obsolescent now and demoted to coolie service as a switch engine.

The other memory is of my first awed glimpse of Laramie's First Family and the mansion that was our equivalent of a manor house. Word had come to the ranch somehow that Mrs. Ivinson would be pleased if my mother would call the next time she happened to be in town. And would she perhaps bring with her some of that currant jelly that everybody talked about?

Edward and Jane Ivinson had come to Laramie in 1868 with the railroad. They were English, though he had been born in the West Indies. He started out as a contractor getting out ties for the Union Pacific, branched out into merchandising, established the First National Bank. They throve mightily. Their wealth was rumored to be fabulous; their beneficences kept apace.

So I found myself trudging up the long walk to the great turreted stone house, which sat majestically in grounds occupying an entire block between Thornburgh (later Ivinson) and University Avenues. I seem to remember that Mama hesitated briefly before marching boldly to the front door; she was better acquainted with the servants' entrance.

One of the Ivinson granddaughters opened the door.

"Why, Bertha! How *nice* to see you!"

She called my mother, nearly twice her age, by her first name! I was outraged.

I try vainly to visualize Laramie's "social matriarch," as Mary Lou Pence calls her in *The Laramie Story*. The picture that comes up, however, is unmistakably Helen Hayes as Queen Victoria at the time of the Jubilee.

I remember little of the conversation. I presume that Mama was questioned about her life on the ranch, and that she in turn wanted to hear all about the girls, who had plagued and teased her when she was their mother's cook and housekeeper. I suppose I was subjected to the usual perfunctory inquisition, to which I mumbled monosyllabic answers. Did somebody bring out port and cookies, as would have been etiquette? I can't recall. Doubtless I peered furtively around while the others chatted, but I remember nothing of the opulence and splendor amid which we presumably sat.

But I do remember Mama's worrying, as we walked back downtown, that Mrs. Ivinson appeared to have been expecting something considerably more than the pint jar of currant jelly we had brought her.

American literature is full of country dances:

The quick feet beating the puncheon floor,
And the fiddle squealing and squealing,
Till the dried herbs rattled above the door
And the dust rose up to the ceiling.

There were no puncheon floors on Laramie River ranches, no squirrel rifles stacked in the corners, and if a song from that distant time were to intrude on my slumbers it would not be "Money Musk" but most likely "Red Wing." But "The Ballad of William Sycamore" catches the sound and the flavor, and *The Virginian* fills in the details, with some fictional embellishment. I shall spare you still another account, which would be different in no important particular.

I went whenever the family went; there were no baby-sitters. Though I may have been towed onto the floor now and then as I grew older, my memories are mostly those of an onlooker — an onlooker who often blacked out just when the revelry was gaining momentum, and woke up in the first watery light to find himself lying crosswise on a bed along with several of his peer group. How he and they got there he could only surmise. One moment he had been sitting on a chair in the living room, couples swirling past, inches from his toes, the nasal scrape of the fiddle, the caller's singsong, the shuffle and stamp of feet, blurring into one droning rhythm; blurring and dimming . . . And the next moment there he and those unchosen companions were, laid out like sausages on a griddle. And beyond the closed door Teed Larson was swinging into "Home, Sweet Home."

Then the long drive home through the early morning chill. Everybody drowsy, except the horses; they, headed for the barn and oats, step out briskly. Dad lets them set their pace. We doze, we wake up when the wagon stops for a gate. Martha or Hattie — they hadn't been wallflowers like me — recalls some incident of the night and we giggle over it. We doze again. The stamp and shuffle still drum through our heads; the squeal of Teed's fiddle interweaves with the matins of meadowlark and blackbird.

We shall be talking it over for a week, or a fortnight, perhaps until the next dance.

Rodeos now are a branch of the entertainment business, a special kind of circus. Big business, too, like football, baseball, golf and tennis. The practitioners are professionals, who follow a circuit stretching from the Mexican border north to Canada and east to the Atlantic seaboard, and spanning a good part of the year. Some may have ranches as home base or hobby, but they don't work at ranching; that's a full-time job.

But it all started with informal tests of skill like the bronc-riding in the dawn flush after a country dance broke up, or Sunday afternoon gatherings at which local cowboys — and cowgirls — matched their skills and settled arguments about whose horse was fastest. Gatherings like the one at Osterman's ranch, when Martha competed in the cowgirl race.

We knew Martha was good, expert and fearless. But we had doubts about Patsy. He was built more like a miniature beer-wagon horse than a Derby winner. And though we had seen him, once under way, overhaul Buck easily, we wondered whether he would have time to work up momentum in so short a distance. It was surely less than a quarter mile.

They lined up, four or five girls, ranging in age from twelve to thirty-plus, on assorted mounts, none as chubby as Patsy. The horses were fretful and skittish. One broke prematurely and his rider had some trouble swinging him into line again. The rawboned bay alongside Pat laid back his ears as if to say, "Don't crowd me, Runt." Pat's ears went back too, and he feinted a short jab. The bay veered off a step. Nobody intimidated Pat.

Finally the starter, having coaxed them into not too ragged a line, yelled "Go!"

Spurred heels dug into ribs. They were off. In a pack, which began at once to break up. The rawboned bay moved out in front. But where were Martha and Pat?

In last place, a length behind.

"Come on, Pat!" Hattie and I wailed. "Come on!"

The gap was two lengths now. But . . . wait a second. Yes, it was beginning to shrink.

Pat was picking up momentum. Martha was crouched over his neck like an Indian. I was sure, from the many times I had raced with her, that she was talking to him, exhorting and encouraging.

"Come on, Pat!" Hattie and I shrieked.

"Come on, Pat!" Martha was crooning into his ear.

Pat came on. His takeoff was sluggish, but his acceleration was sensational. The gap had disappeared. He was third now. No, second. He was pulling up alongside the bay.

"Go it, Pat!" we yelled. "Go it!"

He went it. At the finish line he was a good length in front.

They trotted back to the judges' stand, Martha hatless, disheveled, flushed, grinning, Pat looking rather bored. Martha delved into the pocket of her divided skirt.

"Here's the sugar I promised you."

It was the proudest day of my life, up to then. Maybe ever.

6

Two Minutes of "Miserere"

ONE DECEMBER AFTERNOON Papa brought home from town with the pre-Christmas load an Edison phonograph, vintage 1906 or '07. We watched, dithering, as he assembled it. There was a distressful minute when he discovered that the dealer had forgotten to include the metal derrick that supported the big morning-glory horn. No matter; a string attached to a hook in the ceiling would serve until the next trip to town. He fitted the transmitter into its cradle in the overarching arm, inserted the crank in one end of the box and wound up the spring, took a black wax cylinder from its padded cardboard container, slid it carefully on the metal cylinder atop the box, closed the gate, and moved a lever in front of the carriage. The cylinder began to revolve. Very gently he lowered the needle to the wax.

Out of the morning glory came a voice, tiny, tinny but understandable: "Violin solo, 'El Miserere' from *Il*

Trovatore, played by Mr. Charles d'Almaine. Edison record."

That was an ecstatic moment. We had long envied the Sodergreens, the Nottages and other neighbors who had already replaced the primitive music box that ground out grating noises from a spiked cylinder activated by hand. Now we were as good as anybody. Better, in a way, because our phonograph wasn't a present from doting parents. It was our very own — Oscar's, Hattie's, Martha's and mine, bought with our own money.

We had obtained the purchase price through a somewhat complicated series of transactions. Some time previously, on one of the many occasions when cash was in short supply, Dad had borrowed ten dollars from his aunt, our *Tante* Christie. When he tried to repay the loan she told him "Forget it," or whatever the Norwegian equivalent would have been. He persisted. Finally she suggested, "Well, give it to the children, then."

So we had ten dollars among us. If we had been city children we might have squandered our shares on candy, hair ribbons, toys. Being ranch kids, with little access to such extravagances, we decided (or were persuaded) to invest our capital and watch it grow. Naturally we invested in livestock. She was a heifer calf, and she grew into a cow named Maggie.

But our vision of multiplying wealth — cow, calf, more calves, heifers growing into cows and producing still more calves in a geometrical progression — was not to be realized. Maggie was barren.

When it became clear beyond doubt that she never would be a mother, we regretfully put her on the market. She brought thirty dollars, not a bad return on a ten-dollar investment, particularly in view of the fact that Dad had charged us nothing for pasture, hay or commissions. In fact, I suspect parental guidance throughout the transaction, though the decision to spend our thirty dollars on a phonograph may well have been ours.

For the first few weeks we played it incessantly. Anyway, Hattie, Martha and I did. Oscar soon lost interest, and we bought him out. (Now where did we get the $7.50?) The pattern of our winter evenings changed radically — as television was to change the life style of a later generation. We rarely played casino now. We read fewer books. Our school homework — fortunately there wasn't much of it — suffered. We stayed up later. Once at least Papa, already in bed, called out to Hattie: "Now just two more records (and he specified which ones, his own favorites); then go to bed."

We learned quickly how to operate it correctly: to dust the records with the brush provided for that purpose, to let the cylinder gain speed before lowering the needle, to rewind the spring after every second record. If you forgot, the sound slid down into an ursine growl until you cranked it back into pitch.

The record boxes were identified only by a number on the lid, though the titles were imprinted on one end of the cylinder. It was a couple of years before Mr. Edison thought of listing title and artist on the container. We soon memorized the numbers, and could instantly pick out the selection we wanted. For a good many years, even after we were grown and scattered, we could still do it; we made a game of it when we met.

Our record library grew with every trip to town, until it numbered nearly one hundred and fifty. Its range was wide; our tastes were eclectic; we liked almost anything. I can detect Papa's nostalgia for the sea in the accordion and fiddle numbers — "Sailor's Hornpipe Medley," "Sterling Castle and Harvest Home — Strathspey and Reel." Hattie recalls, however, that the few classic and semiclassic records — "El Miserere," for instance — were also his selection.

Mama liked hymns: "Shall We Gather at the River?" "My Faith Looks Up to Thee," "Sun of My Soul." Both enjoyed dance music, two-steps, polkas and waltzes.

We sampled nearly everything Mr. Edison offered in his monthly *Phonogram*. Much of it, I recognized later, came from the vaudeville stage. Stand-up comedians (though they probably weren't called that): Schultz ("On How to Bring Up Children"); Flanagan (". . . in a Restaurant" . . . "on a Farm" . . . "Flanagan's Motor Car"). Whistlers, who sang the lyric and trilled and warbled the second chorus, with some orchestral help: Helen Trix, in "A Chip Off the Block," and Joe Belmont, "Whippoorwill Song."

And skits, a snatch of dialogue or monologue setting up a situation, a chorus resolving it. For example, "How Matt Got the Mitten":

GIRL (*to audience, confidentially*): Matt's coming tonight, for his answer. I could learn to like him, but his folks are so shiftless.

Then, after Matt has pleaded his case, her verdict:

I don't like your family.
They don't make a hit with me.
I don't want to bother
Lending money to your father
While your ma's relations live on me.
I don't think your Uncle John
Ever had a collar on.
You want me for your wife
But when I get fixed for life
I wa-a-a-ant an orphan!

71

That was the incomparable Ada Jones, pronouncing sentence on Len Spencer, her partner in dozens of records. Len didn't always get the mitten. Often the ending was happy, as in "Meet Me Down at the Corner" ("and bring your heart with you") and "Peaches and Cream":

LEN: Oh I have thought of a dandy scheme.
　　　I'll be the peaches . . .
ADA: And I'll be the cream.
BOTH: Oh, what a beautiful dream!
　　　Hello, peaches and cream!

Eventually Len followed Matt into exile, and Ada teamed up with Billy Murray. Billy was more durable than either. When he died half a century later, at seventy-seven, the *New York Times* described him as "one of the great record sellers of the early days of the phonograph."

That was the heyday of the minstrel show and the "coon song." It was also, as I have noted, a time of unconscious, unquestioning and therefore unmalicious racism. We listened without a twinge of conscience or sympathy to

Rufus Rastus Johnson Brown,
Whatya gonna do when de rent come roun'?
Whatya gonna say? Howya gonna pay?
You'll nevah have a bit of sense till Jedgment Day.
Kase you know, I know, everybody know
Landlawd's a-gonna put us out in de snow.
Oh Rufus Rastus Johnson Brown,
Whatya gonna do when de rent come roun'?

Or the wifely ultimatum:

Pay mo' attention to me, Sam.
Pay mo' attention to me.

72

There's a man in de cemeter-ee, Sam,
What acted ca'less with me.
I'd hate to think you
Might be laid away too,
But I feel it in my bones
It's a comin' to you,
Unless you pay mo' attention to me, man!
Pay mo' attention to me!

Most numerous of all categories in our collection was the popular ballad. I must assume that these songs were popular, since Edison promoted them so persistently. It must have been a transitory popularity; I have never heard any of them on Muzak or the Lawrence Welk show. They were usually sung by a tenor named Byron G. Harlan. They were almost always tearjerkers. I could fill pages with examples, but two will suffice:

If I must say farewell, Kate, let me kiss your lips goodbye.
'Tis better we should part, sweetheart, you tell me with a
*   sigh.*
If I have loved you, dear, in vain,
Just let me kiss you once again.
If I must say farewell, Kate, let me kiss your lips goodbye.

And:

On a night in June, on their honeymoon,
*   Two lovers came to part,*
For a tale was told how her love grew cold,
*   How another won her heart.*
With a tear-dimmed eye and a sad goodbye
*   For him love's young dream ends —*
Till a year has passed, and he hears at last
*   The message his darling sends:*

Two little baby shoes —
How could his heart refuse?
Two little, blue little shoes she sent.
He knew very well what the message meant.
Softly they seemed to say:
"Daddy, come home today.
Don't let your heart break.
Come home for the sake
Of two little baby shoes!"

Looking backward, I am puzzled as to why the musical mood of the first decade of our century should so frequently have been *lamentoso*. It was, if I can believe Mark Sullivan, a time of national euphoria, the era of westward-coursing empire, of manifest destiny. Its symbols were the Roosevelt teeth and the Roosevelt big stick. We "took Panama." We spanked Aguinaldo. We discovered the North Pole, twice. We sassed the British. Our dreadnaughts made a muscle at Japan's front door.

Yet the ballad world of Thomas A. Edison was populated with rejected swains (as in the "Kiss Me Kate" number), jilted damsels ("In a Village by the Sea"), broken marriages ("Two Little Baby Shoes"), and abandoned children ("Nobody's Little Girl"). An impressionable child immersed in so much dolor could hardly escape being conditioned by it.

Sometime around 1910, Edison engineers devised a way of doubling the number of grooves on a five-inch cylinder. Those extra two minutes of playing time allowed for a second verse and chorus, and I learned that ballad writers did not necessarily leave their characters mired in "Miserere." The four-minute records we acquired after the changeover quite often had happy endings.

It seemed obvious to us that the Edison, bearing the portrait and the autograph of the great inventor, must be superior to the Victor, which claimed no more august ancestry than a puppy with his ear to the horn. It also had one indubitable advantage: it used a permanent sapphire needle, whereas Victor's little steel spikes had to be changed with every record.

We assumed therefore that Edison must have the pick of the artists. The *Phonogram* proclaimed Leo Slezak "the world's foremost operatic tenor," and though we didn't own any of his recordings we were proud that he was one of ours, a member of the same team as Ada Jones and Byron G. Harlan. Who was this fellow Caruso?

Again, as when my father stubbornly kept voting for William Jennings Bryan, we had backed the loser. As everybody knows, the disc won out over the cylinder. Columbia changed over, and survived. Edison continued producing cylinders until sometime during the First World War. One of our last purchases was "Joan of Arc, We Are Calling You," with the inspired couplet

*Her sons at Verdun
Bearing the burden* . . .

Shortly afterward the mainspring of our phonograph broke. Our dealer no longer carried spare parts. The Edison and several cartons of records were tucked away in the attic.

Nearly half a century later Oscar cannibalized another vintage Edison, donated by a neighbor, and got ours running again. When my wife and I are in Laramie he sometimes gives us a concert. Ada Jones, Billy Murray and Byron G. Harlan have not lost their magic. We shall not listen to their like again.

7

$40 a Month and Found

COLONEL E. J. BELL SPEAKING:
"Absolutely without a doubt the matter of fact is by the bald-headed Jesus Christ those sonsabitches with the crooked-heel boots and the hairy chaps that won't work and you can't kill 'em 'cause the law won't let you . . ."

The sentence tapers off into sputtering incoherence, as the colonel's utterances were likely to do. The colonel — I have no idea whether he had earned the title legitimately, at some place like San Juan Hill, or acquired it Kentucky-style — was a Little Laramie rancher and entrepreneur with a high quotient of choler and a magnificent disregard of syntax. The context would suggest he was talking mostly of cowboys, but his appraisal would fit a fair number of the nomads who dumped their gear in our bunkhouse during the busy season, fell ravenously on the supper Mama set before them, and caught the stage back to town a day or two later. These were the culls at the bottom of the barrel, shiftless, semiliterate, usually alcoholic. They worked just long enough to buy a meal or two, a skinful of rotgut, and a two-dollar lay, and then caught the next freight out of town.

My father knocked one such down the morning after his arrival, and sent him footing the two miles up to the road. Papa had walked into the barn and found the man kicking a mare in the belly; apparently she had been slow in moving over as he tried to harness her. One thing Dad wouldn't tolerate was abuse of a horse.

Usually you could spot these characters on sight, and would leave them sitting on the curb or propped against a wall on First Street. Sometimes nothing better was available, your need was urgent, and you took a chance. Over the years we had all sorts of hands, good, middling and worthless.

The good ones too you could usually spot on sight. They were clean and kempt. They looked you in the eye and talked terms as man to man. They had suitcases or satchels — war bags, we called them — with a change of clothes; you knew that on Sunday mornings they would do their laundry in the creek and spread it out on the meadow to dry. Their table manners were at least tolerable. And they knew their job; you could see that the first time they backed a team out of the stall and put on the bridles. They usually stayed until the last stack was topped off, and when Papa paid them and they climbed into the spring wagon for the trip to town we were genuinely sorry to see them go. Where they went we could only surmise: north, maybe, where haying was still in progress; then west to the coast for fruit picking, perhaps south for the winter. Next summer they might be on the other side of the continent. Tumbleweed, hustled along by the winds of unrest.

Not all our seasonal workers were Ishmaels. Sometimes

we took on boys from Laramie, or from other ranches with a temporary surplus of labor. One summer Papa brought home two high school lads who had hitched or beaten their way out from Pennsylvania to see the country and earn some spending money. Nice, bright, well-brought-up youngsters, they quickly became members of the family. We hated to see them leave — Hattie and Martha in particular.

The going wage when I began to take interest in such things was $40 a month and found — "found" meaning board and room and a few fringe benefits. My father's scrupulously kept records show that by the turn of the century the wage spiral had already completed several twists. There is an entry for 1894: "Torwald Olson began work on Friday April 15th for ten dollars per month." Torwald's case, however, was not typical. He came from Papa's native valley in Norway, and may have been grateful for a home and a job at any figure while he learned the language and the ways of the country. Other entries are probably more representative:

CHAS. HOWARD commenced work 14th Sept. at 30 per month.
HARRY WINSTON commenced work Aug. 26 at noon 35 per month.
BERT COFFMAN commenced work July 28th at noon for 1 dollar and 25 a day and a load of hay when we finish.
JOHN THOMAS commenced work April 5th at noon. Received 1 lb chewing tobacco 50   ½ lb smoking 25   Flour 25 lbs   Chopped corn 30 lbs.

The last two entries indicate that payment to local men trying to get established on ranches of their own was partly in kind. Purchases made on behalf of hired men were methodically entered in the books and deducted at settlement time.

Many of the names in Papa's records mean nothing to

me, but a few touch off recollections still vivid. For example:

C McClure went to work March 22. Laid of [sic] on 29-30-31st. April 10th $20   April 13   10. Lost two days going to town. Underwear and gloves 1   13; March 23   2   75. (Total) $33.88.

Charlie McClure was my tutor, my constant companion, my best friend, my idol. He was not one of the transients. He must have had roots somewhere in Wyoming or Colorado, though I realize now that I knew very little about his background. Papa took him on, the above entry shows, for the spring work. He stayed through haying and the grain harvest, and came back the second spring. He was quietly competent in everything; good with horses, careful with machinery, trustworthy, diligent, even-tempered.

And he seemed to like children. Anyway, he bore with me. I must have been a nuisance. I was always down in the bunkhouse pestering him, when he might have preferred being by himself. We played cards — first casino, which I already knew, and then more complicated games. Grown-up games — seven-up, high-five, and poker, both draw and stud.

Mama was a little dubious about that. But she trusted Charlie. Anyway, the stakes were only kitchen matches. When I came up from the bunkhouse she would ask me how it had gone, and I would invariably answer: "Charlie won one game and I won the other."

He taught me to make things, too. We whittled out figure-four traps and set them in likely places along the creek, though I don't recall catching any rabbits.

He even took me along when he went a-wooing. He was "going with" the daughter of ranchers living upriver, beyond Woods Landing. On Sunday afternoons he would hitch Dolly and Nelly to the spring wagon and drive up to see her. Sometimes he would invite me to come along. Or did I perhaps invite myself? If indeed I was an unwitting and unwanted chaperon, I don't think I interfered seriously. After the greetings — and Miss Brooks was always gracious — I would wander off to explore the barns and corrals and the nearer meadows, and would not return until she called or waved me in for lemonade and cookies. I remember her and Charlie sitting rather stiffly on the porch, a discreet distance between them, at least when I was in eyeshot. What they talked about I have no idea. Courtship sixty years ago was a stately and leisurely ritual, nothing like today's headlong rush toward the mattress.

Nothing came of theirs. Charlie moved on, whither I don't remember, if I ever knew, and Miss Brooks married a boy from a neighboring ranch.

Then there was Klaus Sevcik, who aspired to be a cowboy.

That was not his real name; though there is only the remotest possibility that he or anyone who knew him will ever read this, I have rechristened him. Klaus belonged to a large family of Central European immigrants who had settled on a ranch down on the flats and who farmed out their numerous sons to neighbors needing an extra hand. He was with us off and on for several years.

He was a big, pudgy, sluggish fellow, though willing and amiable. His English was rudimentary, and thickly accented. We found it and him irresistibly amusing, and with the cruelty of youth and the snobbery of the old-timer we teased and baited him. (We never thought of ourselves as immigrants, of course. Anyway, we were Norwegians, a shade superior to our Swedish and Danish neighbors, and castes above those mid-European johnnies-come-lately.)

Klaus was a romantic. Back in Bohemia he must have read and dreamed about the Wildwest. (Even then Europeans had appropriated the words, melded them into one, wrenched vowels and consonants to manageable equivalents.) His English textbook was the *Buffalo Bill Weekly;* he brought bales with him and replenished his supply whenever anyone went to town. (I used to sneak down to the bunkhouse to read them when he was at work, until Mama forbade trespass.) The opening of one story may give the flavor of those novelettes, now ·collector's items:

Buffalo Bill, the king of scouts, and Pawnee Bill, his pard . . .

If Klaus had come to Wyoming expecting Indians and bandits he must have been sadly disappointed. He may not have made the connection immediately; Europeans are somewhat vague about American geography, as we are about theirs. Certainly the tranquil pastorale of life on the Big Laramie bore little resemblance to Buffalo Bill's world, as imaginatively reconstructed by Street & Smith's anonymous hacks.

But eventually it must have dawned upon him that here he actually was, in the Wildwest, though so far it had failed to measure up to its billing.

One day he accosted Martha and me:

"Oscar kin ride branco, didn't you yet?"

We stared. I said "Huh?" He repeated, painstakingly:

"Oscar . . . kin . . . ride . . . branco . . . didn't you yet?"

This time we got it. Yes, we assured him, Oscar could ride broncos, and when there was occasion he did.

Klaus's broad amorphous face brightened. He studied

for a minute; realizing there was more to come, and scenting sport, we waited. His lips moved, silently trying out phrases. His color deepened a shade. Then he blurted, with the rush of a timid swimmer hurling himself into icy water:

"Maybe sometime I ride branco you think?"

We didn't know, but we agreed to consult higher authority. That meant Mama and Papa. Mama was dubious, but Papa, prodded by Oscar, overrode her demurrer.

So one summer Sunday the whole family, and a neighbor or two, gathered in the shade of the trees north of the house to watch Klaus Sevcik's debut as a branco-buster.

We had one saddle horse that could always be counted on for a performance, the violence and virtuosity graded to the occasion. She was a bay mare named Dixie, a maverick, picked up off the range, her antecedents and previous ownership unknown. She was small, and delicate of build, but her slight frame concealed a seismic energy, as several unwary persons had discovered. In theory she was Hattie's, but Hattie had never ridden her. Martha had, once. Well, more precisely, four times, all in a distance of less than a mile. Three times Dixie unloaded her; three times Martha climbed back into the saddle. Weeping with fury, she swore (through gritted teeth, the *Buffalo Bill Weekly* would no doubt have said): "Damn her! I'll ride her home." And so she did. But even for Martha, intrepid as she normally was, once was enough.

Klaus was an arresting figure as he emerged from the barn. Oscar had lent him chaps and spurs; he had put on his best Sunday shirt and his gaudiest bandanna. I may be wrong, but I choose to recall that he walked with a bowlegged roll as he followed Oscar and Dixie down to the pasture in front of the house. Real Wildwest.

Oscar made sure the cinches were tight, and eared Dixie down until Klaus was solidly seated and stirruped.

Then he released her, and sped her on her ascension with a swipe of his hat across the rump.

Dixie's head went down between her forelegs. Her back humped. She exploded.

The first jump sent Klaus almost to her withers. At the second he was back on the cantle; he had lost one stirrup and was clutching for the horn. On the third pitch he lost contact, and his illusions, for good. He rolled over and over on the turf, and picked himself up. Somewhere in that final split second he must have found the horn and anchored himself to it, because the convulsion that dislodged him loosened the saddle too. At the next jump it turned beneath Dixie's belly; she bucked her way out of it and galloped off. Oscar raced after her, brought her back, and then, so she wouldn't get any mistaken notions — and just possibly to show Klaus what real brancoriding was — saddled her again and rode her to a standstill.

One more entry from my father's personnel records:

OLE VIKLUND started to work Aug. 18 $40 per month.

I remember Ole Viklund very well. Twice he tried to kill me. Maybe he wasn't trying very hard, but he certainly scared the bejesus out of me.

He was a hulking Swede, dark, dour, taciturn, whom Papa had hired to build a new bunkhouse. He had a reputation as a master log worker; he lost no time in demonstrating that it was well earned. Papa and Oscar were pretty good axmen, but Ole was an artist. It was a treat to watch him pare away the round of a big log, swinging the ax with effortless rhythm, until two sides were as flat and smooth as if they had gone through a planing mill. Then he would shape the other sides, notching one, hewing the obverse to a shallow V, so that one log would fit snugly into another, without need of chinking or plaster. You see log houses built that way in the Scandinavian countries; if you find one in America you can safely assume that it was put up by a Swede or a Norwegian.

Ole was a widower, with one son, whom he brought along to the ranch. Ben was a year or so younger than I. He was a nice lad, shy, like a puppy not sure of his welcome, but hungry for friendship. I liked him. I was glad to have a playmate. Then why on God's green earth was I so mean to him?

I didn't really *mean* to be mean. Well, I *think* I didn't, though I'm not quite stack-of-Bibles sure. After all these years my conscience squirms. Was I just teasing, as I supposed — maybe a little roughly, but without malice? Or was there perhaps a mean streak in me, which hadn't had a chance to show itself before, because I had always been the youngest and smallest, at home and in school? And now that I had a younger and smaller companion — more than that, a newcomer, frightened and vulnerable — did the bully in me come into the open?

I shall never be quite sure. But tease him I did, so persistently that his father couldn't help noticing. Ole Viklund was jealously protective anyway. He had already rebuked us — my sisters and me — for mispronouncing his son's name. "You call him Bin!" he said scathingly. "Aye call him Ban!" We scuttled out of earshot, burst into giggles, and continued to say "Ben."

Ben and I strolled into the old bunkhouse one Sunday morning while his father was making their beds. I was chaffing Ben as usual, about what I have no idea. Suddenly I felt myself grabbed from behind. A blanket descended over my head and was pulled tight, shutting out light and air, but not the dust and the reek of sweat.

I wriggled helplessly. I tried to shriek, but the blanket smothered the sound; I got only a mouthful of fuzz. I was frantic with terror.

It couldn't have lasted more than half a minute. Having given me a good scare, Ole released me, and I got the hell out of there. Did I run to the house and yammer to Mama: "Ole tried to strangle me!" I can't recall; perhaps the Freudian censor has expunged the sequel from my memory.

But I hadn't learned my lesson. In a few days the fright faded, and I started teasing Ben again.

The new bunkhouse was going up fast. The sidewalls were finished and Ole was bringing the gable ends in to a peak. He worked from a plank scaffolding that went clear around the building just below the eaves. The scaffolding was a wonderful place to play. One day it could be the stockade around a frontier settlement, with Ben and me beating off a Blackfoot raid; another day a treasure-laden galleon with Blackbeard's pirates swarming over the rail.

We had clambered up one Saturday morning to watch Ole fitting tapered logs into place, and to think up a new game. As usual, I was teasing. Suddenly I heard a roar. I turned to see Ole coming at me, brandishing his ax.

I ran. Where the scaffolding right-angled at the end of the sidewall I stole a glance over my shoulder. He was still coming, and closer. I jumped.

It was, I suppose, a seven- or eight-foot drop. I landed on my feet, tipped over, found my footing again and legged it toward the house. With sanctuary in reach I ventured a look back. Ole had given up the pursuit; he was standing on the scaffolding, Ben clutched tightly against him. He had lowered the ax, but his face was still blood-suffused and bloodcurdling. He shouted something; I didn't understand Swedish but I got the general idea.

Again I don't remember whether I told my parents. If I did, I suspect I got something less than undiluted sympathy. Anyway, Ole stayed on to finish the bunkhouse, was paid off, and went his way, taking Ben with him. I never saw either of them again. So far as I know Ole never strangled or chopped anybody up; if he had, I would surely have read it in the Laramie papers.

But I did have news, a few years later, of the playmate I had liked so much and treated so meanly. Tragic news: poor little Ben burned to death in a bunkhouse fire.

8

Wild West

IN MY YEARS ON THE RANCH I never heard a gun fired in anger. I knew only one cowboy who habitually wore a six-shooter, and I doubt if he ever aimed it at anything bigger than a jackrabbit. Our own ranch had an adequate arsenal of hunting weapons big and small — Dad's .45–70 Winchester and 10-gauge Parker, Oscar's .303 Savage, .22 Remington and 16-gauge Winchester — but the only handgun was an old snub-nosed .44 caliber five-shooter. Papa had given it to Mama to defend herself when he was away on the railroad. I suspect she could have used it effectively had the occasion arisen, but she never needed to.

The Wild West was not, however, a fiction. It was only a generation behind us. My father, as I have mentioned, had seen Big Nose George Parrotte, the last of the notorious road agents, dangling from a telegraph post. Every summer at the Albany County Fair I saw the man credited with having led the vigilantes who, in one violent night, October 18, 1868, hanged Asa Moore, Con Wager and Ned Wilson, and shipped out, FOB anywhere, the satellite pack of gamblers, whores and other scum who had been looting and terrorizing the fledgling town for months.

At eighty-and-something N. K. Boswell still sat his horse erect and easy, his long white beard riffling in the breeze, his gaze ranging the crowd, coolly imperious. After a long career as law officer, sheriff, railroad detective and United States marshal, he had turned to ranching, a dozen miles or so upriver from us.

The range wars — cattle barons against homesteaders, cattlemen versus sheepmen — which are standard material for film and fiction never spread to the Laramie basin. But the Johnson County Cattle War was so recent — 1892 — that even in our corner of Wyoming we learned to speak of it with discretion. Too many prominent men had been involved, or were suspected of involvement. For many years the contemporary account, *Banditti of the Plains,* by A. S. Mercer, vanished from libraries private and public; rumor said that somebody — various names were whispered — had sought out, bought up, and destroyed every available copy. The University of Oklahoma Press reissued it in 1954.

A generation behind, did I say? Well, not quite. My lifespan overlapped that of Tom Horn, though not by much; I was only four years old when he was hanged.

Horn was a professional killer, and apparently he loved his work. He was employed for a time by the Wyoming Stock Growers Association as a stock detective but was discharged, ostensibly because he had proved less interested in collecting evidence against rustlers than in accumulating a body count, but just possibly because his forthright methods were becoming an embarrassment. Afterward he operated on contract, allegedly for five hundred dollars a "case," and for some of the stock growers who had formally disavowed him.

Twice he was picked up for questioning, after ranchers had been "dry-gulched" — shot from ambush — but was released for lack of evidence. When the climate in Wyoming got too warm he took his profession across the border to Colorado. At least two more murders were attributed to him there, but again there was no evidence that would stand up in court.

One may be pardoned for wondering whether the law officers really looked very hard for evidence. Horn's presumptive employers were rich and powerful men.* The murder victims were suspected of stealing cattle — any homesteader who fenced land that the big outfits considered their rightful domain was assumed to be a cattle thief — and rustlers got little sympathy. So for years the killer flourished in security and relative affluence.

Eventually, however, he made a mistake that was to prove fatal. Two mistakes, in fact.

He dry-gulched a thirteen-year-old boy, Willie Nickell, apparently mistaking him for his father; Willie was riding Kels Nickell's horse and wearing his hat and coat. Killing suspected rustlers might be condoned, but murdering a teen-age boy was something else again. At last public indignation was aroused.

Six months later Horn got drunk in a bar and boasted of the murder, in the hearing of two United States marshals and a court stenographer. (Their presence on that particular day was either one of the happiest coincidences in the annals of law enforcement or something else.)

Give the man's employers credit; they did their best

---

* Dr. T. A. Larson, on whose *History of Wyoming* I have drawn heavily, writes: "John C. Coble and Ora Haley have often been identified as Horn's employers by hearsay, though not by any valid proof."

to save him. Seldom has a hired assassin had a more illustrious battery of defense counsel — five of the best lawyers in southern Wyoming. Nevertheless he was convicted and hanged.

Hollywood has unaccountably neglected Tom Horn. To be sure, he never walked down Main Street at high noon, right hand hovering over low-slung holster. He never claimed to be the fastest gun in the West. In fact, I have found no mention of his carrying a six-shooter. His weapon was the rifle. And he avoided confrontations. He preferred to sit snugly concealed in a quaking-asp grove or behind a rocky outcrop until his quarry walked into the gunsights. But script writers and producers have never let facts inhibit them. Other scoundrels, quite as unprincipled, have been fumigated and exalted into folk heroes — Billy the Kid, the James brothers, Butch Cassidy (who was working the same line of country, literally and figuratively, in the '90s). Why not Tom?

For a few years his name was perpetuated by an enterprising manufacturer who brought out the Tom Horn rope, a lariat with a colored strand braided into it. So far as I know, it had no special virtues, but a good many cowhands invested. It was a conversation piece.

All this was history and legend by the time I began to sit up and take notice. In my own experience life in the supposedly Wild West was as tame — no, I reject that cambric-tea adjective; let me rather say tranquil — as life on an Iowa farm, until the spring of my tenth year. Then, for a few days, we found ourselves living on the fringes of melodrama.

It began, for us, with a clatter of hoofs on the road down the bench, the sound of a horse at a dead run. As the rider approached I recognized Axel Sodergreen, from the next ranch upriver. He was riding bareback; that in itself boded something unusual.

He pulled up in front of the house and gabbled out his news.

"Sheriff Bath's been murdered. Up in the timber. They think the feller that killed him is heading down the river. They're getting up a posse. I'm s'posed to tell Hammonds."

He dug his heels into his horse's ribs, and was off again before we could frame a question. A twelve-year-old Paul Revere rousing the countryside.

It is at this point that I enter the story, and exit ignominiously.

If the killer was footing it down the river he would have to come through our ranch, only a quarter of a mile from the house. He must be pretty hungry by this time. Suppose he should sneak up through the brush and walk into the kitchen, demanding food, and a horse to make his getaway?

Papa and Oscar were both gone. I figured it was up to me.

I was in the shed, sliding cartridges into Oscar's Remington .22, when Mama came out of the kitchen.

"Teddy! What . . . are . . . you . . . doing? "

I stammered something, I suppose about hadn't we better be ready, just in case the killer *should* turn up?

"Give . . . me . . . that . . . gun!"

She emptied the magazine, returned the cartridges to their box, put the rifle back on its rack. There was, I believe, a short lecture, ending with something like "And no more of that nonsense!" She went back to the kitchen.

I slunk out into the May sunshine, my lower lip probably lapping my chin. I felt I had been twice cheated — once of being a twentieth-century Paul Revere, again of carrying on the proud tradition of Nate Boswell.

We learned more in driblets throughout the day. Al Bath had been found dead in Bear Gulch, on the Walden road. Apparently he had been shot from ambush, because his own revolver was in its holster, unfired. He had ridden out, alone, to intercept a man named Summers, who was reported to be heading for Laramie on foot after beating up the proprietor of the Walden hotel, where Summers had been working as a dishwasher.

The Laramie River posse rode into our ranch at dusk, and the kitchen filled with men, weary, dust-begrimed, sweaty, thirsty, famished, disgruntled. While Mama and the girls got supper the story came out in blurts and gobbets and rancorous bickering on detail. They had searched the river bottom and the tributary gulches all the way down from Woods Landing, and found nothing. No tracks, no scrap of shirt or overalls conveniently snagged on tightly strung barbwire, no Summers. Nobody at any of the ranches — Bergs, Lunds, Johnsons, the two Sodergreens — had seen anything. There was no sense in going farther, now it was dark. They'd work on downriver in the morning.

But where the hell — excuse me, Mrs. Olson — where is he?

Why didn't he take Al's horse, instead of turning him loose? Feller can't get anywhere in this country on foot.

Aw, you can see a man on a horse ten miles. On foot, he could stick to the brush just about all the way to Laramie. Shucks, we coulda been within ten feet of him this afternoon. We didn't comb every patch of willows. You know that. Couldn't.

Well, he's got to show himself *some* time. He must be pretty hungry by now.

Unless he stocked up with grub before he left Walden. But where's he *heading* for?

It went something like that. I wouldn't pretend to reproduce verbatim a conversation heard sixty years ago by a nine-year-old boy squatting in a corner, groggy with sleep, frightened that any moment his mother would notice him and hustle him off to bed. I do remember that some of the men were voluble, positive it had happened exactly *this* way. Others listened, only now and then grunting a laconic assent or demurrer. Arguments broke out between the assertive ones; everybody's temper was frayed by weariness and frustration.

Once or twice things got a bit ugly. Had they really searched that old barn in Berg's south meadow thoroughly? Who was supposed to? Well, looked to me like he just rode around it and came back. The retort was belligerent. Damn well right he'd searched it. Went in and poked around and looked up in the loft. And if anybody thought he hadn't he could just . . .

It was about then that a stertorous snore rolled luxuriously from the corner by the woodbox. Billy Rice — small, wiry, twinkly Billy Rice from Sand Creek — was making his own comment on the controversy, characteristic and, as it proved, definitive. Everybody seemed to realize Billy had the right idea.

We couldn't sleep so many guests, of course. We put a couple in the bunkhouse; the rest saddled up again and rode down to the Riverside.

They took up the manhunt next morning, starting at our ranch and working down the river. They found nobody. Other posses were busy elsewhere — in the mountains, in the Centennial Valley, and along the Little Laramie, in case the killer had cut north through the timber, thinking to catch a Hahns Peak freight into Laramie.

We learned more details of the murder in the following

93

days, from visitors and from the two Laramie newspapers. Sheriff Bath had started for the mountains that Friday morning, May 29, 1908, in response to a phone call from his colleague in Walden, Colorado, asking him to intercept a man who had felled D. H. Stevens, hotel proprietor, with an iron bar, and was believed to be heading for Laramie. The sheriff set out in a hired car — the law in Albany County was not yet motorized — but changed to a borrowed horse when mud and melting snow made the going too treacherous for wheels.

Late that afternoon two Walden deputies, following the fugitive — at what Laramie accounts snidely described as a prudent distance — found Al Bath's body. Tracks in the mud indicated that the killer had tried unsuccessfully to drag it into the brush. The borrowed horse was gone.

Up to this point there was substantial agreement on what had happened. But here rumor, surmise and conflicting interpretations began to smear the trail and befuddle the chroniclers. The general assumption was that the sheriff had been shot from ambush as he rode — singularly unwary — along the snow-sodden wagon road through the timber. But one member of the posse, noting later that the saddle showed no bullet scars, argued that he must have dismounted, perhaps to question Summers, perhaps to frisk him. Again, singularly unwary behavior for a law officer. Tracks in the mud suggested that the killer had ridden north, toward the Centennial Valley and the Hahns Peak railroad, and the main search first went thataway. Then the borrowed horse turned up near its home ranch above Woods Landing, and the saddle and bridle were found cached nearby. It was this discovery that had brought the fagged, frustrated and quarrelsome manhunters to our supper table.

94

Day after day, as May yielded to June, the search continued, without result.

There were any number of false clues. A report that a man was trapped in a cabin in the Encampment Valley, on the other side of the mountains, brought the new sheriff, Emil Therkildsen, hustling to the scene. Well, hustling is hardly the word, by today's standards. He took the stage to Walden, where the Jackson County sheriff joined him, and they proceeded together by special train to the point nearest the supposed hideout. If Summers had been cached there, he had had plenty of time to get away. The contemporary records are blank. The *Laramie Republican* has no follow-up for a full week, and then only a paragraph noting the return of Sheriff Therkildsen on the Walden stage after tireless endeavors to trace the murderer.

The *Cheyenne Leader* recalled belatedly that a man answering the killer's description had been in its office "within twelve hours of the crime" to ask for travel guidance. A check stolen from Peter Simonson, Pioneer Canal rancher, was cashed in Omaha. WHO SIGNED THAT CHECK? the *Republican* headline asked portentously. A former Laramie man sent a clipping from a Syracuse, New York, newspaper, reporting the death, in a fall from a train, of a tramp who allegedly had told a fellow free rider that his name was John Somers.

And so on.

Al Bath was buried, his death unavenged. It was about the biggest funeral anybody in Laramie could remember. He belonged to one of the foremost pioneer families, and he was liked and respected. The *Republican*'s account of the obsequies carried a shirttail with a one-line head: "Summers Still a Fugitive."

The story was about to peter out for lack of developments when the *Denver Post* decided to get into the act.

The *Post,* under the imaginative direction of two picturesque buccaneers, Fred G. Bonfils and Harry Tammen,
was about the gaudiest newspaper in America. A murder
anywhere in its "empire," as they grandly designated a
territory stretching from Albuquerque to southern Montana — was pay dirt. And the murder of a law officer, by
an assassin who apparently had evaporated into the thin
Rocky Mountain air — well, that was Golconda.

Gene Fowler tells the story in *Timber Line.*

The *Post* at the time was industriously mining another
never-exhausted lode, the common man's hankering for
the mystic. (Is not ours the Age of Aquarius?) Its current
house Mahatma — the word is Fowler's — was an "expo-
nent of advanced thought, magician and table-rapping
king" resoundingly named Dr. Alexander J. McIvor-
Tyndall. By a happy chance the seer was just opening an
engagement at Root's Opera House in Laramie, giving
"demonstrations of the mind, such as thought transfer-
ence, clairvoyance, telepathy, psychometric impressions
and kindred examples of man's supernatural faculties."
The *Post* announced that the Mahatma had graciously
consented to place his occult powers at the service of the
law, confident that he would be able to pick up the killer's
spoor.

Fowler describes the start of the manhunt:

"The blindfolded seer got on his horse, concentrated,
galloped, curvetted and hop-scotched at the head of an
awed cavalcade. The *Post* chronicled his progress; every
spiritualistic sigh was recorded by . . . mounted re-
porters, and even the whinnies of the Mahatma's mus-
tang were construed as solemn evidence of psychic
stimuli."

Alas, the trail was too cold for even his psychometric
nose. At the scene of the crime, he confessed himself
unable "to establish telepathic communication with the

fugitive," as he had hoped, but he did report distinct impressions of the route Summers had followed. (His reconstruction, not surprisingly, coincided with the assumptions already reported extensively in the *Post*.) These were greatly reinforced the following day when he mounted the sheriff's horse. The charger seems to have bristled with psychic vibrations which enabled the Mahatma to describe in detail the killer's route to Woods Landing. But the vibrations faded out where the hunted man had turned his mount loose. McIvor-Tyndall was pretty sure, however, that Summers had headed east. He concluded ruefully that "the murderer is now far away, the faintness of the mental impressions . . . indicating this."

The *Post*, characteristically cynical, had had its circus, degrading tragedy into humbug and farce. Doubtless the circulation graphs throughout its empire had tilted upward for the duration of the show. The Mahatma's failure probably did not disillusion many of the gullible, and it could not have damaged his reputation seriously; he left Denver a few months later for richer pastures in the East.

But Al Bath's murderer was still at large.

The coroner's jury in Laramie announced its verdict on June 11, thirteen days after the killing. It found that the sheriff "came to his death from a gunshot wound inflicted by George H. Summers, alias Henry Ramer, with felonious intent."

With the trail cold, the murder receded into the back pages and the newspapers turned their attention again to the Presidential campaign, just gaining momentum.

There was a brief flurry of excitement a few days later with the discovery that a bunkhouse at Plains Station on the Hahns Peak had been broken into. The intruder had changed clothes for some he found there and left behind a blanket "positively identified" as the one from Al Bath's borrowed horse. But the clue was too stale to be helpful.

George Summers was never captured. How he eluded that cordon of manhunters, which, in the *Republican*'s florid prose, mobilized "as one man, moving upon impulse to find and lodge the fiend behind bars," is only one of the mysteries.

Another is: Who was he? The contemporary sources do not even agree on his first name; it appears variously as George, John and Charles. The coroner's verdict adds "alias Henry Ramer," without explanation. Gene Fowler identifies him as "G. A. Summers, alias Ned Davis, a former convict at the Canon City, Colorado, penitentiary." The *Denver Republican* — calling him "John" — says he "resembled one Mel Long, a Canon City escaped murderer." The first full account in the *Laramie Republican* gives his name as George H. Summers, and says that he had served a year in the Colorado reformatory at Buena Vista for horse theft (he had stolen the horse in Colorado Springs and sold it in Walden), and that he was "believed also to be wanted in Canon City for murder." Before he went back to Walden to take a job at the hotel he had worked for a while at Foxpark, a lumber camp and station on the Hahns Peak railroad, not far from the scene of the murder. There were hints that he had friends there or in Laramie who might have helped him escape.

All this is ex post facto. And none of it apparently was known to Sheriff Bath when he rode out to intercept the fugitive. He knew the man was wanted for felonious assault. Presumably he knew that Summers was armed; the Walden sheriff would hardly have failed to tell his colleague that the hotel safe had been looted and a revolver stolen. But he did not know that he might be facing an escaped convict with one murder already charged against him. And so he rode unwarily to his death.

Perhaps our corner of Wyoming had been tranquil too long. Forty years earlier Nate Boswell would not have been dry-gulched with his gun still in the holster.

9

Solitary Misters

. . . A solitary mister
Propped between trees and water . . .
— Dylan Thomas

O NE SUMMER EVENING stands out in my memory, for good reason. I saw the sun rise in the west. And not only once, but twice, and set there three times before it would stay tucked away for the night.

It sounds contrary to nature, but it wasn't. I was on an errand to a ranch on the slope of Sheep Mountain. When you're close up under an eastward-facing mountain the sun goes down for you while the plains behind are still brimming with light. When you ride away from the mountain you come out of the shadow into the sunshine, and if you look back you see the sun apparently rising, as if your horse were briefly outracing the velocity of the earth's rotation.

My errand was quickly dispatched, and I loped homeward. Sheep Mountain is saw-toothed, and I was riding southeast. Thus I saw the sun emerge through a notch in the skyline, disappear behind a pinnacle, and emerge again in the next notch. From shadow and the first chill of evening into light and warmth; then shadow and chill again; and once more light and warmth for a minute or two before the great east-flowing shadow of the mountain overtook me for good and flooded on across the plains toward the remote saucer-edge of the Black Hills, still candescent.

There is another reason for remembering that day, although it did not become apparent until quite a time later. So many heights of land in the topography of a life slip past unrecognized.

I had gone to the mountain to hire an extra hand for haying. He agreed to come, and I headed home, mission accomplished, without the slightest premonition that in the next few weeks he was going to undermine my faith. All of it: faith in a benevolent, all-wise, omnipresent, anthropomorphic God; faith in life after death; faith in man's special place in the universe as the end product of evolution.

He did it so gently that I felt no wrench or pang. I didn't realize, indeed, what had happened until I returned to Laramie in the fall and had to tell the Reverend Martin Jensen that I wouldn't be able to teach my Sunday school class again.

This is not an *apologia pro vita mea*. My loss of faith is relevant to the story only as a by-product of my acquaintance with a remarkable man.

His name was William H. Garrison. He always introduced himself thus: not "My name's Garrison," as anybody else would have done, but "I am William H. Garrison," or, on the telephone, "This is William H.

Garrison." It tells much of his personality that in a land and a time of casual informality (though not quite as casual as today) nobody ever, to my knowledge, addressed him or spoke of him as "Bill." Even in manure-spattered overalls, shoveling out the cow stable, he remained Mr. Garrison, different from other hired men and other ranchers in ways which nobody could analyze but to which everyone responded instinctively.

He was a small, neat man with a carefully trimmed gray Vandyke. He lived alone in a quaking-asp grove on the flank of Sheep Mountain. There was a spring in the grove and a little creek coming out of it. It watered a small meadow that cut enough hay to winter the saddle horse that was his only livestock. His cabin was a two-room frame structure, tight, snug and neat like himself. Behind the grove the mountain rose steeply; in front the plains flowed eastward in a forty-mile sweep of shifting pastels, dun and buckskin, ochre and lichen-green, bronze and amethyst. By day he could see the smoke of Union Pacific trains, at night the phosphorescence of Laramie, and locomotive headlights coming down Sherman Hill like grounded planets.

I thought then it was a wonderful place to live: a mountain for windbreak, shade and water and pasture, and half of Albany County for a front yard. I told myself that some day I was going to have a place just like it. Maybe a little bigger, but situated like his.

A ranch of that size — if you could dignify it by the name — would of course not support even a single man with few wants. In summer he worked on neighboring ranches. He could drive a team, milk a cow, pitch hay, clean stables. He was steady and undemanding. He could always find employment. He may have earned enough to buy groceries and other necessaries for the rest of the year. We suspected, however, that he had other income.

Inevitably people speculated about him. Where did he come from? Why had he come, to bury himself in a cranny of the mountain, and live like a hermit? Doubtless there were soundings and reconnaissances, perhaps attempts at cross-examination. They could not have been very productive. He was always courtly, but he deftly turned aside feelers about himself and his origins.

Somehow, though, a biography of sorts took shape, how close to the facts I never learned. He came originally from Chicago; that was pretty firmly established. Indeed, his cabin provided corroboration; the kitchen–living room was papered with pictures from the *Chicago Tribune*'s Sunday editions. They looked fairly recent; I assume that he still subscribed. He was reported to have been a well-known lawyer there around the turn of the century.

Why had he given all that up? Here the biography-legend split. Because of a broken heart, one version insisted; his wife had run off with another man. Because of thwarted ambition and wounded pride, another theory suggested: he had been defeated for public office (District Attorney? Congressman?), in an election he had felt confident of winning, and he could not face the humiliation.

As a romantic adolescent I was disposed to believe the first. One clue, possibly supporting that theory, I did uncover, or rather it was laid before me. He showed me pictures of his daughter, now grown and married, and spoke of her proudly and wistfully. The pictures showed an attractive young woman, in the twenties, I should judge, obviously reared in comfortable circumstances, as the novels put it. He never mentioned a wife.

I got to know him fairly well that summer. I suspect he needed someone to talk to. People living alone usually do; until Friday came along Crusoe unburdened himself to his parrot. The evening milking time was our favorite discussion period. In the odorous twilight of the stable, with the milk hissing rhythmically into the pails, the cows rhythmically chewing their cuds, we talked. Mostly Mr. Garrison talked. Not ranch talk — weather, and range conditions, and the price cattle were bringing in Omaha. Talk rather of books and writers and ideas, subjects of which I was learning a little and of which he seemed to know a great deal.

I don't remember how we got started on religion. I suppose conversations usually drift around to religion sooner or later, or at least impinge upon it. (In college, I found that bull sessions always did.)

Up to then I hadn't given religion much thought. I had gone to Harmony church now and then with my parents; I had even "spoken a piece" there. I remember that on his one parochial visit to our ranch the pastor asked me the inevitable question: "And what do you plan to be when you grow up, my little man?" I replied without hesitation: "A soldier." "A soldier of God?" he pressed. I didn't know quite what that meant, but it didn't sound like what I had in mind. I stood mute.

When I was sent to school in town I was put in Sunday school, too. I mastered the catechism, I was confirmed, I was pressed into duty as a teacher. All this because it seemed to be expected of me, and I usually tried to do what was expected, if it did not involve too much effort.

Only twice had I experienced anything like true religious fervor, and both experiences were transitory.

One summer Martha and I, without parental prompting or outside proselyting, decided we should lead Better Lives. For a while our deportment was exemplary. We jumped to do errands at the first word from Mama, and tried to anticipate her wishes. We did our chores punctually, expeditiously and with extra care. We bore with Christian fortitude the teasing of our siblings and forbore to retort in kind. We held long, solemn discussions on ethical and doctrinal matters. We stopped saying "darn" and "doggone."

Since our normal behavior was not particularly delinquent, nobody appeared to notice our reformation. We were understandably disappointed, but we didn't really need approbation; our inner glow was enough. By the same token, when our zeal began to slacken, as it did in a couple of weeks, nobody noticed that either. Our halos came and went without remark.

My second religious experience was more dramatic. I was publicly Saved. I walked the Sawdust Trail, renounced my evil ways, and enlisted in the Army of the Lord.

Happily so many others — a measurable percentage of the population of Laramie — were doing the same thing at the same time that nobody paid any attention to me.

An evangelistic team had come to town for a stay of several weeks. The churches were sponsoring their visit. An old livery stable slated for demolition had been converted into a tabernacle. (The irreverent took to calling it the Barnacle.) The Fife Brothers, and the sister who completed the trio, were good. They were tall and handsome, they had rich, vibrant voices that needed no amplification, they played a variety of instruments, including the xylophone. And they were virtuosi in manipulating that most sensitive and potentially responsive of all instruments, the human emotions.

Their act was a combination of vaudeville, Chautauqua and old-fashioned religion, skillfully orchestrated. In the modern vernacular, it built. Word got around that it was a good show, not to be missed. And of those who came from curiosity, or boredom, or perhaps to scoff, not a few found themselves responding to the climactic call for converts and trudging sheepishly up the sawdust-carpeted corridor.

I was one such. I am not sorry. It is good to learn at an early age the frightening power of mass emotion, the contagion that can turn a throng of individuals into one mindless organism, manipulated by invisible remote controls implanted in the viscera. Having once experienced it, one should have a degree of immunity.

I have no notion how many new members the Fife Brothers (and sister) recruited for the Laramie churches. I do recall that some of the toughest boys in high school stopped smoking and brawling for fully two weeks.

My belief, therefore, had no deep roots in conviction or emotion, and it withered fast in the desiccating breath of Mr. Garrison's logic. I fought back weakly. I interposed buts: "But there must be *some* supreme intelligence . . ." "But it couldn't all have just *happened* . . ." (I have no clear recollection of our serial colloquy, but I am sure I must have advanced all the standard demurrers.) He swept them easily aside. He quoted books I had never read — Renan's *Life of Jesus,* for example — and others I hadn't even heard of. I was no match for him. When the last stack was topped off and he rode away — back to his quaking-asp grove or on to some other ranch that still needed a hay hand — I was an agnostic, though I didn't immediately realize it. Not quite an atheist; I could never be all that positive about anything, even a negative.

I saw Mr. Garrison only a couple of times more. Once I rode up to the mountain to ask how he was getting along; he welcomed me, courtly and aloofly cordial. I think it was on that visit that he talked about his daughter and showed me her picture. Next year we moved to town. I heard of him at lengthening intervals from rancher friends. He was still living in his quaking-asp draw, still a mystery, increasingly a legend. He must have been well into his eighties when he died in the Laramie hospital. I did not know he was there until the death notice came into the office of the *Republican-Boomerang,* where I was then news editor.

I wired a query to the *Chicago Tribune,* something like "Could you use 300 words on death William H. Garrison once prominent Chicago lawyer long hermit rancher Wyoming?" but got no reply. I had hoped the *Tribune* might exhume from its morgue the real story of his earlier career, so that we could learn how close to the mark, or far off it, our rumors and surmises had been. No doubt after so many years the *Tribune* did not consider him newsworthy.

We might not have been much wiser. Whatever the facts were, they probably would not have illuminated his motive for becoming what a later generation would call a dropout from society. A great many men lose wives or elections, but not many of them cut loose from everything and head for the hills. In the few who do there must be a malaise deeper than disappointment or heartbreak.

Perhaps malaise is the wrong word. We should not assume that anybody less gregarious than we are must have a kink in him. Some men, and even a few women, just want to be alone.

The West has always had more than its quota of solitary misters, beginning with the mountain men. Until it was roped down, like Gulliver, with fences and highways and pipelines, it offered magnificent facilities for being alone. Even now you can shake off the dudes and the weekend fishermen and picnickers, if you are willing, and rugged enough, to pack in, ten miles or twenty, beyond the point where the most doughty jeep stalls. But it gets harder every year.

Frenchy Germain (his first name was Auguste) was dead and becoming a legend before I reached consciousness, but Frenchy's mine remained a landmark until after I was in college. His cabin was collapsing, his tunnel had caved in, but the big waterwheel that had powered his operations stood as sturdily as ever, at least to the eye of a passerby on the Woods Creek trail. Old-timers said he had built that waterwheel unassisted, with no other tool than an ax. (When I was old enough to subject legends to critical scrutiny I added to his equipment a saw and probably a hammer and some nails. Even with that qualification, his craftsmanship commanded reverence.)

He never found enough gold to count. Few prospectors in our part of the country did. The flanks of Jelm Mountain are perforated with old shafts and tunnels, boarded up so that grazing stock will not blunder in. Sometimes when I was riding for cattle I would stop to clamber up a pile of tailings, hoping to pick up a nugget the prospector had missed. I found nothing but country rock and fragments of the quartz lead (pronounced *leed*) that had tempted the miner to start digging. "Hungry quartz," Al Mountford taught me later to call it, with the right inflection of contempt.

I never thought of Al as a solitary mister, although he lived a bachelor life in a ghost camp forty miles northwest of Laramie and nine thousand feet up. For one thing, he had a neighbor, a sturdy old lady named Mrs. Morris, who had once been Morgan's postmistress, I believe, and who saw no reason to join the general exodus when the mines gave out. For another, Al was gregarious, a good companion and a wonderful raconteur. He was a stubby little Cornishman, with a bristling moustache, piercing small eyes set deep under fierce eyebrows, and a two-octave voice that he used with histrionic effect. At the climax of a story it would drop to a cavernous rumble and he would end with a basso-profundo "Haw! Haw! Haw!"

Al had a mine, of course. He had bored several hundred feet into the mountain, making a tidy, well-timbered, workmanlike tunnel such as you would expect of a Cornish hard-rock miner. He must have found enough encouragement to keep him going, but I doubt if he really expected to strike it rich. He never did. Mining was his trade, and it gave him something to do during slack times. He worked for wages during the milder months, on ranches or at other jobs. I had met him first when he was cook and factotum for a small geological survey team I joined one college vacation. We hit it off, and we kept in touch for many years afterward. His letters were a delight; his gruff wit, his glee at the absurdity of mankind, came through the misspellings and the shaky grammar. Reading them, I could see his face settle into that familiar ferocious grimace, his eyes glinting dangerously under the bristling brows, and hear again his subbasement "Haw! Haw! Haw!"

I don't think there was anything between him and Mrs. Morris — anything romantic, I mean — though when I went up to Morgan one summer she had Al and me in to dinner. I've never eaten better biscuits.

Come to think of it, I never heard of a solitary missus. Maybe, if such a thing exists, she was one.

I didn't have far to look for other solitary misters, with better claim to the designation. I had two in my own family: Cousin John Larson, who lived on a tiny ranch on the far side of Sheep Mountain, tending a few cattle and a flock of goats; and Uncle Simon, who quit his job in the Union Pacific shops after the last of his three motherless daughters was married, and spent his remaining years on a homestead up Fox Creek. He wasn't antisocial. He was always glad to see us, and he wouldn't sit down to visit until he had stirred up the fire and put the coffee pot on.

Percy Shallenberger does not properly belong in this chronicle. He had nothing to do with the Laramie plains; he lived two hundred or three hundred miles farther north, on a sheep ranch in the foothills of the Big Horns. I did not meet him until a decade or so after I had left the Big Laramie. And though he was a bachelor, and lived alone except for such help as he might require in lambing and shearing time, he was anything but solitary. He had friends all over the world.

He introduced himself by letter. He had read something of mine in a magazine and wrote to tell me he liked it. I replied gratefully and we began corresponding. I was, I learned, only the latest and least of an impressive list of correspondents whose acquaintance he had made in the same manner. He read voraciously; he had plenty of time and few distractions. When he read something he liked, when somebody did something he approved, he sat down and wrote. His letters had a quality that arrested attention; one did not dismiss them with a perfunctory acknowledgment. The Lost Cabin postmaster or -mistress must have been incredulous when envelopes began tumbling out of the mailbags bearing exotic stamps, or the franks of United States senators and congressmen. (George W. Norris, the father of the Tennessee Valley Authority, was one of Percy's pen pals.)

Louis Adamic, the Slovenian-born author of *The Native's Return* and other books, came to Laramie one winter to lecture. A couple of weeks before his arrival I got a letter from Percy, asking me to greet Mr. Adamic for him and express his regrets that he was unable to come down for the speech. When I did so Adamic's face lit up.

"Oh, you know my Uncle Percy?" he exclaimed joyously. He made me tell all about our friend while the crowd queuing up for autographs shuffled and muttered unkind things about Olson's monopolizing the lion.

I met Percy face to face only twice. He was then in middle age, I should judge, a pleasant-faced, graying, soft-spoken man who looked like the bank teller he had once been, rather than a Wyoming sheepman. He brought me a sampling of his record collection, on loan: opera, symphonies, chamber music, all imports. He told me a little about his life, not much. He had worked in a Nebraska bank for a number of years, gotten bored with it, taken out his savings and headed west, and eventually become part owner and then sole owner of a small sheep ranch. And there life really began for him.

I always intended to visit his ranch, but I never made it. A few years later I read in the Associated Press news file that Percy Shallenberger, Lost Cabin rancher, had been found dead in the fields near his house, victim of a heart attack. There was no record of surviving relatives.

A few months later I was notified that he had bequeathed me part of his library. When the books came I found they were mostly history and biography, letters and documents from the seventeenth and eighteenth centuries, with a few volumes of earlier date. I also began to receive catalogues from Foyle's and other English book-dealers; I had apparently inherited his place in their mailing lists.

I wish I had seen his ranch. It would be easier to picture him on a winter evening, poring over the memoirs of some forgotten statesman or courtier, listening to *La*

Sonnambula, or putting down, in his neat bookkeeperish script, his reflections on literature or current events (the New Deal, perhaps? Hitler's emergence?), for some distant friend. A lone man in a lonesome place, but never, I think, a lonely one.

10

In Praise of Horses…
and *Canis latrans*

EVERY FEW WINTERS you read in the newspapers
that a blizzard has blocked all roads in some section of the West, marooned ranchers, set in motion
massive rescue operations to bring food to hungry homes
and hay to starving cattle and sheep. "Operation Haylift"
has been repeated over and over, with dramatic television
shots of Air Force planes dropping bales to herds belly-
deep in drifts, and heart-wrenching stories of catastrophic
loss.

We lived through a few hard winters on the Big
Laramie; indeed, I came into the world at the tail end of
one of the worst in Western history. But I don't remember
anything like this, and neither does Oscar. We agree that
it couldn't have happened in our time, at least not on so
destructive a scale.

The difference can be summed up in a word — mechanization. We did our ranching with horses. Now everybody uses trucks and tractors, except for working cattle.

(They have even tried out motorcycles for that, but not very successfully.) I'll concede that mechanization has many advantages. A tractor can plow ten acres, probably more, while a four-horse team is plowing three. It is undeniably convenient to be able to drive to town in forty-five minutes, for a sack of flour, a mowing-machine bearing, or a movie, instead of jogging for hours along dusty wheel ruts, in a cloud of horseflies. Ranch life now, thanks to the internal combustion engine, is certainly less isolated and ingrown.

But when trouble comes, the advantage shifts to the side of horsepower, the original brand. It takes only a few inches of snow, with a fifty-mile gale hustling it along, to immobilize a truck. Even a tractor can't move over meadows drifted three feet under. Horses can. Not easily, but they can move. In the roughest weather we always managed to break a trail to the haystacks. We usually got gravid cows into the delivery room in good time. We had some loss, of course, but it was never ruinous.

For quite another reason I'm glad I grew up with horses. A Percheron's efficiency rating is doubtless far below that of a Farmall. But no Farmall ever nuzzled your pockets looking for sugar. No GMC ever rubbed a sweaty head against you when you took off its bridle, or nickered ingratiatingly when you opened the garage door.

The first horse I remember clearly was Buck. He was, of course, a buckskin, which is a sort of dusty tan. He stood over fifteen hands, rather tall for a cow horse; he was lean and rangy; he had a fine head and a handsome face, self-possessed, canny, and usually bored. He was a stoic, an introvert, and more than a little of a misanthrope. Perhaps life had made him one, but I think he must have been born asocial. He was seven years old when my father acquired him, and he had a history. He had been an outlaw, one of those rare animals that appear to be unbreakable. Then he was stolen, and it was a couple of years before his proper owner recovered him. The thief may have been a bad character, but he was a good horseman, and he had done for Buck what nobody else had been able to do. The outlaw was now not only a manageable mount, but a trained one, the best cow horse I have ever ridden, as good as any I have ever seen.

You needed only to indicate to Buck what you wanted done; after that you concentrated on staying on top while he did it. He was amazingly swift and surefooted. He could twist and swerve faster than the nimblest yearling. He could think faster, too. It may have been extrasensory perception, but I suppose it was merely experience, based on prolonged study of bovine reactions. Anyway, when the yearling veered to port, Buck was already there on his port quarter; when the yearling braked and tried to cut back, Buck had pulled up on his haunches and was planted squarely abaft. Before the critter knew what was happening he was segregated with the cut and Buck was loping easily back for the next victim.

I have said that Buck was a misanthrope. He was, with one noteworthy exception. He seemed to like children. When Papa or Oscar wanted him they had to drive the bunch into the corral and maneuver him into a corner. Hattie, Martha or I could walk up to him anywhere, put a belt or a hair ribbon around his neck and lead him to the stable. All three of us learned to ride on him, and he was unfailingly gentle with us, untiringly patient. We would clamber on two at a time and he would move staidly across the meadow. When we dug in our heels for speed, Buck accelerated to an equally staid trot. I, being the youngest, had the pillion seat, and I usually fell off. Buck would stop, eye me reproachfully, and wait until I was aboard again.

I don't remember just when Buck decided we had outgrown his tutelage. Anyway, by the time I reached my teens he was treating me like anybody else. If I wanted to halter him I had to corner him in the corral, and once I was on it was my business, not his, to be sure I stayed there. Coming home with the mail one day I dismounted to recover a hat that Martha had lost the night before on the way from town. As I stooped for the hat the reins were twitched from my incautious grasp, and Buck was off. I have said he was the perfect cow horse; I should have noted one grievous imperfection. He had never learned, or never deigned, to stand "tied to the ground," as cowboys call it. With his head cocked a bit to one side, so that he wouldn't step on the dragging reins, he could travel faster than I could pursue. He would let me approach almost within lunging distance, his wise old face bland and innocent, and then whisk the reins out of my reach and take off again. I gave up at last and walked home, two hot and mortifying miles, rehearsing at every step the retribution I meant to inflict. Of course by the time I had caught up Patsy and ridden back my rage had cooled. I gave Buck a few clouts with the bridle reins, but the going-over with a nail-studded two-by-four I had promised him seemed a bit too drastic.

When the ranch was sold we found a home for Buck with a neighbor. He had a few years of retirement, and died a patriarch, died, I am sure, as he had lived — wise, sardonic, reticent, patrician, a Santayana among horses.

If Buck had a friend, it was Patsy. It was a friendship of opposites, for there was nothing patrician about Pat, and he was anything but a misanthrope. He would come from anywhere in the pasture at the sound of his name, and let himself be haltered with apron strings or a hair ribbon. Of course he exploited us shamelessly; his chubbiness was mostly sugar lumps. But he gave full return in affection.

Buck's regard for Patsy was tolerant, protective, an elder brotherly regard. Pat's attitude toward Buck varied between impudence and awe. But when Dixie came into the family — the fractious little blonde who wrecked Klaus Sevcik's aspirations to become a "branco-buster" — she attached herself to Pat with a glutinous affection, rather like a schoolgirl crush. It was feminine, but innocent; Pat was of course a gelding. Pat liked Dixie well enough, but he could live without her. Dixie obviously felt that she couldn't live without him.

In his dilettante fashion Pat was a working horse, and was kept in the home pasture. Dixie remained fractious and undependable, and Oscar decided to turn her out into the homestead across the river. Next morning she was back with Patsy. We took her across the river and checked the fence for breaks. Midafternoon Oscar looked up from his work and swore: "That goddam mare! She's back again."

This time we hobbled her. Next morning she was grazing beside Patsy. The hobbles were still on. A displaced pole showed where she had crashed through the buck fence. We tried cross hobbling — the off front foot hobbled to the nigh rear foot. Same story.

We gave up. From then on Dixie remained in the home pasture with her idol.

Among horses as among men friendships may develop from mere propinquity, and survive through habit. Horses obliged to work together as a team become dependent on each other. You match them for size, gait, occasionally color; you don't consult their preferences, and often they make it plain that they don't much like your pairing. But once the partnership is established it is likely to last.

Tony and Bollie were our oldest team, and by the time I was promoted to full-time duty they were semipensioners. Tony was phlegmatic, uncomplaining; he had learned resignation with the years. Bollie had always been and always would be a malcontent. There was orneriness in the roll of his eye, and Tony was the principal object of his orneriness. If I flicked Bollie with the tip of the line to bring the pusher into motion, he would lay back his ears at Tony. If the pusher pole jogged his leg in turning he bared his teeth at Tony. If a fly fastened on his belly, where the net did not protect him, and where tail and hoof could not reach, Tony was obviously to blame. Tony took it like an early Christian, and never retorted in kind.

Yet when I rounded up the horses in the morning I would find them grazing side by side. And on a drowsy Sunday afternoon they would stand together, in that Damon-and-Pythias pose horses adopt, nose to tail, nibbling each other caressingly, the picture of fraternity and reciprocity, you-scratch-my-back-and-I'll-scratch-yours.

The equine pecking order has nothing to do with size. Diminutive Patsy was unchallenged boss of the horse herd. Belle, twice his dimensions, would move on unprotestingly if he indicated a preference for the forkful of hay she was munching. Sometimes, out of sheer malice, he would go from one haycock to the next, taking a mouthful here, another there, just to see his companions yield place at the tilt of an ear, a show of teeth. He never molested Buck, though. Nobody molested Buck, and Buck molested nobody.

I have remarked that horses are teamed up on the basis of size, gait, and occasionally color. Oscar introduced a fourth factor, nomenclature. He liked to pair the names as well as the horses; indeed, he often predestined colts to a life in double harness in the act of christening them. Dolly and Nelly, Belle and Queen, Tom and Jerry grew up together, were broken to harness together, worked together, and eventually were pensioned together.

Breaking horses, as we did it, was neither so picturesque nor so violent as the procedures you know from fiction and the films. "Breaking," indeed, is the wrong word; it implies conflict, duress, the subjugation of one will to another. That, to be sure, is what happens when a horse that has run the open range for the first three or four years of his life, hardly ever seeing or smelling mankind, is herded into a corral, roped, snubbed down, blindfolded, saddled, and turned loose to exhaust his fright and fury in the effort (usually vain in spite of the newsreels) to dislodge the creature astride his spine, to snap the constriction around his midriff, to spit out the nasty object in his mouth. That procedure, harsh as it may seem, usually works, and none other is practicable on a big ranch. Our ranch, however, was small, and our horses were under fence the year round. If I grew up with horses, it was equally true that horses grew up with me. From birth they were handled, fondled, coddled. They tagged along to the hayfield with their mothers, stealing a sip of lunch when they could. They learned that overalls pockets sometimes hid sugar lumps. They discovered the sensuous satisfaction of being rubbed around the ears and under the jowls — a susceptibility horses share with cats and dogs, and for all I know with jaguars and boa constrictors, though I have never experimented. They never learned to fear or distrust mankind because they had no reason to do so.

Breaking a colt thus domesticated is a process of education, not intimidation. It requires only patience, a gentle hand and a low voice, and the constant reminder to oneself that the colt isn't being obstinate or fractious. If he doesn't immediately do what you want, it's because he doesn't yet understand what you do want. It's up to you to make it clear.

Dago was four years old when we decided to convert him from a draft horse to a saddle horse. At the end of an hour he was trotting sedately around the corral with Oscar in the saddle. He was still a little puzzled, visibly self-conscious, but trying with all his affectionate heart to get the hang of this strange new game. We started by placing a saddle blanket on his back, taking it off and putting it on again half a dozen times until it had lost its strangeness. The same routine was repeated with the saddle. Then, little by little, the cinches were tightened. Dago grunted, and flicked an inquiring ear, but didn't protest. If we were doing this to him it must be all right. Then at last Oscar swung into the saddle, as gently as his 190 pounds permitted, sat there a few seconds, and swung down again, while I fondled Dago's head and talked soothingly into his ear. Twice more; then Oscar gathered up the reins and heeled him gently in the ribs. "Come on, Dago," I coaxed, backing away. Dago followed me. Not one snort, one jump, one tailspin or sunfish or other manner of fireworks. Dull, perhaps, but effective.

It is as meaningless to say "I like horses" as to say "I like people." Both statements betray a lack of discrimination. Affection so general, dilute, and Saroyanesque cannot nourish or warm. You may, at most, confess a predisposition to like people if they give you excuse or encouragement; you don't renounce the right to dislike the lady upstairs who practices Bartók at 11:45 P.M.

My predisposition is to like horses. That is not to say, however, that I like all horses indiscriminately. Even on our ranch we had favorites, and we didn't always agree. Oscar had an unshakable prejudice against horses with Roman noses; he insisted they were innately contrary, and usually stupid. I liked Dave in spite of his nose. Oscar couldn't abide Jinx. I loved her (not with any "Roan Stallion" overtones) because she was beautiful, with a pert, winsome face and a hide like — yes, I'm afraid satin is the proper word. My brother could have forgiven her beauty, even applauded it, but he couldn't forgive her for being smart, too. Not smart in a good, bread-and-butter fashion, as Buck was, but mischievously, capriciously, femininely smart. If Buck was a Santayana among horses, Jinx was a Jimmy Valentine. She used that pretty nose to open gates and pry up the lids of oat boxes. She was always where she had no business being. We finally put a hasp and a harness-snap on the oat box and took to wiring the stable gate shut. Oscar cussed that damn mare roundly and swore he'd work the mischief out of her. I chuckled over her exploits. Like Frost, I am disposed, wherever I encounter it, to respect the least display of mind.

If we had conducted a popularity poll, Ted and Star would have won it easily. They were our crack buggy team; hitched to the two-wheeled breaking cart they could whisk us to town in two hours — less than that if we met an automobile or two on the way. They never accepted the motor age, even after we had a Buick of our own. When a racketing pillar of smoke and fire hove over the horizon, you headed for a siding if you could find one; if not, you took a double wrap on the lines, dug your heels into the dashboard, and set yourself for a ride. After a mile you could usually saw them down to a brisk trot. We came to suspect that their terror was largely simulated, merely an excuse for a romp.

I damned them heartily at times. One morning in late

winter I was trying to feed the cattle. Normally it's a two-man job; this time I was alone. After loading the wagon, I knotted the lines to the front of the rack, chirped gently to Ted and Star, and started to pitch. The next moment I was on my back in the hay and the laden wagon was bumping across the frozen turf. I snatched the lines, pulled the team down to a walk, said various uncomplimentary things, and picked up the fork. One forkful, and they were off at a trot, leaving the hungry herd behind. I braked us to a stop and tried it again.

Finally, a forkful or two at a time, I got the hay unloaded. I made Ted and Star walk every step of the way back to the barn, their chins pulled down against their chests, and every step I told them what I was going to do to them when we got there. Of course I did none of those things. The moment I pulled off the bridles they leaned against me and began rubbing their sweaty heads. You can no more chide a horse when he is using you for a rubbing post than you can quarrel with a woman when she buries her cheek in your shoulder.

Coyotes don't properly belong in this chapter, of course. But no account of ranch life would be complete without some discussion of *Canis latrans*. First cousin of *Canis familiaris*, and therefore close kin to my Shep, who used to escort us to school every morning, leave us at the bridge fifty yards from the door, and be back there waiting when we were dismissed at four o'clock. But how different! Stealthy instead of confiding, treacherous instead of loyal; skulker, predator, thief, killer. And, incongruously, a minstrel of sorts, on moonlight nights particularly. The Villon of beasts, perhaps.

Let's get one thing straight right now. In Wyoming he's a *ki*-ote, not a koy-*o*-tee. Save that pronunciation — closer, I'll admit, to the original *coyotl*, which my dictionary says was Nahuatl — for the Southwest. In our country it would stamp you as a tenderfoot.

In one particular the coyote does resemble the dog. He's smart. Cunning — crafty, if you prefer — words we reserve for intelligence applied to purposes of which we disapprove. But intelligence he has in abundance.

I recall a particularly baffling episode.

Driving to the northernmost meadow one morning in haying time, we saw a coyote in the middle distance. He paused to inspect us, with leisurely insolence, and trotted off. No hurry.

"I'll be damned!" Oscar said. "If we only had a gun!"

Next morning there he was. Same time, same place. A repeat performance complete.

"By God!" Oscar said, "tomorrow by God I *will* bring a gun."

Next day the Savage .303 was tucked out of sight in the bottom of the wagon, cartridge in the chamber, safety on. I was driving, so that Oscar could move instantly to battle stations. This time, Mr. Coyote, we'd teach you a lesson.

No coyote.

Next morning, and the morning after that, the same story: gun ready, trigger finger itching. But no coyote.

Now how did he know?

An incredibly keen sense of smell, which caught the menace of gunmetal and powder at 150 yards? Or ESP?

I lean toward ESP.

Mama used to relate that before my time she had tried to raise turkeys. She gave up after practically all of one hatch had been nipped off in nightly forays by coyotes, even though the young birds roosted on the fence enclosing the yard, not seventy-five feet from the kitchen door.

Coyotes don't insist on turkey; they like chicken too. One day while we were at dinner we heard a hideous squawking from the chicken yard. Rushing out, we saw a coyote trotting up the hill, a pullet in his jaws. Next day we were on watch; sure enough, punctually at noon, he came down the hill, picked out a plump fryer, and trotted off to lunch.

This was a bit too much. By 11:45 next morning Oscar was ambushed behind the fence, with the .303 at the ready, and a free-fire zone across the pasture to the hill.

Punctually at noon the coyote appeared. (Like his cousin Shep, he seemed to have a built-in chronometer.) But for once ESP had failed him. Sniffing no danger, he headed for the chicken house. When he was perfectly silhouetted against the sky Oscar fired.

He missed. Dust spurted up a foot ahead of the marauder, and a second later, as the .303 spoke again, a foot behind him. His reflexes were hair-trigger; he had spun around at the crack of the gun, and by the time Oscar had pumped another shell into the chamber his quarry was going away fast. Osc got off one more shot before he disappeared over the hill.

"Well," my brother said ruefully. "I scared the shit out of him, anyway. I bet he won't be back." And he wasn't.

Coyotean ESP, obviously, wasn't infallible. But it didn't miss once the winter Oscar and I set out traps. We planted the bait enticingly; we buried the traps in snow or covered them with leaves and smoothed away every visible trace of human presence. Visible to our critical eyes, at any rate. Yet when we came by next day the bait would be gone, the trap unsprung, and the story humiliatingly clear in the tracks that skillfully sidestepped the hidden danger.

Our neighbor Art Johnson was smarter. He made quite a little extra money that winter on coyote pelts — $2.50 to $5.00, depending on the market — and the bounty — $5.00. He was willing to share his secrets with us, but no matter how hard we tried to follow his coaching we never caught a coyote.

There aren't many of them left. Forty years ago you were pretty sure of being serenaded as you sat by your campfire or snuggled down into your bedroll. An eerie sound, at once mocking and mournful, a sneer and a sob commingled. In reality, of course, neither. We are incorrigibly anthropomorphic, ascribing our own emotions to every other creature that shares the planet with us. Possibly Robert Ardrey is right, and that moonlight minstrel who sang me to sleep one night in the Shirley Basin, long ago, wasn't snickering at my expense, or grieving over a lost love, but merely asserting his hegemony over that particular creek bottom and the hills cradling it.

It doesn't matter. It was somehow comforting to hear him out there; he was company.

I have written "he" and "him," but it might have been "they" and "them." You're never quite sure; a coyote's howl has a polyphonic quality; one lone animal on a butte may sound like a pack.

It is twenty years since I heard a coyote, much longer since I saw one. The ranchers and the government hunters have pretty well wiped them out, with gun and trap and poison. Of course we paid the penalty, as we always do when we meddle with the balance of nature. The rabbits and other rodents multiplied prodigiously. So man's fantastic ingenuity in slaughter had to be directed against them. Very effectively, too. If you want to be sure of seeing a prairie dog (no *Canis* he, despite the name; he's *Cynomys ludovicianus*), you'd better go to Devil's Tower National Monument, where he flourishes under the benign guardianship of the Government.

It's the same government, of course, that hires or subsidizes hunters, provides ranchers with poison and instructions for using it, and has connived at the extermination of whole species, or looked on benignly while they were exterminated.

The hunter (to do him grudging justice) has his rationale. If antelope, deer and elk were permitted to multiply unhindered, he argues, they would soon exhaust the food supply, and would perish miserably by hunger. In Wyoming now you don't talk of killing game; at least the State Game Division doesn't. The correct term is "harvesting." *Wyoming Wildlife* reports that approximately twenty thousand deer were "harvested" annually in the decade 1960–1970.

The sons and grandsons of men who killed for food now kill — excuse me, harvest — professedly to rectify the balance of nature. The elk's tooth in the watch charm and the ten-point buck looking glassily down from the den wall are merely fringe benefits of that praiseworthy endeavor.

But who upset the balance of nature?

The most ruthless and destructive of all predators, of course, the one that slays not for food but for fun, and for *machismo:*

> *What shall I kill this morning, sir,*
> *To prove that I am I?*
> *The cricket leaping across the rug,*
> *The too inquisitive fly?* *

---

* John Russell McCarthy, "Morning Question," *The New Yorker,* October 11, 1941.

11

How to Succeed
at Ranching, Maybe

THERE ARE TWO SCHOOLS OF THOUGHT about the best
way to make a living, and a little extra, out of livestock.

One believes in a rapid turnover and a quick profit. You
buy a bunch of cattle — calves or yearlings — in the
fall. You feed them through the winter, fatten them in
the summer, on the public domain or under fence, market
them in the fall, and start all over again.

The other school has a longer perspective; it aims not
at the fast buck but at the more modest returns of steady
growth. It is founded on the propensity of any species to
multiply. If you start out — let's take an implausibly
oversimplified example — with twenty cows and one bull,
total twenty-one head, by next spring you ought to have
nearly doubled your original investment. Not quite; the
reproduction rate is rarely 100 per cent, and some allowance must be made for loss.

The progression is not geometric, of course; by the law

of averages half of the calves will be male. But in a few years your original capital will have increased considerably, your annual income from marketing the steers will be substantial, and you will have to buy more bulls.

The one system is speculative, the other organic. You may recognize the parallel with transactions in a more familiar form of stock, the kind listed in the back pages of your newspaper. You can buy and sell for a quick profit, relying on your acumen to keep ahead of the vagaries of the market, or you can put your money in growth stocks.

My father, as the earlier chapters have suggested, operated on the organic system. When he quit the Union Pacific, bought out his partner and moved to the ranch, he sold off all the cattle except six milk cows, at a flat price of fifteen dollars a head. From this nucleus — there must have been a bull on the premises or in the neighborhood, too — he slowly built up a herd.

Those were lean years, before the annual marketings brought enough even to pay the interest at the bank. The records Papa continued to keep, as methodically as he had noted down his runs on the railroad, and mostly in the same notebooks, show some of the ways in which he and Mama scraped together the cash income to keep going.

They sold hay to other ranchers, or pastured and fed their cattle.

March 1 99   6 tons of Hay at 6 dollars per ton $36.00   received by cash $15.

March 11 99   Received 36 head of cattle from Burg to pasture at one dollar per head for month. Cattle to be fed hay when necessary.

March 24 one ton of hay for Burg 28.00 per ton

April 9 took away 19 head of cattle

Took cattle home May 10th

Sold to Harnden 1 stack of Hay Nov. 1st 1902. Length 24, with
18/2½ over 33.
Nov. 1st 1902: Received from Harnden $20.00

Nov.	7	10.00
Nov.	12	10.00
	22	10.00
	28	10.00
Dec.	6	16.10

Butter sales brought in a valuable supplementary income. The Riverside ranch, five miles downriver, was a
steady customer. Though it ran three thousand head of
cattle, it had milk enough only for "the Big House," and
the cowhands creamed their coffee out of a can. But they
ate the best butter, churned and packaged by my mother.
The journals record that between November 8 and March
5 one winter (the years are not identified) my parents
sold 228 pounds of butter plus one gallon of cream, and
received fifty-two dollars. The deliveries are usually identified "the Big House," or simply "B house," and "bunkhouse." I assume the cream went to the Big House.

Another listing:

Butter for D. C. Bacon

April 27 97	20 lbs
May 4	20 lbs
May 5	10 lbs
May 13	10 lbs
June 4	20 lbs

Received payment July 1st [amount not given]

Dan Bacon, of the firm of Balch & Bacon, which owned
the Riverside, was not only our best customer; he helped
my parents in other ways. Oscar recalls that our original

herd was augmented now and then by heifer calves that the Riverside apparently considered surplus. (I can't understand how even a big ranch could have had too many heifer calves; perhaps they were orphans, too young to market and too much bother to bring up on skim milk.)

I never knew Bacon, but my parents spoke of him often, with respect and affection. One senses, in their recollections and Oscar's, a friendship founded on mutual liking but flavored with a trace of patronage. Hans Olson and Daniel C. Bacon could hardly have been more different in background: the one a Norwegian immigrant, self-educated, ex-seaman, ex-railroader, struggling rancher; the other a New England Brahmin, classmate of Theodore Roosevelt, generally considered aloof and crusty. But clearly he and my father found something in common, qualities to admire, interests to share.

He died young. The Riverside was sold and fell on evil days. The Balches moved back East. The Big House burned down. And the Big Laramie had lost the nearest thing to a manor and a squire it was ever to know.

Year by year the offspring of those original six cows — and Dan Bacon's heifers — multiplied. By 1901 Dad could write:

Turned out 69 head of cattle, 16 yearlings of whom 7 were steers and 9 heifers.

When I was old enough to take inventory, we had a respectable capital investment in cattle, horses, hogs, chickens, occasionally sheep, machinery and buildings. We weren't sole owners, I was to learn later. The First National Bank was a silent partner, and a good share of the check that Papa or Oscar brought back from Omaha after the fall shipping went to pay interest. Papa did not live to enjoy the sensation of being free of debt, and the traditional ceremony of burning the mortgage. His life insurance made the last payment.

Obviously our ranch bore little resemblance to the gigantic "spreads" of fiction and television — and of fact, too; witness the LBJ and King empires in Texas. About all we had in common was that we both raised and sold cattle—prime rib roasts and filet mignon and chuck steak and stewing beef for the tables of the ultimate consumer.

The King ranch occupies 970,000 acres of Texas — not to mention even larger holdings in Australia, and sizable areas in South America and Africa. Admittedly this is outsize. But there are quite a few cattle empires that could tuck a European principality or grand duchy into the southeast pasture and never notice it.

We had eight hundred acres under fence, and grazing rights in the Medicine Bow National Forest — subject to annual revision, usually downward, by the Forest Service. The original 640 acres had been expanded by 160 when Dad homesteaded a quarter section south of the river.* (This somewhat chilled relations with our neighbors, the Con Hammonds, who had been eying the same tract. Con and Mrs. Hammond didn't come up so often afterward for evening solo games.)

The great ranches count their herds in the tens of thousands. Even the Riverside ran 3,000 head of cattle. Our bunch fluctuated between 100 and 150. The Riverside cut

* The Homestead Act requires that the claimant "prove up" by building a house and living in it for a year. As the statute of limitations must have run out long ago, I can divulge now that Dad complied *pro forma* by moving the old bunkhouse across the river, log by numbered log, and spending one night in it. This was a practice widely followed and generally condoned in the Winning of the West.

3,500 tons of hay. We stacked 150 tons on an average, maybe 200 in an exceptional year.

Many of the big outfits of the late nineteenth and early twentieth centuries — those that inspired *The Virginian* and other novels — raised only enough hay to feed their horses. Cattle had to fend for themselves. In summer they fattened on the prairie bunchgrass, sparse to the eye, but rich in nourishment. In winter they were expected to forage as antelope and buffalo foraged, digging through the drifts to the frozen tufts they had missed before, eating snow for water after streams and ponds froze over, huddling tail to the wind, or drifting with it. The wind was murderous, and there was no escaping it unless a coulee or a rocky upthrust gave shelter. Stock sometimes traveled a hundred miles, lashed along by that relentless herdsman. If their drift was stopped by any barrier they died. You heard tales of cattle bunched up against a fence, frozen to death on their feet.

Losses were appalling — 30 per cent, 40 per cent, and more. The big outfits could usually take it, though an exceptionally savage winter — that of 1886–1887, for example — might wipe some of them out.

It was a cruel way of doing business. A Montana cowboy named Charles M. Russell caught that cruelty in a watercolor sketch that started him toward fame. It shows a cow, all bones and hide, bracing herself against the level drive of a blizzard, while a few yards away two coyotes, almost as emaciated, bide their time. The title: "Waiting for a Chinook."

Our cattle were under fence well before the first blizzards — except for the few that didn't come back from the mountains — and our loss was rarely more than a few per cent. We tried not to stock more than we could winter safely. We figured a ton of hay per head, with a margin for emergency. In North Park, just across the Colorado border, ranchers doubled that allowance; the snows came earlier, piled up higher, stayed longer, and didn't blow away. I don't remember more than one or two occasions when we ran short and had to buy hay. That hurt; by the end of a hard winter it sold for thirty to forty dollars a ton.

In still another particular, and an important one, we differed from the big outfits. We were farmers as well as ranchers. We grew much of our food, though of course we had to bring the staples from town — flour, sugar, coffee, spices, canned goods to supplement the fruits and vegetables we put down for the winter. Milk, cream, butter and eggs we had in abundance, with a surplus for sale or barter. When we needed meat we butchered a steer or a pig or a sheep, and stowed it* in the icehouse, and sawed off a steak or roast or chops as we needed them. We cured hams with juniper smoke. Our garden supplied lettuce, peas, beans, carrots, turnips, rutabagas, parsnips, radishes — anything that would mature at 7,500 feet. (Not, alas, tomatoes; they came out of cans.) Whatever could be preserved Mama put up in Mason jars. The root vegetables were stored in the root cellar, buried in sand; we kept a kerosene lamp burning there on cold nights. Gooseberries and currants from our hedge and the thickets along the creek and the river provided jams and jellies.

We didn't have much pocket money. I still find it easier to write a check for a hundred dollars than to spend a dollar unnecessarily. But we ate abundantly and well, winter and summer. I sometimes reflect that nobody under forty — no city dweller, at least — knows what good food really tastes like. What do we get now? Vegetables doctored with additives and preservatives, and

* Or more likely a half or a quarter; the rest would go to a neighbor, who would pay back in kind the next time he butchered.

then deep-frozen. Bread without substance or nutritional value; didn't somebody once win a bet that he could squeeze a whole loaf into a ball easily clutched in one hand? Beef overfattened to produce the mandatory "marbling." Bacons and hams quick-cured with chemicals. Everything jazzed up with spices to disguise the homely natural flavor.

Today you drop a clammy green brick into a half inch of boiling water and wait for it to expand into something visually recognizable as the "fresh garden peas" on the label. Try to imagine — or if you were lucky enough to have grown up on a farm to remember — what peas taste like when you pick them yourself. You select only pods still slim but rounding nicely, not yet swollen into tough middle-aged adiposity. You shell them — and what fun it is to slit the pod expertly and scoop the pellets out with one deft sweep of the thumb! An hour or two later you sit down to relish the product, tender morsels cooked in milk and butter, lightly salted and peppered.

You can still hunt up a farmers' market, of course, and buy vegetables allegedly picked that morning. You can still bake your own bread. But how many people bother? The supermarket is so handy, and there are so many other claims on one's time.

Ours was among the first ranches in the Laramie Basin, if not indeed the very first, to raise grain as well as hay on a sizable scale. The early settlers had thought that the high plains were too arid, the soil too lean and stony, the seasons too short for farming. Dad decided to try, anyway. He plowed up part of the benchland north of the house, which until then had nourished only prairie grass, built a network of ditches, and sowed oats, wheat and barley. They flourished.

The word spread. Other ranchers came to scoff and

went away to try it themselves. Ours became something of a showplace. When, a good many years later, a firm of developers and promoters took over the Riverside and began chopping it up into 160-acre plots for sale to land hungry innocents from the East, the Olson ranch was on the grand tour arranged for them.

I remember long caravans of cars driving in, loaded with pilgrims. They gawked at the shimmering reaches of oats and wheat; they visited the granary and dipped their fingers in the bins, not quite emptied of last year's harvest. And they came to the house to see the Medal.

The Medal was a three-inch disc of gold (we assumed; it was yellow, and heavy) representing Third Prize for oats at the National Corn Exposition in Omaha. We were proud of that medal, but always a bit woeful when we took it out to admire. The name on it wasn't Olson; it was John A. Kunkle.

Oh, yes, our oats had won it legitimately. But not the oats we ourselves had sent in. We had chosen our entry with prayerful care, picking it over literally kernel by kernel. We had mailed it well in advance of the closing date, and waited, teetering between pessimism and confidence, for the judging.

We never heard of it again.

A week or two before the deadline Mr. Kunkle, who knew the quality of our grain because he had seen it flow out of his threshing machine, decided suddenly to enter the contest. He scooped up a peck or so, said thank you, and raced off to get his entry in the mails.

When the medal came he was decent enough to hand it over. I don't know how Papa felt. But we children were bitter. We firmly believed — indeed to this day I believe — that if our own hand-sorted sample had reached the judges it would have won First Prize, by acclamation.

As to the pilgrims, quite a number took the bait. They sold everything they owned back in Ohio, or North Carolina, or Vermont, and moved into clapboard and tarpaper shacks on their quarter sections to start new lives. You can still see some of the shacks, the few that haven't been cannibalized, or collapsed to rot back into the soil. The owners are long gone, back where they came from, I suppose, pauperized and chastened by a year or two of semistarvation.

Sometimes, in those night hours when a long-dormant conscience stirs, I wonder why we didn't warn them off. Look, we could have said, you can't *live* in Wyoming on 160 acres. What about water? Do you have a water right? Are there ditches? Is there any open water for stock? What about stock? Where are you going to graze them? Have you got capital enough to keep going until you start selling something?

Nobody warned them, so far as I know. Why not? Maybe respect for the rugged free enterprise on which we were taught our country's greatness had been founded. Maybe the traditional Western feeling that any tenderfoot is fair game; there's no closed season. Maybe we just didn't want to meddle.

All the same, my conscience twitches.

Grain was both a cash and a barter crop. We freighted much of it to town to pay grocery bills. (I try to imagine how the manager of the Laramie Safeway would gawk and stutter now if a rancher drove in with a four-horse load of oats and wanted to dicker.) Some we sold directly to neighbors, some to the livery barns. And of course our own livestock got first call.

There were a few months when a mirage of sudden wealth danced before our dazzled eyes. Oil had been struck in Wyoming. The Salt Creek field in midstate, north of Casper, was already showing promise of fabulous productivity. (The promise was amply fulfilled, although the fulfillment produced a scandal that wrecked a Cabinet and may have contributed to the death of a President.) Geologists were crisscrossing the state in quest of anticlines. Wildcatters were puncturing the prairie with holes, mostly dry. Bobcat-eyed promoters were getting signatures on leases.

One of them reached Laramie and worked his way methodically up the river. We signed. Everybody signed. What we signed I have no idea; I hope Mama and Oscar studied the fine print. There was great excitement, all the way from Woods Landing to the Riverside and Harmony, when a crew actually appeared and started setting up a rig on Sodergreen's ranch, not far from the schoolhouse. Whenever I could I went up and watched the beam wagging rhythmically up and down, bothered the drill crew with questions, hoped I would be lucky enough to be on hand when the gusher came in.

It never did. I don't know how deep they went, but obviously they had no encouragement. One day they pulled their tools, packed up, and moved on. The wooden rig was left to rot away. Obviously we were not destined for wealth. I don't recall being much disappointed.

12

An Empty Place
at the Table

THE MEMORY is a remarkable computer system, with a fantastic storage bank. But its programing can be infuriatingly erratic. It will spew out, unbidden, torrents of trivia — a song heard forty years ago, words and melody complete, the title and plot of a novel by Cyrus Townsend Brady. Then, when you really need help, it lets you down; you choke up tight on the name of the old friend you are about to introduce.

Too often in this memoir I have come across stretches as blank as the interior of Australia on the maps in our geography text.

My brother has appeared often in these reminiscences: Oscar admonishing me, "Get your kindlin', Kid!" Oscar roping the schoolhouse steps; Oscar showing Klaus how a "branco" should be ridden; Oscar tutoring me in the manifold skills of ranching. The memories are detailed and vivid.

But I have no recollection of Oscar's leaving the ranch.

Not just for a night on the town, not to escort a shipment of cattle to Omaha, but presumably for good. Try as I will, I can call up no parting scene, no farewells, no picture of the familiar lanky figure riding up the hill, turning at the crest, perhaps, for a final lift of the hand.

I suppose I could fabricate a leave-taking, but it would be dishonest. I only know that suddenly Oscar wasn't there any more. His gear was gone from the bunkhouse, his saddle missing from its customary peg in the barn, his Dan no longer munching oats in the stall or grazing in the horse pasture, his customary place at the table empty.

It was from Oscar himself, many years afterward, that I learned the circumstances of his departure.

There had been friction between him and our father for a long time. Even I was dimly aware of it, and had witnessed a few flare-ups of temper. Papa did have a temper, that I knew; I had felt its cutting edge occasionally. Oscar, older, beginning to chafe at discipline, and temperamentally less docile, felt it more often.

He recalls, with nostalgic amusement, an early and trivial episode. Our neighbor just upriver, Charles Sodergreen, had dropped by on some errand. Oscar came into the kitchen and called cheerily, "Hello, Charlie."

Today nobody would find anything amiss with that. Everybody uses first names, even in acknowledging an introduction. But at the turn of the century, manners were as stiff and constricting as the foundation garments in the mail-order catalogues. I knew married couples that mistered and missussed each other punctiliously, anyway in public, and quite possibly in the bedroom.

For a half-grown boy to first-name any adult, let alone a man probably four times his age, was unheard-of impertinence. Oscar was fourteen or fifteen, which dates the incident in 1903 or 1904. Charles Sodergreen had fought in the Civil War; on Memorial Day he marched proudly with the Grand Army of the Republic. Our father's outrage was understandable.

"The Old Man sure reamed me out," Oscar says.

Another incident cost him something more than a verbal reaming out. Let him tell it.

"There was one cow I hated to milk. She had such big tits I could hardly squeeze them. So one night I figured I'd stall around, feeding and bedding the horses, until he'd have to take her.

"Well, he saw through my little scheme. When he finished his cows he picked up the pails and walked out.

"Was I mad! I cussed the cow, I cussed him, with every cussword I could think of. I was just about running out of cusswords when the door opened and he walked in. He hadn't gone to the house. He'd been listening just outside.

"He took down a rope and gave me the worst licking of my life."

There were other episodes, none of great consequence, but together building up a combustible residue of resentment. The incident that touched a match to that kindling was so trivial that Oscar himself had difficulty remembering the circumstances.

"We both had hot tempers; we were always jangling. One evening I was banging the milk pails around, and Dad said . . . Now what *was* I mad about? Oh, yes. It was Fair time, and I wanted to go in to the Fair, and Dad didn't want me to. So he said, 'I think it's about time you took out and tried it somewhere else, the way you're always talking about.' And I said, 'All right, I will.'

"Anyway, I rode into town to the Fair. I ran into Charlie Benson there and I hit him for a job at the Riverside. And he said come ahead."

I don't believe it was solely because he and Dad couldn't get along that Oscar left home. That was the proximate cause, but I suspect he would have taken out on his own pretty soon anyway. At nineteen or twenty it's normal to want to see a little more of the world. Indeed, it's an American tradition. That's how the continent got explored and populated.

Papa must have understood. It was the Norwegian tradition too. He himself had left home at fourteen. By the time he was Oscar's age he had been around the world, maybe more than once. I have wondered sometimes whether he too had jangled with his father, and gone off in a huff. He never told us anything that would suggest that. Going to sea was the normal thing for a Norwegian boy to do, particularly a boy who had grown up on a farm overlooking the fjord, with ships passing every day. Certainly there had been no permanent estrangement. My grandfather had come to Laramie himself once, before I was born, to visit, perhaps thinking to stay, but had returned to Norway.

It occurs to me that you don't find in the literature of those footloose times the pejorative language that we — and they themselves — apply now to young people that won't stay haltered. We don't think of Daniel Boone as a drop-out, Kit Carson as a cop-out, Captain Ahab's chronicler as a freak-out. "Call me Ishmael." The tone is pride, not apology.

Drop-out . . . cop-out . . . freak-out . . . The adverb on which those nouns are built implies exodus. We are tempted to say querulously: "All those kids seem to want OUT. Doesn't anybody want IN?" We tend to forget that the mountain men and the families in the covered wagons also were moving out, and that any exodus inevitably involves a TO as well as a FROM, whether or not predetermined.

Is there just possibly something in common between our venerated pioneers and the hairy hordes that now roll like tumbleweed across Europe and Asia, lodging briefly in such unlikely fence corners as Kathmandu and Goa? Go West, young man, and grow up with the country. Go East, young man (and woman); you may find Shangri-La.

Oscar was to discover that the life of a cowboy wasn't altogether what he had expected. Even on the Riverside there were lots of jobs that couldn't be done from the saddle: mowing, raking and stacking hay, pitching it out in winter, keeping irrigation ditches clear, opening and closing head gates — chores that Chip of the Flying U and the other members of B. M. Bower's "Happy Family" never had to perform.* Still, on a big ranch there was a lot more elbowroom and variety. With so many hands to share the work, the daily routine was not inflexible. A man might be mending fence one afternoon, and the next morning setting out with a four-horse team to pick up a load of supplies. Oscar's competence was quickly recognized; more and more often he was entrusted with errands requiring judgment and responsibility.

We were glad he hadn't taken off for the Yukon, as he might have done ten years earlier. He rode up now and then for Sunday dinner. We saw him at country dances, squiring one after another of the marriageable girls in a twenty-mile radius. And once, at the County Fair, we screamed our throats raw as he tried to coax and spur and fan and quirt his mount across the finish line in the wild-horse race. He never made it. After leading the pack all the way around the half-mile track the horse panicked at the sight and sound of the crowd and started pitching again. He was still at it, with Oscar raking him from stem to stern at every jump, when the winners were announced. There is a photograph in the family archives

* B. M. Bower's novels about ranch life in Montana were immensely popular in the first two decades of this century.

showing Oscar in front of the stands, making a handsome ride.

We all missed Oscar. Papa perhaps most of all. I was too young to step into my brother's boots, and there was no way of cutting the job down to my measure, as Mama had often retailored his outgrown shirts.

13

Parents
Aren't Supposed to Die

I come now, reluctantly, to the one episode which, if memory could be amended by purge or surgery, I would most gladly excise. I have carried the shame and the hurt for sixty years.

I had been working in the fields some distance from the house and had come in late for dinner. The family were already at the table. I was famished; I sat myself down without bothering to wash up. Papa admonished me: "Wash your hands and comb your hair."

I glared at him, and saw that he meant it. Resentfully I stalked to the washstand, splashed and toweled sketchily, ran a comb through my hair, and returned to the table. Then, deliberately, I rumpled my hair again.

Immediately I was shocked at what I had done. I had never before shown my father such insolence, defied him so openly. If ever I had deserved a summons to the woodshed, this was certainly the occasion.

But nothing happened. We finished our dinner in

silence. Nothing further was said of my behavior, then or afterward.

Five months later my father died, of the cancer with which, though I had not then known it, he was already sickening.

Childhood is the kingdom where nobody dies.
Nobody that matters, that is . . .
Mothers and fathers don't die.

Long afterward I was to find in those lines of Millay an explanation — or at least a rationalization — for my blindness and lack of comprehension. Surely I must have noticed that my father was not his usual alert, energetic self. He moved less briskly. His voice had lost timbre and authority. More and more often he would go to bed immediately after supper, sometimes without eating supper at all. I didn't think much about that; it had happened occasionally before. If I wondered about such incidents I attributed them to the spells of moodiness that sometimes took possession of him — an upwelling of the melancholia that appeared occasionally in his journal and his notations in books.

I am rationalizing even now. I must try to be honest. I cannot recall anything really disquieting about that summer. If I ever asked Mama whether there was anything wrong with Papa I do not remember it. I must have been cocooned, selfishly and impenetrably, in my own preoccupations. I did my chores. I watered the flower beds and weeded the garden. I helped in the hayfield. In my spare time — and I still had plenty of that — I fished inexpertly, read ravenously, and began filling nickel notebooks with verse modeled on Gray's "Elegy."

I did know, to be sure, that Papa had been painfully hurt in a fall on the ice at *Tante* Christie's house the previous January, and that the injury had continued to plague him. He was alone on the ranch that winter, except for a hired man. Mama had moved the girls and me to town so that we could go to school, and had moved herself with us, because our great-aunt was too infirm to look after us as she had looked after Hattie the previous year. I accepted this arrangement without thinking. Only now, reliving that distant time, do I begin to realize the sacrifices our parents made so that we could get an education, and the ingenuity of their logistical improvisations.

Papa, in town for the night, had gone out to the woodshed for coal, had slipped on the glaze, and in falling had struck his right side against the scuttle. He came into the house in obvious agony. Did anybody suggest sending for a doctor? I don't remember, but I doubt it. People living twenty-two miles from town — at least three hours with a team — and with no telephone, get accustomed to doing without doctors. If there is no visible fracture, or steadily soaring fever, you wait and see if it won't get better by itself. Papa assured Mama next morning that he *was* better. It was probably just a bad bruise. He insisted on going back to the ranch.

I have wondered many times: if he *had* consulted Dr. Hamilton next morning, instead of waiting until months later, might his life have been prolonged? Or was the liver irreparably damaged?

A more observant boy, less deeply immersed in his own concerns, might have asked more questions when Oscar reappeared at the ranch, dumped his war bag in the bunkhouse, and took his old place at the table. If I asked any, they were not searching. My brother was back with us, where he belonged. I assumed that he'd had his fling, and was tired of being a hired hand, taking orders from strangers. The family was together again.

The real story I learned long afterward.

146

He had come back to the ranch to say good-bye before setting out for a much longer journey. The Swift interests were recruiting cowpunchers for their holdings in Argentina. They offered good wages, a three-year contract, transportation both ways if you stayed the three years. He had given up his job at the Riverside the first of July. He planned to stay at the ranch over the Fourth, and then head south, with another cowboy from the Riverside.

He hadn't known that Dad's illness was serious.

"Mama asked me if I wouldn't come back, at least to help through haying. I told her: 'I'll come if *he*'ll ask me.'"

After two years the break was still sensitive. He was too stiff-necked to make the first step toward reconciliation.

"Dad asked me, and I stayed.

"The fellow I was planning to go with did go, along with another man. They were back that winter. If I hadn't received a card from Buenos Aires I'd never have believed they'd been there. So I suppose I was just as well-off. Still, I would have had the trip."

There is a ghost of regret in that last sentence. I hadn't suspected until then that Oscar too had once had the itch for to admire and for to see, the itch that had sent Papa around the world. He was never to get farther from Wyoming than on short trips to Ohio, California and Arizona.

In September, knowing and suspecting nothing, I was packed off to town to enter high school. I cannot remember asking why Hattie and Martha were being kept home. Was it because they were considered old enough to know of Papa's illness, and I was not, and because Mama realized that they would be more useful? Or had family counsel decided that I was never going to make much of a ranchman, and that therefore I'd better get as much learning as possible, in lieu of stature, sinew and practical skills?

For the next few weeks I was busy with the adjustments a high school freshman must make — particularly bewildering if he is a year or two younger and several sizes smaller than most of his classmates, and undisguisably a yokel.

When the Laramie doctors decided that Papa should go to Denver to consult a specialist I still did not suspect the gravity of his condition. Not even when he came back, a few days later, and I visited him at the hospital, saw how gaunt and weak he was, learned that there was to be no operation. I am astonished even now at my obtuseness, my inability or unconscious refusal to recognize that he was dying.

Parents just didn't die.

I don't remember what Mama told me of the Denver doctors' report. Certainly not the truth. Doubtless she felt there was no way in which my knowing would help anybody. They went back to the ranch, and I went back to school. I had no premonition that I would never see my father again.

Of the six Olsons only I escaped the next nightmare weeks. Happily the malignancy was so far advanced that death came mercifully soon. Even so, it must have been a hideous time. Medical science had not perfected any of the palliatives that now postpone and somewhat alleviate the terminal torture. I suppose there was morphine, for a while. After that only endurance, stretched beyond the limits of what anyone could be expected to endure.

One morning my landlady received a phone call from my Aunt Kari. Could I come down to see her? At once?

It was then, as I walked across town to the familiar house across the tracks, that I first began to suspect.

"Your father is dead," my aunt told me.

The day was October 15, 1911. Papa had passed his fifty-fourth birthday less than a month before.

Of the next few days I remember only the coffin sinking into the raw notch spaded for it, the thud of the ceremonial clods hitting the lid, the words of the graveside ritual falling without meaning on minds too numb to receive them. We huddled together, for comfort and for warmth. It was a bitter day. Now and then the wind flung a fistful of snowlike gravel in our faces.

Then it was over. Friends converged on us, stumbled through their speeches of sympathy, backed awkwardly away. The gathering thinned out. Mama thanked the preacher. We looked once more at that notch in the hillside, the mound of raw earth beside it already whitening with snow, and then turned away to go back to Aunt Kari's house.

Though we were to stay on the ranch five years more, I date from that October the beginning of changes that were to come with increasing frequency and momentum. And for the first time I began to realize that change is irreversible.

There was speculation among the neighbors — some of it even seeped down to me — about what Mama would do now. Sell the ranch and move to town? Turn it over to Oscar? Marry again? After all, she was only fifty. She had a good ranch, unencumbered by mortgages. Sooner or later Oscar would be wanting to get married and set up on his own. So no doubt the gossip ran.

Was Mama herself uncertain? I think not. The ranch was home. She and Papa had built it up together, lived there for a quarter of a century. Surely Papa would have wanted her to carry on.

As for marrying again, if the speculation reached her

she must have dismissed it indignantly. Marry again? She had married once and forever. To the end of her life, thirty-five years later, her voice would break and tears would come to her eyes when she spoke to us of "your father."

14

A Tale of Two Houses

THE YEAR AFTER PAPA'S DEATH Hattie and Martha were back in high school. Mama was determined, as Father had been, that we were to have as much education as we could soak up. Resourceful as always, she found us a small housekeeping apartment just across from the school building. We bickered a lot, naturally, but never quite to the point of mayhem. We all had pinkeye. Martha and Hattie got mumps, which I somehow escaped. Mama enriched our diet and simplified our housekeeping with frequent deliveries of eggs, butter, bread and cookies. In June Hattie received her diploma and signed up for summer courses at the University to qualify herself for teaching.

The next fall Martha decided to stay on the ranch and help Mama (another drop-out?), and I was boarded out again. I got home to the ranch oftener, now that we had a car — not just for Thanksgiving and Christmas, but sometimes over a weekend, if Oscar happened to have an errand in town.

It was on one such Friday afternoon, when he came to pick me up at my lodgings, that he told me he was planning to get married.

I wasn't much surprised. It had been evident for quite a while that my brother was, in Hardy's homely Wessex phrase, "in a very coming-on disposition for marriage." He had gone steady for a year or more with the daughter of a rancher living nearer town. Then they quarreled, neither of them would admit being wrong, they drifted apart. Recently Oscar had been squiring the new teacher at the Osterman school.

Oscar and Hannah Vay Dech were married March 6, 1914, in Denver, and Oscar brought our new sister-in-law home to the ranch.

Though Vay had grown up in Nebraska, she had roots in Wyoming. Her parents had once operated the Woods Landing post office and stage station, and Oscar had known her slightly then. She was something new in our experience of schoolteachers. She didn't fit either of the categories with which we were familiar: the local girl, just out of school herself, learning her craft at our expense; the aging spinster, soured and stove-up by decades of trying to break ornery colts to the gaits of learning. She was educated, well beyond the requirements for a license. She read books, and brought a good many with her. (The eight-volume set of Shakespeare I now consult when stumped by a crossword puzzle was hers.)

She brought her piano, too. She played well, and had an extensive repertoire — mostly popular and semiclassic, I think, though I was too ignorant to make distinctions. I remember particularly one composition, the one we always begged for, called "Heart Tones." I have no idea who wrote it, and I have never heard it performed or mentioned since. It was a portentous piece, with great husky chords in the bass, like the tolling of fate, and rising out of them a somber melody, resignation, consolation, and a measure of triumph. Thus at least I interpreted it. I was to find nothing equally satisfying until, a decade later, I encountered the "Pathétique."

It was obvious there wasn't room for all of us at the ranch. My parents had not had the foresight of their Norwegian forebears, whose custom it was to build an extra house to which the old people could retire when the eldest son took over the farm. So once more Mama packed us up — herself, Hattie, Martha and me — and moved us to town.

I still assumed, however, that my home was on the Big Laramie, and when school closed I headed joyfully for the ranch.

I don't think Oscar objected. I was beginning at last to get my growth; I was useful for something more than bringing in kindling and pulling weeds. The decade's difference in our ages seemed less formidable; fifteen and twenty-five have much more in common than five and fifteen. We were friends now. And mostly we worked well together, though I never would approach his easy competence.

Once or twice, however, I had occasion to suspect that Vay might not be as happy to have me underfoot as I was to be there.

One incident I mention only because hindsight identifies it as a portent.

We were in the kitchen one evening, in the relaxed hour between washing-up and bedtime. I don't recall what we were talking about. Certainly not prices at Omaha, or the way the oats were coming along. You could really *talk* with Vay — about books and ideas and ethical problems.

Whatever the topic was, at one point I ventured a mild demurrer. At least I meant it to be mild. But I recognize that I was a feisty youngster, and Vay may have had good grounds for considering it impertinent and me insolent.

She told me so, at some length, and with considerable vehemence, until she broke off into a paroxysm of coughing. Oscar hurried to get her medicine.

Vay was subject to such seizures; she suffered cruelly from asthma. It was agonizing to watch and listen as she struggled for breath. In 1914 doctors didn't know much about asthma; allergenic research was in its infancy, if indeed it had begun. Sometimes, they suggested doubtfully, a change of climate might help.

I was penitent at having provoked the seizure. I was also hurt. I considered setting out for town that very night, on foot. I didn't, of course; it would have been a pretty long walk in the dark. By morning the incident had fallen into perspective, and nobody spoke of it again.

The following June I was graduated from high school, and Mama packed us up again and moved us back to the ranch.

I still do not know whose decision that was, and what the reasons for it were. For once Oscar is no help. I can only speculate.

Mama may well have been hankering for the ranch. The little house on Fifth Street must have seemed cramped to someone accustomed to eight hundred acres of elbowroom and horizons unlimited. By her standards, she was underemployed, with only three to cook for, five small rooms to keep tidy, no chickens, no vegetable garden, only a niggardly strip of flowers. She had time to read again, to be sure, but reading was for evenings, not the middle of the day. We began going to the movies every Saturday afternoon; we never missed an episode of *The Clutching Hand* or *The Golden Giant Mine.*

I myself may have had some part in the decision. Thanks to an early start and the accommodating flexibility of School District No. 8, I was two years ahead of schedule. It seemed a good time to take a break, build up some muscle, and ponder who I was and where I belonged.

Oscar solved the housing problem by remodeling the bunkhouse — the one my enemy, Ole Viklund, had hewn out and pegged together. He partitioned one half into bedroom and living room and fitted out the other as kitchen and dining room. Vay made both bright and colorful. The two-household arrangement worked out pretty well. We cooked and ate separately, except for most Sundays, but we visited back and forth freely. We were likely to gather around Vay's piano of an evening to try out the new songs. When bedtime approached somebody was sure to beg, "Vay, play 'Heart Tones.'"

15

Change and Progress, Perhaps

S O WE WERE BACK ON THE RANCH — all of us except Hattie, who was out teaching school — and life went on much as it had always done. Only when we paused to look back — and on a ranch you don't have much time for retrospection and nostalgia — did we realize how much had changed in our short life-span.

We had new neighbors upriver and down; of the ranches between the Riverside and Woods Landing only two remained under the same ownership as in our school days. The places on each side of us had changed hands twice — Con Hammond to Charles Benson to Art Johnson on the east, Charles Sodergreen to Fred McLaughlin to Tom Durant on the west. Farther up, only the Oscar Sodergreens and the Jacob Johnsons remained, and on both ranches sons had taken over active management. Over on "the flats" — the Pioneer Canal–Harmony country — a few old-timers survived, but there too one saw new names on the mailboxes, new faces at country dances. Only the brands were familiar, more durable than the men who had burned them into quivering rib hide.

There had been changes too in the physical conditions of life, mostly for the better, but not always.

Oscar, whose recollections go back a decade further than mine, remembers that he and Papa, hauling logs down from the big timber, would sometimes hear the distant jangle of harness bells and hastily pull off the road to give right-of-way to freight outfits bound across the mountains to North Park. The jangle neared, and with it the grind and grumble of many wheels, the multiple pound of hoofs. Around a bend a team would appear, and behind it another, and another, and another, hides lathered with sweat and dust, nostrils wide, lungs pumping. Ten span, twenty horses. Then the wagons, coupled tightly together, towering cargoes tarpaulined and roped down. The driver would lift a hand in greeting as the first wagon passed. The lead team was already around the next bend. But for minutes the noise of the caravan drifted back, and the dust hung chokingly in the air.

Everything that North Park needed from outside went in over that road — groceries, furniture, machinery, tools, clothing, whisky. At Mountain Home, on the far side of the pass, five teams would be dropped off and brought back to Woods Landing to await the next load.

By my time the wagon trains were gone. They had been replaced by the Laramie, Hahns Peak and Pacific Railroad, which linked North Park with Laramie and the Union Pacific. The name suggests that the promoters had ambitious ideas. The line later changed its name to the Laramie, North Park and Western, but it never got farther than Coalmont, Colorado.

So long ago it was: people were still building railroads, never dreaming that before the century ran out many of them would have joined the dinosaur.

South of Laramie, just across the Colorado line, you may still be able to see the spoor of the Denver, Laramie & Northwestern — a few stretches not yet biodegraded into the landscape. Once, exploring the titanic jumble of granite along the Poudre River near Virginia Dale, I came across a tunnel, which probably marked its farthest north. The grade raveled out at its mouth; there was no sign that ties or rails had ever been laid.

The promoters were the same crew that chopped the Riverside into 160-acre plots and huckstered them off on land hungry innocents from the gullible East.

I'm sorry I missed those wagon trains. But when I started school our mail was still being brought by stage, and dropped off where the Sodergreen ranch road joined the highway, a half mile beyond the schoolhouse. It wasn't the kind of stagecoach you see in the movies, merely a big wagon with three seats. The driver was a weather-bitten, laconic man named Sid Lawrence. He made the thirty-mile trip between Laramie and Woods Landing six times a week, going out one day and returning the next, delivering and picking up mail, light cargo and a few passengers. He was true to the tradition of the service: neither rain, nor snow, nor dark of night stayed him from his appointed rounds.

Rural Free Delivery put Sid out of business. I recognize now that he was obsolescent, a victim of what economists later would call technological unemployment. But like many others displaced by supposedly more efficient ways of doing things he left a gap.

Now we had to ride five miles for our mail instead of two. Passenger service was terminated; if you fired a hay hand you couldn't ship him back to town on the stage, and only outrageous misconduct — like abusing a horse — justified making him foot it. So you didn't fire him. Sid had always been glad to do small errands. If you needed something urgently you could send in a note to the store and he would bring it out the next trip. The RFD man, being a government employee, couldn't be so accommodating; besides, his one-horse four-wheeled mobile post office had no room for any object bulkier than a mail-order catalogue.

We missed Sid Lawrence. It was some years before the telephone and automobile bridged the gulf his retirement had left.

My first automobile ride took me up the hill a short distance along the two ruts leading out to the highway, and back to the granary. The man who owned the threshing outfit must have seen me hovering around, simmering with curiosity; he called cheerily: "Come on, Kid; I'll give you a ride."

I watched, mesmerized, while he cranked and cranked. I jerked with alarm when the motor hiccupped and caught; the whole contraption shuddered. He jumped into the seat and engaged in a series of manipulations. We started moving.

Funny, I thought. It makes that awful noise when he cranks it, but it doesn't *go* until he pulls that lever and does things with those pedals. Why doesn't he do all that first, and drive off without that racket?

We met cars more and more often on the road to town. Papa or Oscar took a double wrap on the lines and braced himself to throttle down an incipient stampede. In time most of our horses got used to those noisy, stinking trespassers, and contented themselves with a token protest of snorts and flattened ears. Not Ted and Star, as I have recorded, but their stampeding was deviltry rather than panic.

Off the highway, motor travel was still chancy. One summer day a stranger in city clothes, perspiring and mud-spattered, appeared at the door as we were eating dinner, and asked if we happened to have a good strong team.

Oscar told him yes, we had.

"I'm stuck pretty bad."

Oscar told him to sit down and have a cup of coffee, and we'd take a look as soon as we finished dinner. The stranger opted for a drink of water instead; it was pretty hot walking.

We hooked up Belle and Queen, put a doubletree and a long chain in the wagon, and followed his directions to a little-used ranch road just inside the Riverside fence. The car was down over the hubs in meadow-muck. It was a huge, shiny car, the first Pierce-Arrow I had ever seen.

We looped the chain around the front axle, attached it to the doubletree, and hitched on the team. Osc told the driver: "Now put her in low, and when I holler give her all she's got."

The engine bellowed. The wheels spun. Mud sprayed. Belle and Queen crouched to the pull.

"Come on, girls! You can do it."

The car began to move, found traction, spurted forward. Osc swung the team aside as it came up on dry ground, in case the driver didn't stop quickly enough. He did, though, cut the engine and got out.

"That's a great team you've got there."

"We think so."

"What do I owe you?"

Oscar reflected. He knew what hay was selling at, and what steers had brought at Omaha the previous week, but he didn't know the going rate for tows.

"Ten dollars?" he ventured tentatively.

The man pulled out his wallet. We figured we'd never earned an easier ten dollars.

Some ranchers, situated where traffic was heavier,

picked up quite a little extra money during the irrigation season. There was talk, indeed, that certain mudholes never did dry out, even after the water was off the meadows.

Finally we had a car ourselves, a secondhand Buick, 1908 vintage, one of the last models with steering wheel and controls on the right side. It was a five-passenger touring car, with a top and side curtains, which weren't really much use; by the time you got them up the shower had usually blown over. The windshield was vertical, and divided across the middle so that you could open the top section for more ventilation — rarely necessary in Wyoming. There was a bulb horn, which we shortly replaced with a klaxon. The lamps were fed with acetylene from a tank on the running board, and lighted with a match.

The wheels were huge; the clearance must have been close to a foot, a necessary margin on rut roads. The tires were large in circumference, small in girth, smooth of tread, and thin-skinned. Their life expectancy was roughly three thousand miles, and before the speedometer reached that figure you probably would need a couple of new inner tubes.

I'm sure we must have made trips without having to patch and pump, probably a good many. But my memories are mostly of punctures, with an occasional blowout for variety.

There we are, tooling along at a giddy forty miles an hour, the smoke of Laramie already visible. And then that unmistakable tug on the steering wheel as a deflating tire tries to climb out of the rut, or the bump-bump-bump of a rear wheel no longer cushioned from the gravel.

We pull off the road and get to work. Jack up the car; the jack fits under the axle, comfortably accessible on a 1908 Buick. Pry the tire loose from the clincher rim.

Inspect it inside and out, and extract the nail or tack that did the damage. (One summer we ran over a porcupine, and we had flats for a month, every time we took the car out.) Locate the hole in the inner tube, and vulcanize it. Manhandle the tire back on the wheel, and start to pump. Once I counted, and discovered that it took four strokes to raise the pressure one pound, 320 to bring it up to the prescribed eighty pounds.

With the years the hazards and rigors of motoring diminished. Cold patches replaced the vulcanizer. Demountable rims eliminated the patch-and-pump process altogether, unless you had two flats on a single journey. After we had left the ranch, progress accelerated. Balloon tires. Electric lights. Self-starters. Permanently enclosed bodies, eliminating the wrestle with "jiffy" curtains. And antifreeze.

Antifreeze hadn't been thought up then. In winter you threw a heavy robe over the hood and radiator when you stopped for an errand, and went back every half hour or so to warm up the motor. When you got home you drained radiator and cylinder block.

Getting the Buick ready for a winter trip was a major enterprise. First you wriggled under it, on the frigid dirt floor of the wagon shed, to close the pet cocks. You filled the radiator with hot water from the kitchen, two pails of it, steaming into the subzero air. Then you retarded the spark lever, opened the throttle a notch, and began to crank.

You cranked. You cranked. You cranked. Usually nothing happened. You cussed, took a minute or two off to catch your breath — at subzero even the lightest winter oil stiffens to lard — jiggled the spark and throttle experimentally, just to be doing something, and cranked again. If your luck was in, the motor responded at last, with one convulsive belch. Jubilant, you cranked again.

No response. Again. Two belches this time, so vehement that they jerked the crank from your grip; its backspin just missed cracking an ulna. Hurray! She was waking up. Back to the crank. And at last the motor caught, burping raggedly. You hopped to the controls, advanced the spark and fiddled delicately with the throttle until one of two things happened. Either the motor settled down to a businesslike roar, or it sputtered and choked and expired, and you went back to the crank.

We had a couple of tricks in reserve if normal procedures failed. You could unscrew a couple of spark plugs and squirt gasoline into the cylinders. That usually worked. As a last resort — I recall only once when we were driven to it — you could hook up a gentle team and tow the reluctant dragon around the pasture until its sluggish heart began to pulsate.

Sometime in the '30s I noticed that cars no longer came equipped with cranks. I've never felt really comfortable on a motor trip since. What do you do now if the battery goes dead or the starter conks out? Raise the hood to full yawn, like a patient saying "Ahhhh!" for the doctor, and wait for a good Samaritan.

I'm not sure which came into our lives first, the automobile or the telephone. They were not far apart. I do remember our excitement as the line crew worked its way toward us, digging holes, setting poles, stringing wires. The excitement peaked when they fastened the tall varnished box to the kitchen wall, cranked up the central in Laramie, and asked her to try out 783 Black. (It was changed later to 01–R3.) The two bells atop the box responded, and the foreman, after a brief exchange with the voice at the other end, said, "Okay. You're connected."

No need now, if you had something to talk over with

a neighbor, to saddle a horse and lose the better part of the morning. You took down the receiver, wound the crank, and there was Art Johnson or Ole Erickson on the line. If you needed something from town urgently, you could call one neighbor after another until you found somebody who was going in, and ask him to pick it up.

We soon discovered that the telephone had fringe benefits.

It was, of course, a party line. We quickly learned to identify the calls, and it didn't take long to discover which conversations were likely to prove interesting.

If the Sodergreen number rang during the evening there would be a scramble for the phone. Martha usually won. She was adept at easing the receiver off the hook without a betraying click; she would make herself comfortable and settle back to listen, one hand over the transmitter, while Hattie teased for her turn. The schoolteacher, you may remember, usually boarded at the Sodergreens, and if she was young and comely the phone was likely to be pre-empted a good part of the evening. We clocked one conversation at forty-seven minutes. That would be a respectable course record even for a contemporary teen-ager.

Few eavesdroppers were as careful or deft as Martha. When you made a call, especially in the evening, you would hear a succession of clicks as your audience gathered. Once at least my brother was challenged bluntly: "I know you're there, Oscar Olson. I hope you're enjoying it."

Mama didn't approve of eavesdropping, but her expostulations mostly went unheeded. We lacked her strong sense of right and wrong; we would have been honestly astonished to be told that we were violating somebody's right to privacy. We had so much privacy that we did not

164

realize that it was precious, and could not recognize the first erosion.

Certainly life on the Big Laramie was changing. Distances had shrunk, time expanded. Laramie was only an hour away now, instead of three, four or six; neighbors were reachable with a twist of the telephone crank (unless someone else was monopolizing the circuit). A broken part on a rake or mower no longer meant the loss of a man and a machine for the better part of two days. You could take off in midafternoon, pick up the replacement before the stores closed, and be back for a late supper. The importance of foresight and planning diminished. If we ran short of something it was easy to whisk into town and replenish the stock. And once we were in town, our errand completed, why hurry home? The hired man would do the chores. Why not stay over for a movie?

The time came when we didn't need the incentive or excuse of an errand. Sometimes we went unashamedly, just to see the movie. With Mary Pickford, or Doug Fairbanks, or William S. Hart only an hour away, who could begrudge us a night on the town — even if it meant a very late bedtime?

When we did stay home, which was mostly, the evenings were brighter. Now we supped and washed up and read in the purring radiance of a gasoline lamp. The kerosene lamps, with the quavery yellow flame jigging at every stir of air, the wick contrarily sprouting little horns that sent licks of soot up the chimney, were relegated to the bedrooms and the bunkhouse.

We had come a good way into the twentieth century. But we still hoisted water from the well by hand and heated it with fuel hauled down from the tall timber. The womenfolk still boiled and soaked and rubbed the dirt out of clothes as their peasant grandmothers had done. We

165

still slithered down the snowy path to the privy to do our business on zero nights. The Rural Electrification Administration, and propane gas, and water piped into the kitchen and the bathroom, were still decades away.

Our horizon unquestionably had widened, our mobility had increased dramatically. But we had lost something, too. Self-sufficiency, surely. And the pleasures of isolation, which are real, though not everybody appreciates them: the satisfaction of battening down hatches and knowing that nobody is likely to hammer for admittance. The motor age has been hard on the solitary mister. If he survives, it is more likely to be in a slum garret than in a quaking-asp draw on the mountainside.

And, strangely enough, with the coming of the motor car we lost something of our security. In my childhood nobody on the Big Laramie thought of locking doors when he left the ranch for a few hours, or days. Indeed, we didn't even have a key. The code of the country decreed that if a traveler found nobody at home he was entitled to walk in, build a fire, make himself a meal, and go his way when he was ready — just so he washed his dishes, put things back where he had found them, and replenished the woodbox.

As rut-roads evolved into graded highways and the first pioneering gas buggies grandsired a streaming, screaming progeny, that gracious tradition perished. We began to hear of ranch houses along the highway being broken into, looted and vandalized. Down on the river off the main-traveled roads, we felt reasonably safe. But as the incidents multiplied we took heed. We had keys fitted, and when we went away for any length of time we were careful to lock up, and tuck the key away where (we assumed) nobody else could find it.

A couple of years ago I passed a summer cabin in the Colorado mountains that displayed a professionally painted sign facing the road:

WARNING! THIS HOUSE IS BOOBY-TRAPPED

16

The Round of the Seasons

I REMEMBER MY SABBATICAL as a good year. I was no
longer on the fringe of things, tagging along with my
elders, bothering them with questions, helping in whatever small ways I could, no doubt making a nuisance of
myself. At last I was a full-time member of the crew, a
regular hand — and as competent a hand, I could persuade myself, as most of the $40-a-month transients,
though certainly not of the caliber of Charlie McClure.

This seems to be a good place, therefore, to pull the bits
and pieces together and fit them into a coherent account
of the ranch routine through one full year. Not any particular year; though this chapter draws largely on that
fifteen-month sabbatical, there will be a number of flash-
backs. Call it, if you will, an archetypal year.

Spring

People used to say, with a sort of rueful pride — perhaps they still say it — that Wyoming has only two seasons — July-August and winter. There have been years that almost justified that sardonic simplification. Snow has been known to fall on the Fourth of July. The worst storm I ever experienced was in May, 1927. It snowed for two days and nights, four feet in all. Dozens of fishermen and picnickers who had gone to the hills one sunny Sunday morning were trapped, and several persons perished.

Still, by the first week of March you begin to hope that this winter is going to end eventually, as every past winter, however stubborn, has ended. The groundhog saw his shadow, of course; he almost always does, even though he may scuttle back into his burrow rubbing a frostbitten nose. That means six weeks more of winter; we add a few for good measure, knowing that the groundhog legend originated in a climate considerably more clement than ours. (I think we really believed in that weather-wise groundhog. I didn't know until I read Edwin Way Teale's *Winter Across America* that you could use him for a bowling ball without awakening him before his inner alarm clock went off.)

But already the days are appreciably longer. There are mild spells when the icicles along the eaves drip and dwindle and begin tinkling down. The drifts sink visibly; the path to the stables is a bog. Along the creek, willow bark begins to take on a honey warmth as the sap works upward. You start looking hopefully for the first reconnoitering pussy-willow paw.

The cattle still have to be fed daily; it will be a long time before there is green grass to sustain them. We take a saddle horse along to the fields, and after the hay is spread out one of us rides through the herd looking for cows about to calve, and weak animals that need special care. We have a maternity ward in the shed by the barn, and we try to bring expectant mothers to shelter a day or two early. Even so one of them eludes us occasionally, and we find her hidden in the brush, proudly licking the new baby dry. She eyes us balefully, and shakes her lowered head to warn us away. If their hideout is snug and dry and the weather mild, we say "Good for you, old girl," and leave them. Otherwise we load the calf in the wagon and take it up to the shed, mama bawling anxiously behind.

Cows usually manage the delivery process by themselves, competently and without fuss. Not always, though. For one grisly afternoon and evening Oscar and I struggle to extricate a calf that has "come wrong," and will come no farther. Our expedients, increasingly desperate — I shall not describe them — are in the end unavailing and we lose both heifer and calf. I am to remember that dreadful lesson in obstetrics for the rest of my life.

The calves are still dropping, but so are a few of the old-timers and the weaklings. Sometimes, when the daily count comes out one short, we find the missing animal lying down at the edge of the willows. As we approach she makes a brief struggle to get up, and then drops back, her great eyes watching us with the docility of the doomed. Sometimes we can help her to her feet by taking a grip on the tail, well up, and boosting. (Tailing her up, it's called.) Once afoot she can stand, in a rickety fashion; she may nibble at the hay we place in front of her. We leave her, and hope: hope it won't snow or turn cold, hope she'll be up and taking nourishment in the morning. With luck, she may make it. The odds are against her. Most likely she'll be down again next day, too weak to stagger to her feet, too far gone to show interest in food. A couple of days later we strip off the hide — it may bring a few dollars — and drag the carcass across the river for the coyotes, maybe burying a couple of traps alongside in the hope of recouping a fraction of our loss with the pelt and bounty.

If we can identify the poor risks while they're still on their feet and get them under shelter we may pull them through. The spring blizzards are the killers, striking when cattle are gaunt, their energy spent in the struggle with snow, wind and cold. March is the cruelest month, but April can take its toll too.

So the winter routine continues, but along with it the spring work is getting under way. The farming equipment has been tinkered into shape in the slack hours between feeding and evening chores. The work teams are brought into the stable to be "oated up" for the hard grind awaiting them. (In winter we keep up only one team for feeding, and a saddle horse for general purposes, including fetching the mail.) The days are crowded now, and longer. No dozing luxuriously until seven; we are up at daylight, and reveille gets earlier and earlier as the days lengthen.

We aim to start plowing as near the first of March as possible, but that is never a firm date. One year we were turning furrows the last week in February; another year we had thirty-below-zero temperatures for five successive nights in March, and it was near the end of the month before the frost was out and the fields were dry enough to work.

Once you start, nothing short of a blizzard stops you. I have sat on a gangplow with earlaps pulled low, chin tucked deep into sheepskin collar, gloved hands almost too stiff to hold the lines and manipulate the levers, feet numb under overshoes, shoes and heavy wool socks, face stinging with the slap of snow, wind-stung eyes weeping icicles. And another year, or a couple of weeks later that same year, I might be in shirt-sleeves, under a sky of morning-glory blue, sun June-warm on face and shoulders, meadowlarks and blackbirds tootling deliriously in the cottonwoods, the plowshare now and then turning under a tuft of flowers.

On such days plowing is fun. The twin furrows curl brown and fragrant from the moldboards. The four horses plod steadily across the field, heads nodding rhythmically, great muscles flexing under satiny hides. They know their job as well as you know yours, rather better. The pair on the off side trudge uncomplainingly in the furrow, seeming not to begrudge their teammates the solider footing on stubble. Once the first furrow is carved out, they will keep on course without guidance. For the length of the "land," as a tract laid out for one continuous plowing is called, you can leave the job to them, while you soak up sunshine and spring scents, listen to the meadowlarks, and let the fancy roam.

After the plows come the harrows, to break up the clods and crumble the soil to a consistency hospitable to seed. The seeder is an ingenious device that cuts a swath of shallow grooves in the soil, feeds the grain into them at proper intervals, and then covers it up and tamps it down. When Oscar finishes with a field the pattern is as beautifully accurate as if strung on a loom and then stretched out flat. After the grain is up you could fire a rifle between the rows and never nick a shoot. My weaving, alas, looks as if it had shrunk and warped in the wash. No matter how hard I try to drive a straight course, picking a distant tree or fence post as marker and keeping it squarely between the heads of the team, I always seem to wobble. It's just as well that I am usually relegated to the harrow, where accuracy doesn't matter so much.

We try to have all the grain in the ground by the first of May. Spring is racing on, and there are never enough hours. Feeding is no longer necessary; the cattle forage ravenously for the young grass. Now the meadows must be dragged, to distribute the fertilizer the herd has been depositing, down payment on next winter's board. The garden has to be plowed and planted, and the potato patch, on a spur of the bench west of the house.

In the mountains the snowpack — ten feet or more deep if the winter has been generous — is squeezing out millions of tiny rivulets that merge and swell and go whooping down gully and ravine in seething yellow freshets clotted with flotsam. Our creek spreads out into the flats above the stables; the greening willows are knee-deep in water.

The river runs brimful for a day and then breaks over the banks. The nearer meadows are a shallow lake; here and there a graveled knoll remains, a temporary island. The Big Laramie, ordinarily placid, is showing us a new personality. Suddenly he is a barroom brawler, loud-mouthed and truculent. I go to sleep with his voice in my ears, a besotted guttural recital of grievances and menaces, incoherent and endless. We don't take him seriously. In a few days he will sober up and become his normal soft-spoken companionable self, like a cowboy returning to the ranch after he has blown his winter's savings.

Sometime in the last half of May — it depends on how rapidly the snow in the timber is going out and the young grass coming in — we turn the cattle out to summer pasture. The sooner the better, to free the meadows for their proper function of growing hay for the next winter. Our range is the Medicine Bow National Forest in the mountains to the west. Each ranch has its quota of permits, the number of head determined by a formula that presumably seems fair to the forest supervisor but rarely satisfies any rancher.

Early one morning we set out, two men, or a man and a

173

boy, and some 150 beef critters of assorted ages, genders and patterns. It is not an orderly parade. The cattle were perfectly content, thank you, in those lush meadows, stuffing themselves on young redtop and timothy, with buttercups for garnish. Unlike their two-legged tormentors, they have no folk faith in the greater luxuriance of distant pastures. They would just as soon stay put, indeed, a little rather. They try to break back; for the first mile or two you keep spurring off after defectors, swinging your lariat. At gates they bunch up, Alphonse and Gaston of the Sunday funnies many times multiplied. Sudden little Donnybrooks break out. Two bulls decide for no reason whatever that now is the time to settle, once and for all, that little matter of priority. A cow old enough to have learned better manners aims a murderous stab at the flank of a heifer ambling alongside. If the aggressor had not been dehorned long ago there would be blood and bowels in the dust.

Our horses are lathered and our throats raw by the time we have the herd strung out along the highway, two miles and six gates from home. Fortunately there is always a natural leader in every bunch. Usually it is an old cow with a hieroglyph of brands on ribs and flanks — her life's odyssey for anyone with lore enough to read it. She sets out at a swinging stride, and the others, figuring perhaps that she must know something they don't, fall in behind. The calves trot bravely along. The big +E seared into their rib hide yesterday is still raw; blood has crusted the V-shaped notch in one ear; the skin twitches around the wounds. They seem, though, to have pretty well forgotten that traumatic experience. The plodding pace bores them. They skip off to explore; they frisk and buck and butt. If there is a momentary holdup, back they hustle to the maternal udder: ten seconds' pause for refreshments.

Cute little fellows: sturdily built, straight-backed,

174

sleek hides well cushioned (no skim milk in *their* diet!).
Mostly red — which is really a brown varying from near-
sorrel to a deep russet. Mostly white-faced, as Herefords
should be. (We say Hurfurd, a pronunciation that would
grieve an Englishman, but usually we call them white-
faces.) But a sprinkling of nonconformists: brockle-faces,
unorthodox patches of white, black-and-whites with the
rangy build of Holsteins, and one pure black that certainly has an Angus ancestor not far back. Our range
cows are a mixed lot, as on most ranches, though our bulls
are pedigreed Herefords. Unless you run your stock under
fence the year around a certain amount of miscegenation
is bound to take place. Cattle have no color prejudice.

At the old Berg place — now Ole Erickson's — where
Jelm and Sheep Mountain come almost within nuzzling
distance and river and meadows have scant space to
squeeze between, Oscar spurs ahead and sets Old Faithful
on a new course. At once we are in the mountains, and
climbing steadily. Our trail follows Fox Creek, sometimes
splashing through the swollen stream itself, sometimes
high up in the greasewood and contorted pines of the
canyon side. Along the river the cottonwoods were filmily
green; as we climb, the leaves shrink and curl back into
the buds, until the aspens are again the gray of bleached
bones. Snowbanks crouch in northward-tilted gullies.

Around noon we reach our destination, a plateau well
above the creek and rising westward to timbered mountains. There are stretches of sagebrush, green scraps of
park, clumps of aspen and willow, juts of granite, here
and there a solitary pine carved by wind and ice to the
likeness of a troll. We dismount, loosen cinches, slip out
the bits so that the horses can graze, and unwrap our
lunches in the lee of a granite outcrop. Thus sheltered, and
drenched by the midday sun, we could almost imagine
ourselves six weeks ahead, in July. But at these altitudes

the wind never gets farther down the calendar than March.

The cattle have settled down to lunch too. Settled isn't quite the word, though. They sniff, nibble, move on to nibble again.

"Pretty thin pickin's," Oscar comments. "They'll keep drifting down until the feed gets better." Indeed, a few are already working their way toward the gully leading to the creek bottom.

We turn them back before we head homeward. For the next week I stay at Erickson's, riding morning and afternoon to pick up truants and shove them back into the hills. It is a week when spring comes on at a gallop, summer spurring behind. Leaves explode, grass seems to grow while you watch. By Saturday the cattle have forgotten the home meadows, and are moving up into the timber, following the tender young grass at the edge of the melting snowbanks. We can forget about them now until fall.

Summer

After the seed is in the ground and the stock are in the mountains there is a breathing spell. We still get up at five and put in a fourteen-hour day. But the pressure is off; the sense of urgency has eased. Nature is doing most of the work now. The grain is inches high, and so is the grass in the meadows. The milder winds of June flow across the fields in lovely sinuous rhythms. The potatoes are getting ready to blossom.

In the mountains the cattle are quilting winter-honed ribs with firm sound flesh. Those frolicsome calves are growing at a rate that might make you think they were impatient to qualify as baby beef. The bulls — one to every twenty-five cows, Wyoming law stipulates — are applying themselves conscientiously to their task of begetting T-bones and prime rib roasts.

Of course nature welcomes a helping hand. Head gates have to be manipulated, earth dams built or removed, to bring water evenly to oats and wheat and barley. Weeds must be chopped or uprooted. A horse-drawn cultivator keeps the furrows clear in the potato patch, but somebody has to follow with a hoe. As for the vegetable garden, I've already described that tedious and never-quite-won war.

Early summer is a time for mending and patching. Just about everything man puts up starts falling down, by imperceptible degrees, as soon as he turns his back. Fences, for instance. There are miles of fence on an eight hundred-acre ranch. One of my jobs is riding fence (which has no kinship, of course, with being ridden on a rail). I saddle up Buck one morning, tuck a claw hammer, a pair of pliers and a handful of staples in my jumper pockets and tie a sack of spikes to the pommel. We slosh through the meadows — churning up a Job's plague of mosquitoes — and cross the ford to the "homestead" on the bench beyond the river. There we plod along the fence, keeping a sharp lookout for fallen poles or sagging wire. I say "we" advisedly. Buck, sagacious and experienced, understands our assignment just as well as I do, and often spots a gap in our security cordon before I see it. Usually repairs are a simple matter of spiking a pole back or replacing a missing staple. Our fences are mostly the pole-and-buck variety — two poles and a strand of barbed wire on one side, another wire on the far side, to keep stock from rubbing the poles loose. I make a mental note of any rotting poles or wobbly bucks. If necessary we'll come back with the wagon and replace them.

Then there are gateposts to be reset and gates to be rehung. We boast that you can open any gate on the ranch from horseback. Ditches choke up with silt and debris. Dams undercut by high water have to be re-plugged with stone and sod and brush.

Compressed thus into a couple of paragraphs it may sound like unalleviated toil. I don't remember it that way. We kept busy, but the pace was unhurried, the tasks were varied enough to preclude boredom, and often their completion brought a glow of accomplishment. There's solid satisfaction in spiking a rail into place to close a break in a fence, having a gate swing smoothly and latch snugly after you have reset a sagging post. And we were working not in a stuffy basement or a cluttered garage but in a shop measuring forty miles long and as many wide, with a roof of that Rocky Mountain blue that lowlanders refuse to believe when you show them pictures. "Hmph, Kodachrome," they sniff.

When we stop for a breather there is Jelm, massive and benevolent, with crinkles of heat along his flanks. The wind, cool on sweaty foreheads, brings a medley of fragrances. There is sure to be a meadowlark somewhere nearby. Maybe a pair of goldfinches (in our ignorance we call them wild canaries) flick through the branches in a dizzy polka of love or war.

The summer moves toward its climax, harvest. By the first week in July, sometimes sooner, we set about getting the haying machinery into shape. Sickles are ground and worn blades replaced. Rakes and sweeps get corrective and preventive dentistry, with new teeth fitted where necessary. Nuts are tightened, bearings greased, harnesses checked for worn straps and broken snaps and buckles. The head gates have been closed so that the meadows can dry out and the hay ripen. Horses are brought in to be "oated up" for the toilsome weeks ahead.

178

And finally comes the great day when cutting begins, exciting to me even at sixteen as it was at six. Then it was Papa who drove the mower into the field below the house, lowered the sickle bar, clucked the team into motion. Now it is Oscar, and the very last summer I am able to join with another team and mower. The grass folds back over the sickle in a constantly breaking wave, green and russet, specked with the froth of daisies and wild caraway. The scent is sweet and pungent. By late afternoon the meadow below the house is a rug of broad swaths of paling green, following the irregular frame set by the creek, the fence and the corrals, but converging toward the center.

In good weather hay cures fast. By noon next day it is ready to be raked into windrows and then into cocks. The third day we load it into the hayrack and stow it away in the mow and the cribs around the corrals to feed horses and milk cows.

That much we manage by ourselves. Now the action shifts to the larger meadows, and a much-augmented cast is required. Oscar drives to town and comes back with a crew, or as much of a crew as he has been able to recruit among the itinerants lounging in front of the saloons, flophouses and brothels along First Street. They drop their gear in the bunkhouse and fall ravenously on the steak and potatoes and fresh peas and stewed tomatoes and apple pie laid out on the kitchen table, now stretched with every extra leaf in place.

Next morning Oscar gives out assignments on the basis of claimed experience and his own appraisal of each man's probable competence. Mowing demands skill; a clumsy or careless "hand" could break a sickle bar and slow up cutting for a couple of days. Stacking also is an art, and requires brawn as well. But almost anybody who can drive a team can operate a rake. By seven o'clock the crew is on the way to the field.

If the weather holds haying goes fast. A stack a day is our objective when we have a full crew: two mowers, two rakes, one or two sweeps, one man on the stack unless the hay is exceptionally heavy and close by, in which event someone is detached to help him stow it away. The mowers work two days ahead of the rest of the crew, a field or two away. From the stack they look like mechanical toys crawling around the perimeter of the distant meadow. Nearer by the rakes are scooping up the dried swaths and spinning them into fat hawsers of bleached green. After them comes the sweep, a wide, low structure with long tapering teeth, polished by friction with the turf. The sweep straddles the windrow, a horse on each side; the teeth slide under the hay and roll it up into a mighty fragrant prickly hillock. When the hillock threatens to topple backward on the driver he brings it in and deposits it on the apron of the stacker.

The stacker is simply an inclined plane of wooden slats supported by a massive rigid structure of beams and trusses. To get the hay up the incline we use a pusher — an elongated T-shaped structure with what looks like a panel of fence at one end and two horses at the other. The cross-bar of the T picks up the hay on the apron, the horses buckle down and dig in, the load moves up the slant in a churning mass and cataracts onto the stack. The sweep driver backs the pusher down to its waiting place and goes out after another load. No fear that the pusher team will take off across country. They are semipensioners, too old for mischief, capable of the brief output of energy required but content to doze and switch at flies between loads.

We are proud of our stacks. We look with contempt at the shapeless mounds piled up by some of "the Missourians" out on the flats. (Whether all or any of them actually came from Missouri I can't say, but our attitude toward them was much like that of a Proper Bostonian toward shanty Irish.) Our stacks are geometrically accurate, rising plumb-line true for seven or eight feet, then tapering to a wedge. The art is in "topping out" the stack, pulling the sides in symmetrically while the ends remain vertical, until the builder stands astride a gable roof as he pats the last forkful into place. Then the stack is fettered against the winter gales with a ridgepole and four sets of hangers straddling it.

The man on the stack scrambles down. The apron, hinged, is folded up against the incline, and two teams detached from other duties drag the ponderous structure to the next setting.

Five o'clock in the morning is a shivery hour even in August. Dew winks on leaves and grass; my boots leave wet tracks on the path to the barn. Old Buck lifts his long sardonic face as I enter and gives me a bilious look, misanthropy, world-weariness and resignation mingled. His ears go back at the touch of the cold blanket; he inhales deeply, blowing himself up to maximum circumference, as I hook the cinch ring into place and haul on the latigo. It is a ritual protest. He knows he won't get away with it; he will have to exhale soon and when he does I shall tighten the cinch properly.

I keep the reins tight as I swing into the saddle. Buck is nineteen or twenty, but he will still bow his head on a chilly morning, given a chance. (Bow his head is a euphemism for living up to his name. Actually he isn't called Buck because he bucks, though he used to be notorious, but because of the color of his hide.) As it is he tries a few crow hops before I get him strung out and headed across the meadows toward the river.

My job is rounding up the horses, turned out at night to graze. I love it. This is surely the best hour of the day. Everything fresh, crisp, honed to an edge. The sun is still hidden, but its uptilted rays are burnishing the summit of Jelm. Buck's hoofs flick little bursts of glitter from the wet grass. Birds spurt up at our approach; farther away they are fluting and fiddling giddily.

But where are the horses?

Hiding out, of course. Buck and I begin a methodical search of the woods along the river. The first little park is empty. We push down a narrow cow trail; a low-bent bough gives me a wet slap across the forehead. We emerge into a larger opening. Empty too.

No, not quite. On the far side a coyote stands broadside, eying us over his shoulder with insulting insouciance. Not until we are halfway across the park does he turn, deliberately casual, and trot off into the undergrowth. His manner says plainly: Nobody is going to panic *me*.

We find the horses on the south side of the river, near the east fence. They know their game is up. A whoop and a swing of my hat are enough to turn them toward the barn. We come up through the meadow at a trot, Ted and Star, the buggy team, frisking in front. I herd them into the corral, fetch halters and stable them, buckle on the harnesses while they munch their oats. On the way to the house I overtake Oscar and the one hired man who knows how to milk cows and is willing to do it. I never cease being grateful that I have drawn the horse-wrangling job.

Our breakfast is not for weight watchers. We sit down to oatmeal, pancakes, meat, potatoes and gravy, bread and butter, coffee, with thick yellow cream. Plates and cups are emptied and refilled. But there is no lingering afterward. By seven we are on the way to the meadow.

Back to the house at twelve for dinner; out again at

one; back in time to unharness and turn out the horses, wash up for supper, which is at six. By the time the cows have been milked and bedded down and the milk separated and the calves fed and the pigs slopped you'd think we'd done about enough for one day.

But there's still one vital job waiting: sharpening sickles. A mowing machine will use up two a day in heavy grass; since we have two mowers running now, four sickles must be rewhetted before the crew goes back to the field in the morning. A sickle is a six-foot steel bar with a lot of wedge-shaped blades, about two-and-a-half inches on a side, riveted to it. Every one of those has to be ground separately, and each has two edges. If you find one worn down to a crescent shape you chisel off the rivets and replace it with a new one. By the time the four sickles are ready for use again dusk has gathered and it's bedtime.

In fine weather haying goes briskly. In August, alas, weather isn't always fine. You can't put up hay wet. If you do it rots. Even a heavy afternoon shower will suspend operations for a morning, perhaps a day. Only the mowers chug methodically on, their distant clatter dampened and thickened. If the rain persists even the mowers give up. No sense in having more hay on the ground to spoil.

Hay hands, unfortunately, keep on accumulating wages, whether they work or not. They continue eating, just as voraciously. We try to keep them busy at odd jobs — hauling manure from the corrals to the meadows already shorn; fencing the completed stacks; strengthening dams.

There was a story current in those days — possibly from a minstrel show — of the colored plantation worker who was overheard saying. "Mo' rain, mo' rest." "What's that, you black rascal?" his employer snarled. "Why,

Marse Henry, I say 'Mo' rain, mo' hay for de hosses to eat." I'm afraid that I, like that black rascal, used to be furtively glad to see gravid Ethiopian clouds building up to north and east.

An afternoon shower is a temporary setback, not serious. A night of rain, or a night and a day, begins to be worrisome. A succession of rainy days may be calamity. Happily, Wyoming weather is volatile, rarely all bad or all good. I remember harvests that dragged on into September; I remember a few stacks that were put up too wet and were all but worthless when we dug into them next winter. But usually we got the hay up in pretty good shape, and had a little to spare when feeding stopped in the spring.

The day comes when the ridgepole is hoisted to the top of the last stack and the hangers strung across it. That night Oscar figures out each man's time, deducting any purchases made for him on trips to town. Next morning the men are driven back to Laramie, and we see no more of them.

It never occurred to me to wonder where they went after they were deposited, $40 or so richer, on First Street. When I was older, and had begun to examine First Street with a more knowing eye, I had a pretty shrewd idea: saloon first, then whorehouse.

Fall

Snow has been known to come as early as the first week of September. Happily it doesn't stay long. Between that first cautionary visitation and the serious onset of winter you can usually count on six weeks, maybe more, of fine autumn weather, clear, crisp, delightful.

We put them to good use; there is much to do. Grain to be harvested and threshed. Haystacks to be fenced. Roundup, branding, and shipping. Woodcutting and hauling. A last trip to town to stock up with groceries. That is the chronological sequence, roughly, but there is considerable overlap.

The mowers are tucked away in the wagon shed and the binder comes out. A binder is a mowing machine plus; it not only cuts the grain but wraps it into neat cylindrical bundles, about as thick as a ten-year-old boy, knots twine around them, and drops them gently on the stubble. Three horses pull the binder, one man drives, another comes along behind and assembles the bundles into shocks.

You grab a sheaf in each hand and prop them against each other — butt ends down, of course, kerneled heads tight together. Two more sheaves, similarly braced, make a sort of cross; four to six others are tucked in around the original four. Properly constructed, a shock will stand up against even a Wyoming wind. Now and then the knotter malfunctions and a bundle drops without its cincture. You wrap a few long stalks around the rest, twist the ends and tuck them in. That's the classic technique; you can see it in a Brueghel painting.

Grain in the shock is fairly weatherproof, for a while. You can leave it — the field an encampment of wigwams, like a convocation of pigmy Sioux — while you tend to other urgent chores. It isn't bird-proof, though; the crows are gorging themselves. As soon as we can manage, therefore, we haul the grain in and stack it near the granary, to await the threshing crew.

When I was a small boy threshing was about the most exciting event of the year, except for Christmas. I remember the outfit coming to the ranch in the evening, whether because it followed a fixed itinerary every October, or because the impressions of the first visit remained indelible. We hear its approach long before we can see it — a distant clank and rumble beyond the crest of the hill. Louder and louder. A massive bulk materializes, black in the thickening twilight, a smoking monster with a fiery glow in its belly; it drags behind it an even massier bulk.

The traction engine grunts cautiously down the hill, the separator lurching behind it, and is directed to its berth near the grain stacks. Pails of water from the ditch quench the fire in its belly; a neglected spark could send a whole season's harvest up in flames. The engineman comes to the house for a wash, a late supper and a bed in the bunkhouse. The rest of the crew will report in the morning.

Threshing is in part a communal enterprise. The operator of the outfit is an entrepreneur, who makes the round of the ranches every fall, but most of the work is done by us and our neighbors, helping us as later we shall help them. They ride or drive in early next morning and help position the separator. The engineman starts the fire and begins to build up steam. The sun is still low, the frost thick in the shadows, when he engages the gears, the drive belt takes hold, and the separator clatters into action.

I wish I could reproduce here Adolf Dehn's watercolor, "Threshing." It would give you a better idea of both the mechanics of the operation and the look of it. The engine — an early-model tractor, coal-burning, with huge cogged wheels in the rear, smaller wheels in front, a tall smokestack exhaling sootily — stands well back from the inflammable grain and the still more combustible chaff. A long flat belt connects the drive wheel to the separator, which is tucked snugly among the stacks. Men atop the stacks pitch the sheaves onto a toothed conveyor belt leading down into the separator. What goes on there, a complex mincing and sorting and sifting, I never really understood. What comes out is a steady gush of kernels from a spout on one side, a fountain of pale chaff from the tall exhaust pipe on the other.

It's hard, hot, dusty work, whether you're on the stack pitching bundles or at the spout catching that torrent of kernels in gunnysacks. Fortunately there are breaks — in the literal sense of the word as well as the figurative; the belt may squirm off the drive pulley and have to be worked back into place. Every so often the chaff spout must be redirected; the stuff piles up fast, being fluff with little substance. When two stacks of sheaves have disappeared into that voracious digestive system the separator is moved to the next two, and the engine shifted accordingly. There are pauses, therefore, to permit long gulps of water from jugs standing in the shade.

The crew are a tired and grimy lot when they troop to the house at noon, scrub away some of the smear at tin basins in the dooryard, fall ravenously on the food waiting on the kitchen table. Again I turn to art for assistance. Grant Wood painted the scene — making it a little too neat and lyrical — in "Harvest Dinner."

Dehn's watercolor catches the outdoor setting admirably: the glow of straw and stubble against a delicately fleeced autumnal sky; the greasy gray-purple engine smoke contrasting with the pallid, almost transparent chaff spray; the threshing crew tiny against the mountain masses of grain and straw. He gives it a look of pageantry. And it is as a sort of pageant that I remember it. I was always sorry when it was over and the engine, clumsily mobile again, clanked up the hill, the separator clattering clumsily behind.

The days are shrinking faster. We get up in semidarkness; the morning star is an ice chip in the seepage of dilute lemonade above the eastern hills. Frost crunches underfoot as we go to the stables. When we come out with the milk pails the light has strengthened; we see a skift of new snow on the upper reaches of Jelm. As the sun reaches the mountainside the aspen thickets glow yellow, touched with red. The cottonwoods and alders along the creek and the river, the willows on ditch banks and in fence corners are yellow too.

The cattle are straggling down from the mountains now, retreating before the snow. The highway channels them past the ranches along the river; somebody has to ride out every day to bring in those bearing our brand — 1/3 in my father's time, +E after Oscar takes over. Weather does much of the roundup work for us. The great communal sweep pictured in novels, movies and Charlie Russell's paintings, with scores of riders from dozens of ranches fanning out over thousands of square miles of prairie, mesa and creek bottom, wouldn't have worked in the densely timbered, deeply canyoned labyrinth of the Medicine Bow National Forest. And it isn't necessary. We can count on snow and cold to bring the stock out of the hills, and since the downward migration tends to follow watercourses it's easy to collect them.

We help each other out, naturally. When we pick up a few head belonging to Ericksons, or Johnsons, or Sodergreens, we shunt them into their home pastures as we come by. They would do the same for us. If one of ours turns up farther away word will reach us eventually, and someone will ride over to bring the stray home. Some cows are like some people: they've got to see what's beyond the next ridge. Big Laramie cattle have been known to drift as far as North Park in Colorado, thirty or more miles away. When that happens it's sometimes easier to let the finder ship them with his own stock, and mail you a check.

A few never do come back. We have to figure on some loss, two or three per cent if no worse. We can only guess what became of them. Natural causes, perhaps — an encounter with a bear, a crippling fall, or lightning. Or human villainy. One of those hobo steers might have found himself in the corral of a homesteader with no conscience and a knack with a running iron, just like in the story books. We also suspected, though with no evidence, that lumberjacks cutting ties for the railroad occasionally feasted on fresh beef at our expense.

Roundup is the rancher's harvest time. Beef is his main cash crop; the others — grain, potatoes, garden stuff — are subsidiary or subsistence products. The crop is now reaped, though still ambulatory, and it's time to get it to market. So we saddle up again, and begin cutting out the animals destined for the feedlot, the slaughterhouse, and eventually the butcher's block. Steers, primarily, two- and three-year-olds. And agey cows; they will bring a few cents a pound as "canners and cutters." Perhaps one or two old, unhappy bulls, past their procreative prime. The rest of the bunch go back to the meadows, to multiply and mature for another season.

One morning Oscar and the hired man set off for the twenty-two-mile drive to the Laramie stockyards, where the cattle will be fed and watered and loaded into cars bound for Omaha.

Someone from the ranch has to go along, of course, to look after the stock and deal with the brokers. Oscar remembers the expedition as an adventure, a welcome digression from ranch routine. The cowmen ride in the caboose with the train crew. They play cribbage or poker, they swap anecdotes of the summer's mischances, they speculate dolefully on the way prices always seem to drop disastrously the day Wyoming cattle hit the market.

Most likely there will be a bottle or two circulating. At stops for watering they get out to stretch their legs and see the town; not much worth seeing, though, in these flat, drab Nebraska hamlets.

Once, Oscar remembers, the train stopped unaccountably in the middle of nowhere. He and a companion walked ahead to see what was the matter. Suddenly the train started, and began picking up speed on the long downgrade from Sherman Hill to the Platte. They managed to grab a ladder and scramble to the top of a car, where they were stuck until the next stop.

It was, happily, a mild night. My imagination embellishes Oscar's laconic recollections. I postulate a moon, three-quarters full. It gives definition to the sleeping farmland, wakening a creek or a stock pond to a momentary silver-and-pewter gleam, silhouetting a house, a barn, a cottonwood grove against its own stylized shadow. The clank of the wheels, the chuff of the engine, their own voices are the only sounds, except now and then a dog barking, the bawl of an insomniac calf. At long intervals a distant light shows that somebody else is awake. Why?

Sixty years afterward Oscar would still recall that night nostalgically. Somehow those few hours had taken on a quality of magic; they endured, insulated from time, immune to corrosion.

Marketing beef-on-the-hoof is different now. Buyers come to the ranch and make offers. When a deal is struck they load the cattle into trucks and drive off — to the stockyards in Denver or to feedlots in northern Colorado, where they will be fattened on beet pulp before being shipped farther for slaughter. The long, dusty drive to railhead, the clanking amble across Nebraska, the grime and sweat and turmoil of the stockyards, more cowmen and cattle milling around than a fellow had ever seen at one time before, the night on the town afterward — all this is only legend now.

"There ought to be some ducks up the crick," Oscar says one mild October afternoon. "Let's see if we can get a few."

I fetch my recently acquired Winchester 16-gauge and we set out.

The creek coils lazily through the meadows, seal-brown in the shadows, silver where the low sun strokes it. Leaves shiver down to weave a rusty mat in the eddies. We move cautiously across the springy stubble, peering around each willow clump before we proceed.

There the ducks are. Six of them, cruising sedately in a broader stretch where a head gate slows the stream. As we emerge from cover they make off across the pond with a skutter of frightened wings, and are airborne. Up come our guns, following that whickering flight. I hear Oscar fire as I try to bring my chosen quarry into the sights. I squeeze the trigger; my shoulder drinks the recoil. A miss. Oscar fires again; out of the tail of my eye I see a feathery rocket wilt in midair and plummet down. By the time I have pumped another shell into the chamber they are out of range. Oscar is wading out to claim his trophies. Mallards both.

"You want to lead 'em more," he instructs me. "Unless you catch one going away."

He tucks the mallards into his hunting jacket's capacious pockets and reloads. We move on upstream. A quarter of a mile farther on we flush four more. This time I do better. With the report of the Winchester I see my target wobble, collapse in a sudden disintegration of flight, plump down in the stubble. Oscar has dropped his also.

When we come home we have seven. We shall feast on duck tomorrow and the day after. In our afternoon of sport we have contributed to the household economy, as those evening fishing trips contributed. There is a valuable by-product, too. Mama saves the duck feathers to stuff pillows. Small wonder that someone brought up on duck feathers finds foam rubber conducive to either insomnia or nightmare.

Roundup over, cattle in the meadows, cleaning up the nooks and crannies the mowers couldn't reach, stacks tightly fenced to discourage trespass when the browsing gets sparse. Ice fringes the creek of a morning, and the path to the stables is flint under boot heels.

It's time to get in the winter's wood. That means a week in the mountains felling logs, another week or two hauling them home. Bright and early one October morning Oscar and I set out.

The lumber wagon has been stripped to the running gear; the skeleton is draped with chains. Mama has filled a grub box with hams and a slab of beef, potatoes, cans of tomatoes and peas and beans and peaches, many loaves of bread, an earthenware jar of butter. Our road takes us along the highway to Woods Landing and there turns up Woods Creek. It is only a wagon track, deeply rutted, jolting over boulders, tilted dangerously by granite outcrops. Leafless cottonwoods give way to leafless quaking asps, quaking asps to jackpine and patches of lodgepole. The climb steepens. Belle and Queen buckle down to the pull; we stop now and then to let them catch their wind. Snow appears alongside, scraps at first, then drifts, pitted and dingy; occasionally the wagon track cuts through the taper of one. Oscar peers vigilantly into the dense timber. "We just might spot a deer," he says.

At midmorning we come out into a clearing, cinctured

with a rachitic rail fence. At the far end is a huddle of gray buildings. We unhitch, water and stable the horses, and unload. This is to be our home from home for a week.

The cabin is musty; the air swims with motes when we swing back the shutters. There are six bunks, double-decked; a plank table, a rusty range, a cupboard holding cooking utensils and dishes, some of them complete, two chairs, two benches, a woodbox, a cracked mirror. The walls are of rough log, the bark flaking off and the plaster visible between.

Chimney Park might be called a condominium; we share ownership with several other ranchers, and use it while cutting wood and riding for cattle. I have been here before, and the memory is embarrassing.

When I was ten or eleven my father brought me along while he and his co-owners were putting up a new horse barn. The first afternoon I set out to see what I could see from the top of a rounded hill half a mile or so to the west, the one bulge in the flat forest horizon. It proved a disappointment; whichever way I looked there were only more trees, miles and miles of them. I might as well head back to camp.

That wasn't as easy as I had figured. In a few minutes I realized I was lost.

The trouble was that going away from a hill is quite different from going toward it. As soon as you've turned your back on it, it's no use at all as a landmark. Whichever radius of the 360 spoking out from its hub you follow, it will still be behind you.

One thing I can say for me: I didn't panic. I experimented cautiously with a change of course, a few points farther to port. And when I came out on a dim road — an old, old road, grass and kinnikinnick high between the ruts, a bleached tree-carcass slanting across it — I was bright enough to know that even abandoned roads go somewhere. And shortly the frightening stockade of trees thinned out and I was back in Chimney Park.

My absence had been discovered, and the whole crew were out looking for me. Dad gave me hell.

Back to 1915.

We eat a cold lunch and then walk the four miles to the ranger station at Fox Park to get our logging permits. Next morning early we go to work. A quarter-mile through young growth, twice a man's height and bristle-thick. Then up to a knoll where the timber thins out and thrusts skyward — slim, smooth shafts of copper red or lichen gray, ten, twelve or more inches at the base, reaching up and up until they sheave out into a flat crown of boughs that knit with others to roof the knoll into an immensely lofty room.

Oscar is the axman, I the trimmer and sawyer. Power saws, which can gnaw their way through a twelve-inch pine in one shrieking minute, are far in the future. We fell trees much as Solomon's builders felled the cedars of Lebanon, though our tools probably are better. First a notch on one side, well down; we despise slovenly work-men who leave tall stumps. Then a horizontal cut on the opposite side, a diagonal slash down to meet it, flaking off a wedge. Deeper and deeper, until the triangular slash approaches the shallower notch on the up side. The tree begins to tremble. One last deep cut. A crackle, a louder crack, a shiver all the way up to the lofty crown. Oscar steps back, leans his weight against the bole. The slim red column sways, rebounds briefly, and bends slowly, with haughty condescension. It seems to lean on air, so leisurely is its descent, but instant by instant it gathers momentum, and with a crescendoing rush comes down, scything lesser growth in its path. The impact vibrates up through our knees. A slow rain of dust and needles and powdered bark sifts down.

Now my job begins. While Oscar moves on to another tree, I chop away the branches and saw the trunk into manageable lengths. We take a break now and then, for a cigarette and a breather. In a minute the sweat congeals and we shiver into our sheepskin coats. We lunch on sandwiches and tepid coffee.

It is uncannily still, except for the snore of the wind in the ceiling far above. The creatures of the forest have vanished, burrowed deep into their winter cells or flown southward. In summer or early fall there would be camp robbers — gray jays — darting boldly in to snatch a morsel; they will fly right into a cabin and share your dinner if permitted; and chipmunks sitting up and chittering for handouts. Now the high country is empty, shuttered and battened down against the approach of winter. I cannot help feeling that we are intruders, and wondering how long our trespass will be tolerated.

The days pass. Mornings of plush-thick frost; I have to break a disk of ice from the water pail before I can fill the kettle. Noons of tepid sunshine. Nights of sharp cold and silence. Once or twice we hear a wolf howl in the distance; the night closes over the sound like water around a sinking stone.

We harness up the team, with a doubletree and a chain, and I begin snaking logs down to the road where the wagon can reach them. Slowly the pile grows. I take a turn with the ax myself, trying to match Oscar's casual competence. My first few stumps look like the work of an apprentice beaver, but with practice I improve.

One morning there is a glaze over the sky, and the air is unexpectedly mild. Osc sniffs appraisingly. "Weather coming," he says judiciously. "Let's load up. We've got enough to take us through the winter."

By midmorning we are ready to move. Logs piled high between the four uprights that fit into the brackets that normally would hold the wagon box, chains snubbing them tight, with a sapling pole inserted like a stick in a tourniquet, its free end roped hard down. The grub box and the bedrolls are strapped on. Osc and I scramble up to our perches at the front of the load. All snug. Osc loosens the brake and slaps Queen and Belle lightly with the slack of the lines. "Get a move on, girls. We're going home."

I feel a wet spatter on my cheek. The predicted weather has arrived.

Wood hauling is a grueling business, for man and horse. Up before daybreak, on the road with the first meager intimation of thaw in the black ice of the eastern horizon; back long after dark, with horses to be watered, stabled and fed and the logs unloaded before the eighteen-hour day is over. (The womenfolk have done the milking and separating, of course.) It takes a week or more to build the pile of logs behind the bunkhouse to dimensions Oscar considers adequate.

In the early years we had our own power plant to saw them into stove lengths — a big waterwheel straddling the creek. Eventually it became too decrepit for further repair. Thereafter we depended on an itinerant power saw, belonging, like the threshing machine, to some rancher with the capital and the enterprise to set himself up in a service business. One autumn he passed us by for some reason. That winter Osc and I sawed our firewood by hand, and I learned that the sage — was it Thoreau? — who remarked that wood warms you twice, first when you split it, again when you burn it, was one count short. Before you can split a chunk you have to saw it off, and that will work up a sweat even at 30 degrees below.

One more task remains before we are ready for whatever menaces the winter can muster against us. We must stock up with provisions, the staples our own efforts cannot supply: flour, coffee, tea, sugar, salt, canned goods. Our shopping list would have appalled the lady who was just ahead of me at the check-out counter this morning, her cart piled to capacity. We buy in bulk, by the sack, the crate and the barrel. And we are mighty careful to check and recheck the list for possible oversights; you don't trot back for a package of raisins or a can of baking powder when the store is twenty-two snowy miles away.

The trip takes two days — six to eight hours each way; a team with a load travels much slower than a walking man. We usually have a load going as well as coming. Ours is in part a barter economy; we deliver oats or wheat to the Gem City in payment for the groceries we bring home; sometimes we sell hay to the livery stable that boards our horses.

With that wagonload of booty tucked away in the cellar we can say cheerfully: "Let winter come." It will anyway, with or without our permission.

Winter

In this season of shrunken daylight it is six-thirty or seven o'clock before the house begins to stir. Mama is up first, of course, putting a match to the kindling in the range, opening the draft in the heater so that the smoldering chunk will blaze up and thaw the glacial air. We menfolk hustle into our clothes, layer on layer, pull on overshoes and sheepskin coats, caps and mittens, fetch the milk pails from the cellar and set out for the stables.

The air sears the skin. The packed snow squeals underfoot, except where the chivvying wind has spread a fresh dune across the trodden path. Some mornings there is no longer any path; we flounder knee-deep, heads bowed to the drive of snow; we keep close to the fence for guidance until the corrals and stables emerge from the smother.

At the corral we separate, Oscar going to the cow stable, I to the horse barn. When the door rolls back there is a chorus of nickers. It's nice to be welcomed, even though I know the welcome is really for the breakfast I am about to serve. Ted and Star nuzzle me ingratiatingly as I come into the stall, forget me the moment the oats are in the box. Buck, as always, waits impassively, too honest, perhaps, for any pretense of affection, more likely too misanthropic. He gets right down to the business of eating without, as Oscar would put it, saying thank you, go to hell, or anything else.

I climb to the loft and push hay down into the mangers, I harness the team, and then join Osc in the cow stable. It is warmer there; seven cows radiate a lot of heat. Osc is a fast milker; I am not. I am accordingly grateful for the division of labor. I couldn't swear that I didn't dawdle a bit over the feeding and harnessing in the hope that he would be started on his fifth cow by the time I reported for duty, leaving only two for me.

In winter we linger a little over breakfast. We savor that second cup of coffee; Oscar has a cigarette. Then we don our work clothes and set forth again.

The cows have finished their breakfast too; we turn them out into the corral or the small pasture adjoining it, where they can get water. In bad weather they will shelter in sheds along one side of the corral. We clean the stables — rather, I clean the stables, now that I am no longer in school. It's a messy job. Extraordinary how much excreta a cow can rid herself of in one night. The shallow wooden channel sunk into the floor behind the stalls is an open sewer of urine and ordure. I push it down toward the door and shovel it through a square shuttered porthole set there for that purpose, mop out the trough with the soiled hay, and spread fresh bedding for the coming night. The same chore has to be done in the horse barn. Horses, though, are cleaner by nature. For one thing, their fecal matter is solider, and therefore easier to dispose of. For another, they are fastidious; they will not willingly foul themselves. A horse will detour around a pile of fresh manure; a cow will walk right through it.

I like feeding cattle. This particular morning the snow still lies deep on the meadows, though the wind has scrubbed the bench-rim bare. Therefore we take the hay sled. The runners have frozen fast; Oscar swings the team first to one side, then to the other, to jerk them loose. Ted and Star break into a trot as we come down into the meadow. The runners make a pleasant country-fiddler music. It's a good morning. Cold, to be sure, the dry cold that crinkles the nostrils, but for once windless. The sky is blue and hard; the mountains glitter in the flat shafts of the low sun.

The cattle are trickling out of the brush along the creek, where they bed down at night. Their bawling augments as we approach, a hundred variations on a single theme. The vanguard drops into file behind. We pull up beside the stack; I hop off and pry loose the poles closing the gap in the fence, and Oscar backs the sled in, hard against the stack. We clamber up and begin forking the hay down.

When the sled is itself a haystack, rack and horses invisible under the mountainous load, we drive out, nail up the fence, and start off across the meadow, heaving great forkfuls overboard. When the rack is empty the herd is strung out in a ragged horseshoe.

Breakfasting cattle are a laboratory study in pecking orders. The dominant types get the first forkfuls, of course; at the far crook of the horseshoe you find the

Milquetoasts, the meek, who may eventually inherit the earth but for the present get the leavings. The distribution is not necessarily an accurate graph of hierarchy, however. I have seen some cantankerous old critter bully her way clear around the horseshoe, grabbing a mouthful from every clump, horning prior claimants aside, just for the hell of it.*

In the course of a winter you get pretty well acquainted with a bunch of cattle. Identities emerge from the milling mass of shaggy red-brown hides and broad white faces. They are no longer merely so many units of property, beef on the hoof, eventually money in the bank. They are personalities. By January you know that the ragged procession emerging from the brush to greet the breakfast cart will almost certainly be led by the brindle-faced veteran with a crumpled horn and the brands of a dozen outfits on her ribs, and that right at her heels will be a one-time pet skim-milker, now a coming three-year-old with the fetus of her first calf bulging her belly. She has long since forgotten me. But some of last year's skim-milkers still recognize me; occasionally I drop off the sled to greet one, rubbing his ears and stroking his neck while he nuzzles me, dimly remembering that I was once his mother-substitute.

Feeding is not always the pastoral idyl I have pictured. There are days of wind and snow — wind so violent you are afraid, with reason, that it may lift the rack from the wagon bed, wind that rips the hay from the fork so that you have to pitch two loads to fill the rack once. On such days we feed as close to the creek course as we can drive,

---

* It's tempting to assume some etymological relationship between *bossy*, "U.S., a cow or calf," and *bossy*, "Colloq. Inclined to play the boss." But the dictionary will have none of it. The first comes, obviously, from the Latin, *bos, bovis*, the second, surprisingly, from the Dutch *baas*, meaning master. Where, though, did the Dutch get that word?

where cottonwoods and willows break the wind. Other mornings we may find a stack half snowed-under, with a flying buttress on the leeward side, ten feet through at the bottom and packed solid. We utter the ritual blasphemies, and start shoveling.

Feeding the cattle is a full morning's work. By the time we have watered and stabled and fed the horses, dinner will be ready. Like breakfast it is a leisurely meal. But there is always some work waiting. Manure must be hauled from the corrals and stables; we spread it on last year's stubble to nourish next summer's oats and wheat. The three horses we keep up in winter — a team and a saddle horse — empty the haymow surprisingly fast, and every few weeks we replenish it. These are good-weather jobs — good weather meaning anything short of a blizzard. On blizzardy days we find tasks indoors: harness mending in the barn, small repair jobs in the carpentry shop or at the forge.

The pace, though, is relaxed, and in midafternoon we usually come in for coffee and a snack. By the time we finish the sky is red behind the skeletal cottonwoods and the evening chores are waiting.

Splitting firewood is my job, as bringing the kindling used to be. I like it. The trick is to use a short-handled ax, and a fairly dull one. You prop a chunk of wood on the chopping block, which is a mighty stump, flat on top and sitting solidly on or in the ground. You appraise the. chunk judiciously to find the cleavage plane — identifiable by the largest of the fissures radiating out from the center — and bring the ax down. If your blow is on target, and if you're lucky, the chunk should split neatly into halves. If it doesn't, you swing chunk *and* ax — now deeply imbedded — overhead, and bring them down in reverse order, the head of the ax underneath. That usually does it. Now you split the halves, steadying the chunk with the heel of one hand while you slice off stove-size segments. Once you get the rhythm it goes fast.

By the time the wood and kindling are in, the west has charred and it's time for the evening chores. The horses have to be watered and fed, the cows roped into their stalls and their mangers filled. We milk by lantern light. After more than half a century I can't be sure how much of the picture that materializes is authentic Laramie River cow stable, how much is filched from Dutch and Flemish painting — the dramatic chiaroscuro, shadow dense as tar around the core of radiance which flickers as the flame is teased by icy trickles of air. Whatever its genesis the picture, supplemented by touch and sound and smell, is nostalgically pleasant. The warmth of the cow's flank against head and shoulder; the rhythm of the milk jetting into the pail, metallic at first, thickening as the twin streams work up a cushion of foam; the contented crunch of multiple mastication; the complex fragrance of warm milk, and cow, and hay, and stable odors best not analyzed too closely but from long familiarity not repellent.

When you're young, December is the longest month of the year. Not just because the days keep shrinking until there's no more than a nubbin left between sunup and sundown, and you can't help wondering once in a while: what if this year, or some year, the shrinking didn't stop and shift into reverse? A scary speculation, even if you realize it's nonsense. No, the trouble with December is that those shrunken days — anyway, the first twenty-three of them — crawl past so sluggishly.

Our thoughts and speculations began to focus on Christmas with the arrival of the winter supplies. Tucked in among the flour and coffee and sugar and canned goods would be other packages, of intriguing shapes and dimensions, which Mama and Papa whisked past our avid scrutiny and tucked away in their bedroom. We knew we weren't supposed to snoop, but we couldn't resist an occasional peek. Martha was quite shameless about it. She never unwrapped anything; she knew she wouldn't be able to duplicate the clerk's expert packaging. But she hefted and palpated, and usually had a pretty shrewd guess what was inside — though which book, or what color apron, even her hypersensitive fingertips couldn't deduce.

We followed some of the Norwegian Christmas customs. Mama didn't have time for the traditional seventeen varieties of cakes and cookies; in Norway Christmas starts early in December. But she always made *lefse* and *fattigmand* and *julekake*. *Lefse* is an unleavened bread rolled out thin and baked in great flat sheets on top of the stove. Cut into manageable segments and lathered with butter it's wonderful, if you like it; I do. *Fattigmand* is cooked in deep fat, like a doughnut, but it's much more delicate, being a thin twist of dough fried crisp. The name means "poor man," and is a condensation of *fattigmands bakelse,* poor man's baking. That's a misnomer. Though like most Norwegian pastries it's not cloyingly sweet, it's nothing for weight-watchers. *Julekake* is simply raisin bread, only better than you're likely to find in any store.

On Christmas Eve Norwegians eat *lutefisk.* That's dried cod that has been marinated in a solution of lye until it's a gelatinous mess. Mama, Papa and Hattie loved it; Oscar, Martha and I didn't. For us nonconformists Mama provided something else, usually spare ribs. Christmas dinner was all-American — roast turkey and the fixin's, plum pudding and/or mince pie, and a lot more.

A couple of days before Christmas Papa used to saddle a horse and set out for the foothills of Jelm. Hours afterward, depending on weather and the depth of snow, he would return with a six-foot spruce strapped behind the cantle. Decorating the tree was the children's job, though of course Mama helped. The decorations were mostly homemade — strings of popcorn, paper cunningly snipped into patterns that opened out into filigree when stretched, lop-sided stars scissored from whatever colored materials we could find. The only store-bought items were the little sconces that clamped on the boughs and the candles that fitted into them.

It never occurred to us to worry about fire. I wonder why no ranch house, to my knowledge, ever burned down. I do remember seeing a neighbor's tree blaze up suddenly while we were paying a Christmas-week call. There were a few minutes of excited scurrying, but no damage. Of course we were careful, and there were always two brimming pails of water in the kitchen if need arose.

The Christmases I remember most vividly, however, were two that looked for a while as if they were going to be complete washouts, or worse.

One winter it stormed so fiercely all week that there could be no thought of going up to the mountain. We kept hoping, day after day, but Christmas Eve came with no break in the weather. We kids were desolate. Christmas without a Christmas tree! That wouldn't be Christmas at all.

We moped around until Mama could no longer stand our woebegone faces.

"We're going to have a tree," she announced decisively.

She got an ax, went out in the yard, and chopped down a cottonwood sapling.

"There you are," she said. "Decorate it."

It wasn't my idea of a Christmas tree. Spindly, leafless, a skeleton without symmetry or life — really, it was worse than no tree at all. Lugubriously we set to work draping and garnishing that ungainly scaffolding. As we worked we began to cheer up. It turned out to be rather fun, trying to make something out of such unlikely material.

Another year it looked for a couple of hours as if we would be spending Christmas Eve in the schoolhouse, and maybe Christmas Day as well.

A storm had blown down from the north in midmorning and augmented steadily. By four o'clock the snow was heaped halfway up the windows. When we scraped a peephole we could see only a churning maelstrom the consistency of cottage cheese. The teacher decided she wasn't going to turn us out into that.

We took inventory. Fuel: adequate; happily the wood was piled alongside the schoolhouse in easy reach. Food: a couple of sandwiches and one hard-boiled egg left over from various lunches. The outlook was dismal.

I don't remember how long it was before a stamping on the front steps roused us from our gloom. The door opened, and in came a swirl of snow, and Father. He was cocooned in white; his eyebrows and moustache were ice-fringed. He shook off some of the snow, strode to the stove and held out his hands to the warmth.

We were very glad to see him.

A few minutes later Albert Sodergreen joined the party, and the rescue was complete.

We found our way back to the ranch, as Papa had found his way to the schoolhouse, by following the fences, until Tony and Bollie, knowing where shelter, hay and oats were waiting, took command. When they stopped suddenly their muzzles were touching the barn door. We waited while Papa stabled and fed them, and then followed him to the house, floundering through drifts as high as we were. Suddenly a pale luminosity thinned the smother, and we were at the kitchen door.

It was a very merry Christmas.

"As the days begin to lengthen the cold begins to strengthen." An old saying; Mama used to quote it. And a true one. By mid-January, though there is only a barely perceptible difference in the morning, twilight is appreciably later. But night after night the mercury shrinks deeper in its tube — zero, ten below, thirty below. There are days when it never climbs back into the plus zone.

Water holes freeze over and have to be chopped open morning and evening. One winter the creek froze to the bottom; the dammed-up water backed up into the corrals and froze there. Around the hole where I watered the horses morning and evening the ice built up, two feet, three feet, maybe more. I chiseled out a slippery staircase to the open water. The horses didn't like it; they had to be coaxed, begged, pushed and yanked until thirst overcame their fear of the treacherous footing.

Once I yanked too hard on a halter rope, and skidded into the water. I left the team to fend for themselves and legged it up to the house. By the time I reached the kitchen my overalls looked like Ivanhoe's armor.

By late January or early February the ice on quieter stretches of the river is twelve to eighteen inches thick and ready for harvesting. We chop a hole big enough to admit the saw, measure off a grid of rectangles, perhaps two feet by fifteen inches, and begin dissecting. Two long cuts first, then cross-cuts, until block after block breaks loose and can be hauled out and dragged aside to await loading. That's a two-man job, one on each end of the block, with tongs firmly set, to tow it up the ramp and slide it into the wagon. At the icehouse the blocks are stacked neatly in tiers and packed in sawdust. It's good insulating material. The block I shall dig out some Sunday next July, to be crushed for the ice-cream freezer, will be smaller than when it was tucked away in February, and rounded at edges and corners. But some of last winter's ice will still be there at the bottom of the discolored sawdust when we bring in the new crop.

We hang quarters of beef and halves of hog in the icehouse to freeze solid during the winter. When the spring thaws come we gouge out caverns in the ice and bury the meat. We had our own deep freeze before city folks enjoyed that convenience.

As children we learned to skate on the marshlands west of the stables, weaving in and out of the wizened reeds and cattails and gaining confidence and maneuverability. But the best skating was on the river. When my sisters and I tired of watching the ice cutters we would set out to explore — warned by Papa to keep away from the riffles and watch out for air holes. The going was smoother downriver, where the wind had scoured the snow away. But we liked skating upstream, even though sometimes we had to clump through drifts stretching from bank to bank. The dense woods pinching the river in were a little scary, perhaps, in their silence and immobility, but it was a pleasant tingling kind of scariness.

The silence was never complete. Even on the calmest day there was wind somewhere aloft, strumming the stiffened boughs, loosening a concretion of snow so it came down with a feathery impact. There were other winter wayfarers afoot; we crossed their tracks, the rabbit's double-quote followed by an exclamation point, the clear firm claw print of a crow, other scribbles, Sanskrit or Mandarin, that we could not identify. Sometimes we heard a scutter in the brush, but rarely did we catch a glimpse of the scuttler. Our skates had signaled our coming in ample time to send the timid to shelter.

Not all my winter memories are that pleasant.

One day in mid- or late January Oscar and I set out for town with a load of oats and a four-horse team. We had known, from the moment we first poked our noses outdoors, that it wasn't going to be a pleasure trip. For a week the temperature hadn't climbed above zero; at night it must have been far below. But the sky was clear, the wind for once was on a holiday, there were no visible or sniffable auguries of any blizzards within pouncing distance. It seemed like a good time to get those oats to market and bring back a few things for the family larder.

We walked most of those twenty-two miles, stamping our feet, flailing our arms, massaging cheeks and noses. The cold was skewering. It pierced to the marrow, through sheepskin coat, horsehide jacket, sweater, flannel shirt, woolen underwear. Hands stiffened in fleece-lined leather mittens.

How did the horses stand it? They plodded on uncomplainingly, their breath congealing as it left their nostrils, rime crusting thickly on the bridles.

The landmarks inched past: Nelson's ranch, Halfway Hill, Seven-Mile Lakes. A lunar landscape in which nothing moved. We met nobody, we saw no stir around the infrequent ranches, no sign of life except thin trickles of smoke. Who would be abroad in such weather, once the essential chores were done? Did anybody, scraping a peephole through an ice-furred window, watch our passing and ask the question, perhaps adding his comment: "The goddam fools!"

We had subsided — at least I had — into an apathy of misery, the anodyne the body somehow generates as a last defense. I didn't feel the usual lift when the University Tower pricked the horizon and the town materialized around it, a drab sprawl, exhaling dirty smoke into the dirty sky. I had never before realized how insignificant it was in that great expanse of prairie, camel color — a mangy camel — except where snow mottled it with a leprous white. You could imagine that the cold had shrunken it physically, the weight of that iron sky flattened it against the inhospitable land it occupied on sufferance.

No such morbid fancies for Ted and Star, Belle and Queen. Journey's end was in sight, and journey's end meant a warm stable, a rubdown, water, oats, hay, rest. They quickened their pace; on the slope down to the river the lead team broke into a trot, the wheel span following. We rumbled across the bridge, fretted for five maddening minutes at the crossing while a string of freight cars shunted indecisively. Ted and Star made a dutiful show of stampeding when the switch engine chuffed past, but their hearts weren't in it. Then up Grand Avenue two blocks, right on Third Street two more, and captain, my captain, the fearful trip was done.

I carried the souvenirs for quite a while. I had frozen both ears. Not too badly; they didn't drop off, though they hurt like hell when they began to thaw. We used the standard treatment, vigorous massage with handfuls of snow, which doctors now say is the worst thing you can do. They burned and itched for a couple of weeks, and to this day they remain sensitive to cold.

17

Poisonweed
and Other Portents

YES, IT WAS A GOOD YEAR. But looking back, I can
recognize portents.

Shortly before turning-out time that spring we had
learned that we would have to find summer pasture
for a good many of our cattle somewhere else than in the
Medicine Bow Forest, where Olson stock had grazed as
long as I could remember. I am tempted to make a dramatic incident of this: Curt notice from the forest supervisor that our allotment had been cut by one third. Family
consultation, dour with dismay, sizzling with outrage. Im-
passioned appeal to the supervisor: Look, the Olsons have
been running cattle on the Medicine Bow ever since the
Reserve was established. What do you mean, pushing us
out to make room for these pilgrims? Frosty turndown.
Anguished consideration of possible alternatives. And out
in the meadows one hundred and fifty Herefords waiting
(with no impatience whatever) to be taken off the green-

ing timothy and redtop and turned out to forage for themselves.

It would make a pretty story. But Oscar, faithful to the facts, tells me it didn't happen that way at all. We had lost our grazing allotment through a misunderstanding. We had assumed it belonged to the ranch, more or less in perpetuity. It didn't. It was ours only as long as we used it faithfully; the Government couldn't and wouldn't hold your quota over for a season, keeping out some other bunch that could have fattened on that precious pasturage, if for some reason you didn't need it. One year — was it the year after Papa's death, when, Oscar recalls, we sold most of the cattle, "probably to clear up the debts"? — we didn't apply, and our priority lapsed. The supervisor hadn't always enforced the regulations rigorously. But this year things were tight; we were cut back.

So what to do? There weren't many choices. Renting pasture would be ruinously expensive, even if we could find any not yet bespoken. There remained the country south of the river.

The plains between the river, Jelm Mountain and Red Mountain were mostly public land, except for a couple of ranches close up to the foothills. They were also poisonweed country.

There are several plants that can kill livestock, but to us poisonweed meant larkspur. Not the garden variety, though distant kin. It's particularly dangerous in May and June, because it greens up early, and looks delicious to hungry heifers. If they gorge on it they die; you find the corpses bloated to hogshead proportions, legs sticking out like pegs.

Happily poisonweed didn't grow everywhere, only in scattered and fairly well defined patches. So that summer it became my job to patrol the danger areas and shoo away any animals that might drift too close.

I liked the job. In late spring and early summer the high plains are intricately embroidered with the pinks and blues and lavenders and whites of demure flowers, whose existence you would never guess a few weeks later. Chokecherry blossoms fill the draws with drifts as white as those that melted only a fortnight ago. Previously I had known the prairie only in midsummer and fall, when its beauty was muted, a pastel of shifting lights and shadows. I had never realized that for a week or two every year it could be a garden.

It would have been blissful, ambling through that garden on a June morning, except for one thing. I had to keep repeating, so I wouldn't forget, the short course in veterinary surgery Oscar had given me before I set out.

Place your thumb on the patient's hipbone and measure one hand-width toward the ribs, another hand-width down, and jab in your knife, deep. Then cut an X on the under side of the tail, an inch or two from the root, so that it bleeds well.

That was the drill in case a cow or steer should slip through my one-man cordon and eat of forbidden fruit. The stab in the belly is supposed to relieve the bloat, the slash under the tail to drain out the poison along with the blood. If you get to the victim soon enough, that should save him.

I never had occasion to perform the operation. I never saw it done. I don't know whether it is sound medical procedure or merely folklore. I still wonder whether I could have driven my knife in deep and true, or would I have flinched and bungled?

That fall we couldn't count on the first heavy snow to bring most of our cattle home, as we were accustomed to do when they all grazed on the forest. So one crisp October morning Oscar and I rode off to join the Red Mountain roundup.

Just south of our homestead quarter we came across a scattering of cattle — Oscar's +E and Art Johnson's TV brand — and decided to get them under fence while they were handy. Buck and I were pelting hell-bent across a shaly sidehill, trying to head a refractory bull, when suddenly sky, prairie, Jelm and bull cartwheeled. I picked myself up, dazed but undamaged, and saw Buck scrambling to his feet a few yards away. The bull was disappearing over the hill; Oscar was loping back to take a body count.

We all seemed to be intact, although Buck had cactus spines in his poll, and my coiled lariat had been uprooted from the saddle pommel. But in a mile or two Buck began to limp. By the time we got to Boswell's ranch on the upper river, where the roundup rendezvoused, he was limping so badly that it was obvious he, and therefore I, would be of no further use. After dinner I dolefully watched Osc and the others ride off to comb the breaks along Red and Bull Mountains, and then headed for home.

I walked most of the ten miles. Buck's sprain, or whatever it was, had stiffened. His limp was now a hobble, and he stumbled nearly every step, so badly I was afraid he would fall. I got off.

Cowboy boots are not made for walking. Cowboys notoriously despise walking any farther than from bunkhouse to barn. By the time we reached the south fence I was hobbling almost as badly as Buck. I turned him loose in the river bottom, soaked my blisters for a while in the cold water, and trudged ignominiously up to the house, toting saddle, blanket, bridle and humiliation.

Let me backtrack. One midsummer morning we learned that we had something new to worry about. Well, not really new. We worried about it every year, sometimes with good cause, sometimes not.

Oscar had set out after breakfast, rubber-booted, shovel on shoulder, to see how the oats were coming along, and to rechannel the water to any patches that looked thirsty. The oats were doing fine. But the runnels between the rows held only mud, already beginning to dry. The lateral that fed them was empty too.

A break farther up? Oscar hoped so; that could easily be mended. But he didn't really believe it. When he reached the main ditch, and found only a trickle of water among the boulders, he knew that we were in trouble. Our head gate had been shut.

Watching the spring runoff come down, brimming the streams and flooding the meadows, you'd never think there could be a shortage. But once the snowpack had melted the flow shrank rapidly. By the end of June the gravel bars in the river were bare and head gates were beginning to shut down.

The average annual precipitation in our corner of Wyoming is twelve inches. Walter Prescott Webb, in *The Great Plains,* contends that any terrain getting so little moisture is in effect desert, unsuited for cultivation. He thereby excludes most of the high plains east of the Rockies, to the outrage of Chambers of Commerce in the mountain and prairie states.

Since the first permanent settlement there has been constant litigation — interstate, intra-state, local — over water rights. Wyoming, Colorado and Nebraska have bickered interminably over the North Platte and its tributaries, one of which is the Big Laramie. Six states have claims on the majestic Colorado, which heads in the mountains of Wyoming and Colorado, traverses Utah and

Arizona, and flows along the borders of Nevada and California. The thirst of the lower basin states, particularly California, is insatiable. The dams built to satisfy it have submerged forever some of the most beautiful country in the world, and the reservoirs already overtax the river's capacity.

The flow of the Big Laramie had been allocated long before I was born. Our water right dated from 1884, which sounds like a pretty good card but could be trumped by several others. When the flow drops too low to satisfy everybody's needs, the ranches with higher priorities get first claim, and the water commissioner shuts and padlocks your head gate, leaving your meadows and grain fields to parch.

This had happened to us before, and might be expected to happen more and more often as settlement grew denser and water consumption increased.

There was nothing we could do about it, except cuss. And perhaps pray; any succor would have to come from aloft. There was one consolation: the lower hay meadows shouldn't suffer too badly. It would soon have been time anyway to shut off the water so the hay could cure properly. But the grain — even if it didn't burn up it was bound to be short.

Was it because the ditches were dry when they should have been brimming that Oscar decided we should grub out the principal feeder channel? I may be wrong about the timing, but I remember the episode well.

It's always an ugly job. You use the plow first, to loosen the accumulation of silt, willow roots, dead branches and other litter, and reshape the channel. You follow up with a scraper, scooping out the debris and dumping it on the bank. That sounds simple, but it isn't. The nose of the plow keeps locking in a nest of willow roots. The scraper glances off a hidden boulder and loses purchase; as the tug lessens the team surges forward. You cuss them out roundly — as if it were their fault, as if they didn't hate the job just as much as you do.

The day was hot, steamy hot as it rarely gets in the high country. There was no wind. The mosquitoes and the deerflies settled like a gray fungus on the horses, wherever the flailing tails could not reach. They settled on us, and feasted heartily before we could free a hand for a swipe. That torment can make the most docile team refractory, the most equable temper incendiary.

My job was to drive the horses while Oscar manipulated plow or scraper. He was steering the scraper when a boulder tilted the blade upward. As the tug slackened the team spurted forward. The jerk wrested the handles from his fingers and one of them caught him a crack on the jaw.

"God damn it, Kid," he yelled, "can't you hold those horses?" He gave me a cuff that sent me sprawling.

Weeping with fury, I squalled:

"God damn you to hell! I'm going to kill you."

I scrabbled around for a weapon, and heaved the first thing my hand touched, a sizable cow turd. It glanced off his cheek, doing no damage. We grappled indecisively for a spell, then broke away. There was work to be done.

We didn't speak more than was functionally necessary the rest of the afternoon, but by next morning the incident was as good as forgotten.

Generations of Wyoming ranchers have complained that in June and the first half of July, when you need moisture, the weather is likely to be remorselessly fine, Noah's forty days and nights contrariwise, whereas as soon as you get out the mowing machines the sluices open. It wasn't quite that bad this year. There were a few showers during the growing season, and a couple of near cloudbursts in the mountains briefly refilled the ditches. The hay crop was about average; we topped out the last stack on schedule.

The grain was short, particularly on the knolls, but it had headed out satisfactorily. We had the wheat and perhaps half of the oats cut and shocked when, in the first week of September, the sky dumped six inches of wet snow on us.

The shocked grain dried out well enough to be threshed, but the uncut oats were flattened. We salvaged what we could with a mowing machine, but much of it was left to the crows and the blackbirds.

Next winter we were to learn that we had been a bit too impatient in getting the sweeps started again after one rainy spell. We opened up a stack, skimmed off the weathered outer crust, heaved up a forkful — and loosened a belch of dust and the stench of decay. We delved deeper. No better. Instead of crisp green-brown, still breathing a ghost of blossomy meadows, we pried loose great clots the color of tobacco, the smell of mold. Cattle turn away from such garbage; there is no virtue in it, no nourishment. If nothing better is offered they will get some of it down. But it will not fuel them against the cold. We cut a cross section with the hay knife. Still the same tobacco color, the same musty stink. We gave up, and moved on to another stack, hoping for better luck there, and for a mild winter.

That was the winter when the war in Europe moved perceptibly closer.

The guns of August had echoed only faintly on the Big Laramie, remoter than summer thunder and surely of less portent to us. Sarajevo was in the headlines for a few days, and then disappeared. The Balkans were far away.

Our school geography had given the area only a few paragraphs. Somebody always seemed to be getting assassinated there, anyway.

We had no notion of the rickety scaffolding of alliances on which the peace of Europe was precariously balanced. When the scaffolding collapsed we were of course shocked. England, Germany, France and Russia were not the Balkans. We talked it over desultorily when we came in to the stacker for a drink of water. Of course it would be over quickly. And anyway it didn't involve us.

We began quite soon to take sides. In that Scandinavian concentration there were a few families of German origin, who were jubilant as the Kaiser's armies ground westward. Our sympathies swung quickly to the Allies — violated Belgium, indomitable France. We even forgot our century-old grudge at England in admiration for her "contemptible little army."

Little by little the war, far away though it still was, began to affect us. Prices went up. Beef on the hoof at Omaha, oats on the scales at the Gem City or the Star Barn. That was fine. But also groceries, shirts and shoes and overalls, sickle blades, rake teeth, nails and staples. A new phrase came into the language: the High Cost of Living, quickly abbreviated to HCL.

Word reached us one day that buyers were canvassing ranches on the Little Laramie, seeking horses for the British army — saddle stock for cavalry, draft animals for artillery. They were reported to be paying fantastic prices, two hundred dollars a head and up.

A week or two later they drove into our ranch.

There were two of them, a horse dealer, from Cheyenne or Denver, and a British officer. I seem to remember a trim belted tunic, tapered breeches tucked into highly-polished puttees, a brisk, peremptory manner. But I cannot swear to it; in the intervening half-century I have seen too many World War I movies. The face that materializes atop that martial elegance is unmistakably a construct — Errol Flynn, David Niven and perhaps a touch of C. Aubrey Smith.

We had brought all the horses up from the meadow and turned them into the round corral. I was stationed at the gate to let the culls through. Oscar joined the Englishman in the corral, to answer questions, to keep the horses moving so that they could be inspected in action, to shoo the rejects to the exit. The womenfolk had come up from the house to see the show. Martha was perched, characteristically, on the top rail, so as to miss nothing; Mama and Vay watched through the poles.

It was immensely exciting.

The first eliminations went fast. His Majesty's Army had no use for mares, yearlings and two-year-olds, or superannuated pensioners. I was kept busy swinging the gate as Oscar cut out the discards; I had to move nimbly a couple of times to nip off a dash for freedom. The corral, still muddy from snow, was churned into a bog. The Englishman's boots and puttees had lost their shine; his uniform was spattered with mud and manure.

We could see that this man knew horseflesh. He watched shrewdly as the survivors trotted past, Oscar keeping them strung out in a ragged orbit. A shake of the head dismissed another and another. Oscar cut them out and I swung the gate open, shut, open, shut. Only ten were left now. Then eight. Then six.

The Englishman said something to Oscar, and my brother went to get halters.

It must have been about then that my excitement began to wear thin. Up to now this had been an adventure, a spectacle, a chance to play a role, minute and brief, in that distant European drama. Now, suddenly, I began to realize just what we were doing.

The temptation to invent is strong. I could so easily identify a moment when that realization broke upon me, an incident that precipitated it. Perhaps it actually did happen that way. While Oscar was getting the halters, the horses, chivvied for an hour or more, continued to mill restlessly for a while, and then quieted. Isn't it quite possible that one of them, seeing me waiting by the gate, came over to say hello, to nuzzle my shoulder in the hope that I might have a lump of sugar in my jumper pocket, to ask wordlessly what the hell was going on?

I must be honest and admit that I don't remember. I do remember watching Oscar set out for Laramie next morning, leading the four horses the Englishman had finally selected. I can still see the little cavalcade, black against the tatters of the last spring snowfall, as it trailed up the hill and disappeared, Ted and Star frisking as usual.

Yes, we had sold Ted and Star. The Englishman had been greatly taken with them; he had offered a premium price.

I don't recall protesting. I am reasonably sure I didn't venture to protest. It was Oscar's business, and I was accustomed to accept his judgment. I kept my grief to myself; I doubt if I betrayed it even to Martha, who must surely have shared it. Eventually the hurt dulled, as most hurts do. But it awakened at intervals, when I read of the battles writhing meaninglessly back and forth across the mud of France and Flanders. I told myself it was most unlikely that Ted and Star were anywhere near that carnage, but I could not always suppress the grisly images my book-fed fancy generated.

Long, long afterward I learned from Oscar why he and Mama had felt it necessary to sell them; learned too that it hadn't been easy for him either.

"They were eight or nine years old, and we had others

coming up. And no doubt we needed the money. I don't remember how much we got for them."

He added: "I do remember leading them to the stockyards and turning them loose. I didn't kiss Ted and Star good-bye. It hurt."

18

Good-bye to the Ranch

PORTENTS THEY WERE, but only by hindsight — that spurious wisdom that comes too late to guide and can only mock. I continued to assume that the ranch would be there whenever I needed it. My sense of belonging had been intensified by more than a year of total immersion. I liked being a ranchman. If you averaged up good and bad you found it a satisfying life.

When I entered the university that fall I enrolled unhesitatingly in the College of Agriculture. I bought a new four-dimple Stetson, the mandatory uniform of an Ag. student, and signed up for courses in Agronomy, Zootechny (it had nothing to do with running a zoo; the textbook was *Types and Breeds of Farm Animals*), and — also mandatory — a hideous hybrid called Agricultural Math.

Everything seemed normal when I went home at Christmas. I got back into overalls and jumper, took over my customary chores, helped Oscar feed the cattle, and was ridiculously pleased when Duke, the big, blond, blaze-faced colt I had made my pet the previous summer, came up to greet me and have his ears rubbed.

I do not recall any warning or intimation that it might be my last Christmas on the ranch.

That was a seismic spring. The country was moving toward war, at the awesome pace of an accelerating avalanche. The emotional climate was feverish and confused: disbelief, dismay, excitement, impatience. I shared the excitement, and perhaps the impatience. It began to look as if I might have use for the new skills I was practicing every afternoon as an ROTC private — "Squads right — march! . . . Column right — march! . . . Company, halt! Fix bayonets!" I learned to yell bloodthirstily as I drove my blade deep into the target dummy's straw entrails. That for those poor Belgian babies!

The familiar world was coming apart everywhere at the same time. It must have been just before April 6, 1917, that the sale of the ranch was completed and Mama came to town to find us a new home.

I was too numb — and once more, perhaps, too pre-occupied — to ask many questions. More than half a century later I learned from Oscar the multiple answer to the big question "Why?"

There were several reasons. The old worry about irrigation water. The relatively new worry about summer grazing. Vay's health. She did not thrive on the Laramie River. Her asthma was worse there than it had ever been elsewhere; when she was coaxed back to the Osterman school for a couple of months to replace a teacher who had left in midterm she found immediate relief. In summer, and particularly during haying, she suffered grievously.

Oscar, who had an understanding with Mama, though

no formal contract, that he would eventually take over the home place, began to doubt that he would ever be able to pay out. Maybe, he reflected, he and Vay might do better on a ranch in Colorado, somewhere not far from Denver. On trips there, he recalled, he had seen young cattle that could be bought cheap, fattened up, and marketed whenever they were ready, instead of being dumped in the fall when everybody was shipping.

It was the ancient mirage of richer pastures beyond the horizon, the vision of "gold and green forests" that had brought our parents to America.

Oscar believes Mama was not reluctant to sell. He recalls (something I never knew or suspected) that there had been talk of selling even before Dad died, at the time when the Riverside and other big properties were being carved up into bite-size and sold at forty, fifty, sixty dollars an acre. In 1910 such figures were dazzling. And tempting.

I cannot resist the taunting "if." If they had sold out then we would not have been living at the Christie house next winter. Papa would not have gone out for coal and slipped on the ice. He might have lived for many years longer.

Seven years later nobody was paying sixty dollars an acre. Charles Neal's first offer was seventeen thousand dollars. Mama held out for twenty thousand dollars, and got it. With the land and the buildings went the machinery, wagons, harness, some of the horses, a few cattle, and Father's 1/3 brand. (A few years ago, the property, considerably expanded and modernized, sold for well over one hundred thousand dollars.) The cattle, which were Oscar's, were sold separately.

Twenty thousand dollars. A niggardly return, one might think, for more than a quarter century of toil and frugality. I doubt that Mama applied that arid bookkeeper calculus. A ranch is not merely a capital investment; it is a way of life. I remain persuaded — from everything I remember and from what she said afterward — that she had found it a good life.

Did she look back as the car reached the top of the hill for the last time — back to the house, now stripped and empty, where she had lived for nearly three decades? Did she say anything, in reminiscence or farewell? I cannot testify. I was spared that leave-taking, as I had been spared so much else. She had firmly overruled my wish to help with the packing and moving. They could do very well without me; I must not miss any classes.

Oscar writes: "I don't recall any emotion that showed. I think she was glad, and looked forward to an easier life." Yet I wonder. She was never given to emotional display. She was a stoic by disposition and long habit. But she felt deeply; of that we had had ample evidence. It must have been a cruel task, clearing the house for its new occupants, deciding what to pack, what to discard. Even now, when people change residence so casually, there is always a twinge of regret as one looks around the empty rooms, and then walks out and closes the door. Martha, who had helped with that last housecleaning, might have told us more. But Martha is not here.

Mama and Martha had us pretty well settled when I was summoned to move my few belongings to our new home. It was a green shingled bungalow at the eastern edge of Laramie, two blocks from the University. Mama had brought most of our lares and penates from the ranch: the tall glass-doored bookcase (a few books had unaccountably disappeared en route); the bedroom suite she and Papa had bought when they were married; the wicker rocking chair in which she had sat so many evenings darning and mending; the Norwegian chest that had been her trunk when she immigrated. (The legend inside the lid is dated 1799, and indicates that the chest had belonged then to one Ole Simensen, probably her great-grandfather.)

Oscar and a good neighbor, John Pearson, had moved it all to town, Oscar driving a hayrack, John a box wagon. Of that last journey over the road he had traveled so often, laden or light, with a plodding four-horse team or with Ted and Star stampeding in simulated panic at every encounter with the motor age, he remembers only one incident. About halfway the kingpin worked up and the front wheels slid forward, letting the rack drop. Osc and John found a fence-buck and a pole — possibly borrowing them from the fence along the right-of-way — and with the buck for fulcrum and the pole for lever lifted the rack, slid the wheels back, replaced the kingpin and were on their way again.

We had left behind many things that we would regret abandoning. How could we foresee that half a century later many of the homely utilitarian tools we had used unthinkingly would be collectors' items?

The kerosene lamps I had filled and trimmed daily, for instance. The barrel churn, the dash churn, the coffee-mill, the bootjack. Papa's shaving mug. The branding irons — Papa's **1/3**, Oscar's **+E**. The decoy ducks we touched up with fresh paint every fall before we sent them forth on their quisling mission.

Not long ago I saw a display of decoy ducks in a Washington bank window, with a sign: "America's earliest folk art." I am reasonably sure that none of them had ever lured live mallards or redheads within shotgun range. Today's working decoys are — of course — stamped out of plastic. These, I learned, are fabricated for collectors by a few survivors of the ancient craft. Some of them had price tags in three figures.

I have sometimes reflected that a young man wanting to assure himself a competence on retirement should start collecting things. Anything and everything, one of each, however meaningless or ordinary. Fifty years later a few of them would be money in the bank.

It probably wouldn't work. How many of today's gadgets will still be functional five years from now, let alone fifty? And if any should survive, through some miscarriage in the mechanism of planned obsolescence, who would want them?

Artifact n. [L. *ars, artis,* art + *facere, factum,* to make.] A product of human workmanship, esp. of simple primitive workmanship.

What gives a decoy or a bootjack its value to the collector is the visible presence of a human fabricator, attested by its simplicity, even its crudity. (I concede that moustache cups and kerosene lamps do not have quite the same genealogy. But they were not stamped out of plastic in quantities of one hundred thousand or a million; somewhere in the process living hands touched them.)

If the twenty-first century has artifacts it will be because the grim vision of science fiction has become reality, and a few stunned survivors of nuclear warfare are learning, because they must learn or perish, the ancient skills of handicraft.

Mama could not leave ranching completely behind her. She insisted on having a chicken house and enclosure built at the back of the lot, and populated it with Rhode Island Reds, possibly to the dismay of our neighbors. We had fresh eggs at breakfast for a couple of years, no more. The chicken house became a storage shed, the chicken run a vegetable and later a flower garden. Though we could no longer replenish the borders with humus from the river bottom, Mama's thumbs were still green.

She was to live in that house for thirty years, until her death, at eighty-five.

19

You Can't Go Back

FOR YEARS I clung to the delusion that some day, somehow, I would make my fortune, buy the ranch back, and restore it as it used to be. Even after it became clear that I was never going to make a fortune, Oscar and I kept looking for a "spread" somewhere on the Laramie River that could be bought for nothing down and a substantial assist from the Farm Credit Administration. We found one, upriver in Colorado, that met our every specification — ample water, luxuriant meadows, timbered mountains to south and east, and a magnificent panorama west down the river valley. The price was reasonable. But the Laramie banks were politely but firmly discouraging. Even in the best days of the New Deal you couldn't buy a ranch without some capital or collateral.

Oscar had never found that dream place outside Denver. He had farmed for a few years in northeastern Colorado, with moderate success, then settled in Denver.

There he turned to carpentering, a trade he had picked up as one of the many skills a rancher needs.

After Vay's death in the spring of 1925, in the twelfth year of their marriage, he moved back to Laramie. Her long struggle with ill-health had been ended by pneumonia. Perhaps it was a merciful death. She had undergone one operation for cancer and had begun to suspect a recurrence.

Oscar got back to ranching for a while in the '30s, and so did I, as a sort of silent partner. (I too had returned to Laramie, after seven years as an itinerant newsman — Oakland, San Francisco, New York, Denver, Casper — and was then news editor of the Laramie *Republican-Boomerang.*) Oscar leased the old Wright place on the Little Laramie — it had once been a stagecoach station on the Overland Trail — and we pooled our resources to buy a few cows. We found a brand nobody was using, the Coffeepot — Σ — and registered it under the name of Olson Brothers. Oscar and Mary, his second wife — a ranch girl from the Laramie Peak country — ran the place, and took in summer guests to provide most of their income.

It was a living, and they met some interesting people. Stuart Palmer, creator of the spinster detective Hildegarde Withers, stopped off en route to Hollywood and in two days sampled more aspects of ranch life than most dudes attempt in a month. But it was a precarious existence, and there was no room for growth. After a couple of years they moved back to town and Oscar took up carpentering again.

Martha too never got over her hankering for ranch life. It was a hankering that fortunately her husband shared. Harry Miner had been a cowboy, riding for a big spread in the Encampment Valley, when he first came courting. Through three decades of working in oil refineries, in

Laramie and Casper, he clung to the vision of a place in the foothills where he and Martha could begin living as sensible people were meant to live. On his days off and during vacations they explored, all the way up the Wind River Mountains, across to Jackson Hole and the Tetons, north from Cody into Sunlight Basin.

Their only son had a different goal. Lee loved the outdoors too. He was a crack skier; there is a downhill run on Casper Mountain named for him. He also loved books, and Strauss waltzes, and a dog named Trouble. But most of all he loved drawing pictures. He was in art school in Chicago when he was called into service. The Army, in its inscrutable wisdom, made him a medical corpsman. His letters from North Africa were illustrated with delightful sketches of Moors and Berbers. They kept coming for some time after the telegram reporting him missing in action.

For two years Martha clung to the conviction that he was alive in some prison camp. She did not give up hope until, several weeks after V-E Day, a letter from one of his comrades, just released, told her that Lee had been mortally wounded in a German ambush near Salerno. He is buried in Anzio-Nettuno cemetery southwest of Rome.

After Harry's retirement he and Martha took up the search for that dream ranch more intensively. Not quite full time; much of Harry's boundless zeal and energy was directed to the cause of conservation; he was state president of the Izaak Walton League and a member of the national board. They found some likely looking places, but none that quite fitted their specifications. They were still looking two years later when Harry, tough, resilient, indestructible Harry, who thought nothing of driving all night after an elk hunt and going directly to the refinery for an eight-hour shift, had a heart attack in the middle of the night and died before he reached the hospital.

So Martha too came back to Laramie. She brought with her the two saddle horses she and Harry had been boarding out a few miles from Casper, for use when they finally did find that place in the foothills. They were, I suspect, also surrogates for the son buried in Italy. For ten years Martha visited Shorty and Ginger at least once a week, in all kinds of weather, bringing offerings of oats and range cubes. They would come at the sound of the horn — loping up with a flourish at first, less and less friskily as age stiffened them — empty their pails greedily, submit to being fondled and crooned to and brushed free of flies, and then would amble off. Cupboard love, no more, but for Martha that was enough.

She was no longer a tomboy, of course. She wouldn't have dared to jump impulsively on Shorty and pelt across the meadow bareback. But she was still good company. When I visited Laramie we bird-watched and rock-hunted together. And she could still quote poetry by the furlong. We spent hours prompting and cueing each other, all the way from Barnes and *Stepping Stones* up to Frost and Millay.

The horses outlived her, but only a couple of years. After her death, at seventy, Oscar and Hattie had taken over their weekly provisioning. When Shorty and then Ginger became too rickety to face another winter it was Oscar's grim responsibility to have them destroyed.

Hattie had returned to Laramie on her retirement from government service. She had given up schoolmarming after a few years and taken up bookkeeping. (We might have guessed that would be her destiny, 'way back in School District No. 8, where she first displayed her inexplicable affinity for numbers.) After a venturesome look at Alaska, and a longer stay in California, she had joined the Veterans Administration, and worked successively in Casper, Cheyenne and Denver.

Her recollections of our childhood were invaluable to me in writing this chronicle. But she was not to see them in print, as I had hoped and expected. She died, three months before her seventy-ninth birthday, while this book was being put into type.

Even before we were too old to undertake new ventures Oscar and I realized that our dream of becoming ranchers again was unrealistic. Our kind of ranching was obsolete. We knew horses; we didn't know tractors. I suppose we could have learned — Oscar at least, if not I. Everything now is mechanized — plowing, cultivating, fertilizing, irrigating, harvesting. The gain in time and efficiency and the saving in manpower are obvious. But the capital investment is correspondingly heavy.

A few years ago Oscar and I stopped at a small ranch to ask directions. The area between house and barns, and well out toward the road, looked like the display lot of a dealer in agricultural equipment. Some of the machines I recognized; there were others whose function I couldn't even guess. We speculated: how much money was tied up in all that hardware? Fifty thousand dollars? Probably more.

There wasn't a horse in sight.

The irrigation problem has not diminished. The water table is sinking steadily; the evidence is plain in the skeletons of cottonwoods along dry streams and ditches; the saucersful of brackish water where there used to be considerable lakes.

Yet the few ranchers we know — sons or grandsons of our contemporaries — seem to prosper. Some fly their own airplanes. Quite a few go to Arizona or California for the worst winter months, leaving somebody else to pitch out the hay, keep the water holes open and milk the cows — with milking machines, of course. The union scale for ranch hands — when you can find them — has quintupled, from forty dollars a month to two hundred. The fragméntation that began with the Riverside has been reversed. As the original owners die off or move to town or California, the big outfits buy up their holdings. The big outfit may be a corporation with headquarters in Denver or Omaha, or a prosperous lawyer or banker in Cleveland or St. Louis. A ranch or farm can still be a good investment. The government will pay you for fallowing land that was never productive anyway, and your operating loss can be charged off against taxes.

Ranching is even being computerized. I'm told that the eastern outfit that owns the famous old Two-Bar, north of Laramie, tags every cow and her calf with a number. Thus pedigrees are kept straight, an accurate record is provided of fodder consumed per beef yield, and inferior stock can be weeded out. I shall be interested, if I am still around, to learn how it works. I wonder whether the University of Wyoming's College of Agriculture now teaches computer techniques.

I suppose it was inevitable that every cow and bull and steer and heifer would eventually have a social security number.

I try to get to Wyoming for a few weeks every summer, now that I'm retired. Back in the '30s my wife and I had fully expected to spend the rest of our lives there. She had come out from Chicago to teach violin at the University and had fallen in love with the country. But when the Republican-Boomerang changed hands the new publisher had other ideas, and I went back, reluctantly, to New York. The war rescued me from the Herald Tribune copy desk and ferried me to London, and after the war the transition from psychological warfare to peacetime

234

propaganda and eventually to diplomacy was a natural one.

Louise and I still find it hard to explain why we seem to have taken root in a Washington suburb, without a mountain in sight. We were luckier during our seventeen years in the Foreign Service. We could usually look out the window to some local equivalent of Jelm: in Oslo, Holmenkollen; in Athens, Hymettus; in Reykjavik, Esja.

Our ranch has changed hands perhaps a dozen times since 1917. Recently it has had a succession of absentee owners. Over the years Oscar and I have visited it occasionally. When the current owner or manager could be persuaded that we, as early settlers, had preferential status, we have sometimes been permitted to fish there. ("Just don't trample down the meadows" — as if we had to be cautioned!)

It's amazing how well I remember that river. Sometimes, when worry or weariness or aging bones keep me awake, I revisit it in imagination. I start at the Sodergreen fence and fish downstream. I fish painstakingly, with all my remembered cunning — every hole, every riffle, every stretch where the current, dark and sleek, slides under an overhanging bank, and there must be a rainbow waiting for delicacies to shake down. I splash out through the shallows to drop a Royal Coachman seductively at the far side of the swimming hole where we used to wash away the sweat and heat prickle of a day in the hayfield. I let the fly drift warily toward the fallen cottonwood a few rods downstream, its root mass exposed like a huge cluster of spiders, its trunk, the leaves still green, almost bridging the river. Warily, because I have lost more than one trout and a good many flies and leaders in that underwater cheval-de-frise.

It is better medicine than Seconal. I always fall asleep well before I reach the Hammond fence.

I don't think I'll go back to the ranch again, now that they've pulled down the old house. I can't blame them. The new houses — there are two — are bigger, handsomer, and doubtless much more convenient. That low, cramped structure, with the hops and morning glories softening the weather-bleached logs, the phlox and sweet william and verbenas brilliant along the footings, was not a historic monument. The Overland Trail gave it a wide berth. Nobody of distinction, President, general or outlaw, ever slept there — not even Bill Nye, Laramie's one celebrity. But for eighteen years it was my home.

I saw the ranch a couple of years ago through binoculars, from a perch high on the slope of Jelm. We were antelope hunting, Oscar, Jack Hassett and I. (At least Oscar and Jack were hunting. I had gone along for the ride, hoping the antelope would stay out of range. Obligingly, they did.) From the rocky outcrop that sheltered us against the brusque September wind we could look all the way to the Laramie range, across a tremendous sweep of buckskin-colored prairie shading at the far rim into blurred amethyst. The cottonwoods along the river were still yellow. They hid the house, but we could make out the corrals and the shape of the fields, and the lesser vein of the creek bending down to the river.

It looked much as it had looked when I climbed Jelm sixty years before. At that distance, the changes that seemed to me so great dissolved. By lowering the binoculars and looking through narrowed lids, I could rub away houses and corrals and fences, and imagine I saw the plains and the river valley as the Indians might have seen them — that nameless tribe that left its indelible signature in the great circle on Ring Mountain.

The plains still dwarfed the patches of green and yellow and bronze that had been chipped out of them. The contours of the mountains were the same as always. You would never suspect that there was a hundred thousand dollar house with every modern convenience tucked into the thick stubble of Boulder Ridge. And the river, though fifty years of spring freshets had reshaped its course in minor particulars, was the same river that I had listened to on spring nights, and not significantly different from the stream where Jacques La Ramie may have set his traplines before the Sioux scalped him.

It was comforting to find that much permanence in a quicksand time. And yet I worry. We mark the earth with ruin. As I write this, strip miners are at work only a hundred miles north of Laramie. Their monster mandibles are gnawing away the tender pelt of the prairie to gouge out coal for our insatiable generators. When they move on they leave desolation, hideous and complete.

I pray that they may spare the Laramie plains. There is some ground for hope. The very poverty in mineral resources that starved out the early prospectors may be our salvation. I find comfort also in an unlikely quarter, the census. Wyoming is one of the few states forced to admit shamefacedly that their population is dwindling. Perhaps these high prairies may still nourish life when most of our planet has become uninhabitable.

At any rate, I can be reasonably confident that they will last out my time.

Acknowledgments

Recognizing that one's own recollections are bound to be fallible, I have checked mine wherever possible against those of others, and against the few printed records relevant and available. My brother and my sisters helped immensely, setting me right on points where my memory tripped or faltered, and contributing much enriching detail.

Of the published chronicles I am indebted particularly to the following:

History of Wyoming, by T. A. Larson. Published by the University of Nebraska Press, Lincoln, Neb., 1965
The History of Albany County, Wyoming, to 1880, by Lola M. Homsher. Privately printed, Lusk, Wyo., 1965
The Laramie Story, by Mary Lou Pence. Privately printed, Laramie, Wyo., 1968
Timber Line, by Gene Fowler

The files of the *Laramie Republican* and *Laramie Boomerang*, Laramie, Wyo.

For any errors — and there certainly will be some — only I am responsible.